The Closer You Get

Rose Grey

Printed in the United States of America.

Simply Romance Press
26 Homestead Ave., #5
Warren RI 02885.

ISBN-13: 978-0-9994247-8-0

ACKNOWLEDGMENTS

Thanks to my author friends at Rhode Island Romance Writers, NECRWA, FTHRW, Romance Writers of America and to the Last Call Girls. You know who you are. The input, guidance and support you share with such warmth and generosity of spirit mean more than you can know.

Thanks to Judy Roth for her editing savvy and incisive advice.

Thanks to Tara at Fantasia Frog for being the most patient cover designer ever.

Thanks to my family far and near. You're the best.

Finally, thanks to the many authors far and near who spent years of their lives creating the books that filled my childhood and adulthood with wonder. Because of you, I could escape into another world and come back with tools to help me understand the world I lived in.

This story like all my stories is dedicated to my husband who demonstrates the essence of love every day through word and deed.

By Rose Grey

Durrell Brothers Trilogy:

Waiting For You

All Of Me

The Closer You Get

Hot Pursuit

Not As Advertised

The Closer You Get

"HOLY CRAP."

"Language," Jessica Piers admonished automatically before looking up and nearly saying the same thing. She could see why twelve-year-old Liam was impressed. It was a car worthy of some serious admiration. Burgundy red, muscular and screaming mid-life crisis, it probably belonged to one of the wealthy summer residents. The beginning of June was a bit early for tourists, and the antique auto shows popular in the Boston area were not a thing on Demerest Cove because of the cost of transporting the vehicles to the island by ferry. But she couldn't think of any year-round resident who drove an antique like this one.

As a party planner, Jessica made a point of being familiar with potential clientele in her small town as well as the clients already on her list. She squinted, but the car had already pulled past her broken down sedan to park in the long shadows on the side of the road, and she couldn't see the driver. She guessed it would be an older man. Usually the people who went for old cars were the ones with fond memories of them.

She looked at the car's trunk critically. It was oddly shaped. Probably impossible for a tuba, she thought with an internal sigh. So there would be no point even going to the middle school band concert now. But beggars couldn't be choosers. She put on her game face and tried to infuse her smile with warmth and gratitude. It wasn't hard, since she was grateful. Until the driver opened his door and unfolded himself from the vehicle.

"Candy? Candy Piers?"

Those long legs strode toward her and for a moment, hearing him say the name she had used back then, in another world, she was transported back to high school. Ronan Durrell looked almost exactly the way he had looked as a teen,

better, actually. He was still slim but more muscular than he
had been as a youth. Cool green eyes assessed her broken
down sedan. His hair was darker blond now, and when he
ran his fingers through it she noticed a scar on the back of
his left hand. It hadn't been there when she had last seen
him. She would have remembered. She remembered everything about Ronan.

"Candy, what happened?"

His tone sounded impatient. For a moment she thought
he had read her mind, and she almost snapped, "A baby. Isn't
that what usually happens when a person is pregnant?" But
before she could embarrass herself beyond saving, Liam
bounded forward, his usual diffidence with adults forgotten
in the face of the coolest car ever.

"Sweet set of wheels, dude! What kind of car is that, anyway?"

She could see the moment it clicked. Ronan looked at
Liam, then at her, then back at Liam.

"It's a Bentley R-type Continental from 1952," he said
finally. "Do you need me to call a mechanic?"

She held up her cell and shook her head. "Doyle's isn't
open until tomorrow morning. I'll have it towed then. We're
fine."

He frowned but did not argue the point.

"I'm guessing you folks need a ride." He looked at Liam.
"Are you old enough to drive?"

Liam's shoulders slumped. "Not for another three years.
I can get my learner's permit then."

"Maybe you'd like to drive it around a parking lot, sometime? I mean, if your mom says it's okay."

Liam's eyes shone at the thought and for a moment Jessica despised Ronan. He surely understood how difficult it
was for her to see him again. And using Liam as a weapon
was beneath him. Or at least she had thought it was. She had
never known Ronan to be purposefully cruel, so she couldn't
understand what his game was now. She started to shake her
head no, absolutely not, but before she could speak, Liam
stepped back so he stood next to her.

"Thanks, but I don't think I should."

Liam's tone was steeped in longing, but he tucked his hand in hers and squeezed not so much, she thought, out of a need for comfort as out of a need to comfort her. His willingness to give up on something he clearly prized to protect her was a mark of his maturity. And that, more than anything, infuriated her. She had promised herself twelve years ago that her son would have a complete childhood. But despite her best intentions, he still sometimes took on the role of protector. She gave his hand a squeeze back and took a deep breath.

"I know Liam would love to," she said.

"Really, Mom?" Liam's face glowed at the prospect.

"As long as you keep up with your chores," she added.

"Totally!"

Ronan gave her a long look as Liam ran to rummage through her car. "You okay with that?"

She shrugged lightly. "You and I may never be friends, but we've known each other too long to be strangers."

He nodded curtly.

"I'll need my music," Liam called out cheerfully. "And my tie. Oh. And my tuba."

Ronan's eyebrows shot up. He strode to his car and unlatched the back, revealing a surprisingly generous space.

"Good thing the Bentley is ideal for tubas. Where are we going?"

"Middle school," Liam said, opening the back door of the Bentley reverently. Jessica couldn't seem to move her feet toward the car. A vision of sitting next to Ronan as he drove her to Boone's Ice Cream the day he first got his driver's license flashed in her memory. For a moment, she could feel the cracked leather of the seat under her bare legs, smell the wild summer roses that tumbled along the side of the road near her house. Or what had once been her house. She swallowed and forced herself to loosen her grip on her purse strap.

"Liam, you can sit next to Mr. Durrell. I'll sit in back."

Ronan shot her a sharp look but said nothing. Instead, he slid behind the wheel and reminded Liam to buckle his seat belt.

"Do you have more cars like this?" Liam asked.

Ronan chuckled. "Kind of. My brothers and I bought The Grand Hotel a few years ago and it came with a fleet of antiques. But no one has time to drive them much. Max and Aidy prefer newer more dependable cars, so if I don't take the Bentley out when I'm in town visiting, she never gets exercise."

"Where do you live?"

"Liam." Jessica shifted uncomfortably in the back seat. "Don't pester Mr. Durrell."

Ronan's eyes met hers in the rearview mirror.

"On the pestering scale, this ranks low," he said mildly.

He glanced at Liam, "I live in Boston. But my brother Max and his wife Aidy are expecting. Once my little niece or nephew is born, I'll probably visit more often. The island is a good place for a kid to grow up. I went to school here when I was about your age."

Jessica stiffened. The image of Ronan as a recurrent presence in Demerest Cove was disturbing. Instantly, she regretted having given permission for the driving lesson. It would have been easier to make the interaction a one shot event if Ronan lived far from the island. Across the country would have been ideal. But even Boston was okay, as long as he stayed there.

"Did you know my mom back then?" Liam twisted in his seat to look at Jessica and then jerked back with a gasp. He managed to grab the folder of band music as it slipped from his lap, but the contents slid out and scattered at his feet. And then, as he leaned over to gather them, his eyeglasses slipped to the floor as well.

"No," Jessica said firmly.

"Yes," Ronan said at the same time. His eyebrows rose as he registered her response.

"Not well," she amended.

"I seem to remember spending some time together," he said.

"I don't," she said.

She had never been so grateful to see the school building looming ahead. At least Liam had been too busy gathering his sheet music to press the point. She reached for the door as the Bentley slowed to a stop, already considering how best to thank Ronan without allowing for any continuing conversation. But before she could begin, Ronan turned to Liam.

"I can drive around back to let you off near the stage door so you don't have to walk so far with the tuba."

"That's okay," Liam responded quickly, "you can let me out at the front door. I'll be fine walking, honest."

Ronan's eyes met Jessica's in the rearview mirror.

"Stay in the car a moment," he said.

Jamming a rumpled cap from the glove compartment onto his head, Ronan trotted around the long nose of the car with an officious air. He opened Liam's door with a flourish and then did the same for Jessica, pointedly ignoring the open mouths of the slowly gathering crowd of children and their parents. Striding to the back of the Bentley, Ronan heaved out the tuba. He pulled a tissue from his pocket and gave the worn case a thorough dusting before setting the tuba gently at Liam's feet. From the corner of her eye, Jessica could see Liam's face, flushed, his embarrassment tempered by sheer delight.

"Thank you," he stammered.

"All part of the service, Master Liam. I'll look forward to hearing you play."

"Go on in, Liam." Jessica kept her tone level with effort. "I'll meet you in the lobby after the concert."

She waited until her son had disappeared into the crowd of newly impressed classmates before turning on Ronan.

"Why did you *do* that?" Her voice was grim, loud enough for Ronan to hear, but just barely. The island gossipmongers would be chattering as it was. She didn't need to give them more to work with. But still.

He shrugged. "It won't hurt Liam to have something to boast about. That's like currency in middle school."

She raised her brows. "How many children have you raised?"

He raised his hands in a placating gesture. "If I did wrong, I apologize."

She bit her lip and looked away for a moment, tapping her foot. Sometimes being a grown up didn't seem sufficiently satisfying to justify the frustration. Finally she shook her head and let out a ragged breath. "No. I apologize. You've been kind and I appreciate it."

She didn't want to shake his hand, but in the moment there didn't seem a better way to close the conversation. The evening was cool and a damp breeze was picking up, promising a drenching spring rain. Her fingers were chilled. Even so, she could feel a kind of heat when he clasped her hand in his. Something about the touch of his skin against her palm quickened her pulse. She snatched her hand back as though she had touched an electrical charge and marched away from him toward the school's entrance. Before she could disappear into the now quiet lobby, he spoke. "You'll need a ride home."

She stopped and turned her head but kept her hand on the door's push bar. "Thanks, but we'll get a lift from one of the other parents."

He shrugged and pulled the cap from his head, running his other hand through his hair. But she didn't wait to hear his response. Because the touch of his hand still lingered on her palm. And she could smell rain coming. And because more than anything else in that moment, she wished he would stay.

CHAPTER 2

JESSICA SANK TO the carpet and scrunched into the knee-hole under her desk, yanking her purse behind her. The problem with running a business was you couldn't control who walked in the door. But Demerest Cove was composed of two types of people. The ones who had money and the ones who didn't. Lynne Mullin, for all her flaws, had money.

Moon Shell Events couldn't afford to turn away any potential business. But party planning for Lynne would be in and of itself a disaster. Primarily because Lynne hated her. Which begged the question – why was she here?

"Don't come back, Carl." Jessica silently beamed the thought to her only full-time employee. "Not yet."

Technically Carl was on break, but Jessica knew he had gone for muffins so he was likely to return soon. Her only hope was that he would become engrossed in conversation with a new friend and would lose track of time. Lynne would leave, irritated at the lack of service. And Jessica would be able to move on with her day. That was the best-case scenario.

"Hello? Isn't anyone here? What kind of business *is* this?"

Despite herself, Jessica's back stiffened. She didn't have a facility, of course, just the little two-room store front. And she would never be able to compete head to head with The Grand Hotel or its adjunct the Retreat Center. But lots of people planned to run their anniversary parties or smaller wedding receptions in their homes or in rented halls. And that was exactly the sort of need Moon Shell Events excelled at meeting.

Lynne's foot, undoubtedly shod in a pointy-toed spike heeled Louboutin, the sort Jessica privately called witch shoes, tapped impatiently.

"Total incompetence."

The shoes clacked away across the glossy wood floor of the reception room. Jessica let out a sigh of relief as the bell over the door tinkled. She crawled out from under the desk, only to duck back under cover when she heard Carl's voice. Shoot.

"Ms. Mullin. What a pleasure to see you. What can we do for you today?"

Carl's Jamaican accent always reminded Jessica of honey. Or maybe that was just his sweet personality. He was tall and lanky, his dark skin a perfect foil for his warm sparkling eyes. His long dread-locked hair, which he kept bound in a pony-tail for work, had been a topic of interest when he arrived on the island, and his preference for men had been intriguing too, but the locals had been won over by his engaging smile and easy manner – which he was exercising now with some success. Lynne defrosted rapidly as she began describing her plans for a family reunion party in response to Carl's friendly questions.

"It's too small a function for The Grand. So I thought I'd see if you had availability. But your girl, Candy, wasn't here, which I'm only telling you because I think you ought to know if your employees are slacking off."

There was a pause. Jessica snorted at the thought of Carl's expression and belatedly covered her mouth.

Carl paused. "You must be thinking of my boss, Jessica Piers," he said finally.

"Yes. Well. Just because Candy Piers changed her name doesn't mean she changed her personality. She's not the sort of person I want involved in this event. Or any event I'm at, really. But you can handle my party on your own, right? I'm just doing a light lunch. It's an informal gathering and I don't expect a big crowd."

Carl coughed gently. "I'm sure we can arrange something to your satisfaction, ma'am."

"That would be wonderful. It will be a lovely get-together with the right sort of people. And Candy simply doesn't –"

Her voice trailed off, probably in deference to Carl's ex-pression rather than any sense of the inappropriateness of her comment. Lynne and her friends would never forgive what they considered Jessica's intolerable breach of propriety.

Initially, their comments had hurt Jessica, back when what her mom's friends thought mattered. When what Mom thought mattered. But now, as long as their nasty opinions didn't affect Liam or his twelve-year-old life, Jessica didn't care.

By the time Carl sauntered into the back room, box of muffins in hand, Jessica had crawled out from her cubbyhole. He looked down at her, grinning.

"Turns out, wealth doesn't make a person classy. Who knew? Lynne Mullin sure hates you. What did you do, despoil her only son?"

She shook her head and massaged her aching calf. Carl had come uncomfortably close to the truth. Lynne's hatred was just something Jessica had to put up with. Like seasonal allergies. Or an occasional bout of food poisoning. Too bad there was no antibiotic to combat spite.

"Old business," she said. "And not resolvable, unfortunately. I could have dealt with Lynne myself, but the moment I saw her at the door, I knew I would blow it. The last thing we need is bad publicity, and Lynne is always looking for a way to provide it."

Carl gave her a puzzled look but didn't probe further. He dropped the sheaf of notes he had taken on her desk.

"I'm sure you heard most of our conversation. I quoted a generous fee and she made noises about going elsewhere, but we all know there is nowhere else to go on the island unless you want The Grand. And even though the Durrell's charges are more than reasonable given what they provide, looks like Lynne doesn't want to pay that much. I'm betting she'll be back with a signed contract and a check."

Jessica brushed off her backside, collapsed into her swivel chair and stared at the pages without touching them.

"We don't have to take the job, you know. She's pretty awful." Carl pulled his own chair over and sat next to her. "We've got our regulars and there are probably some more weddings coming our way this summer. Want me to call The Grand and see if they can take her on? Max and Aidy Durrell are pros at handling difficult customers."

"No." Jessica contained the reflexive twitch she always had when she heard that name. "I don't do business with the Durrells."

"You may want to rethink that. I just learned the Durrells are developing a venue for smaller events as a complementary site to The Grand. It'll include a chapel, a couple function rooms, a kitchen, offices, a garden venue too. Word is, the price point for the new event space is going to be a lot lower than they charge for The Grand."

Not good. People already talked glowingly about attending weddings in the classic rose garden overlooking the ocean in the shadow of The Grand. A second smaller facility with an additional garden setting, nestled in the woodsy grounds near the big hotel, would provide a fabulous location for elegant entertaining. But the side effect would be devastating for Moon Shell Events, which depended on customers who couldn't afford The Grand.

"When is the new venue supposed to be ready for bookings?"

"They already have the plans and permissions. End of August."

Three months. Worse and worse. Moon Shell Events had several commitments from brides and grooms for the summer, but she knew from past experience those commitments could be and often were changed at the drop of a hat. Last year alone they had lost two bridal receptions and one anniversary party to The Grand when the hotel offered a special all-inclusive deal for afternoon events.

"We'll just have to ramp up outreach," she said finally.

Carl gave her a long look. "That's like rearranging the deck chairs on the Titanic. At this point, we only have one good option."

"Not happening."

"Accepting Max and Aidy's offer of employment would benefit us as well as them," he persisted. "I don't know what happened between you and that family, but I do know you're letting your past dictate your financial future."

He took a deep breath and let it out slowly. "Jess, you know I love working with you. It's been a blast. But I need to have a job. If you are making a unilateral decision to drive Moon Shell Events off a cliff rather than accept a perfectly reasonable alternative, I'm going to start sending out my resume today."

Her mouth gaped open for a minute and she shut it with a snap. Carl was a flexible person as a rule. That was a big reason why she had decided to hire him. But once in a while, he dug his heels in and when he did, he was positively immovable. The worst part of it was he was right. Her throat felt tight as she spoke.

"Please don't say that. I know there's a solution, I just – I haven't figured out what it is yet."

"Tell Max and Aidy you've changed your mind," Carl insisted. "With this new venue, the Durrell's need for the kind of event coordination we do will be even greater. But they can't afford to wait long. If you don't take Max up on his offer, he'll bring in someone from off the island to do the job instead of us, and you and I will both be out of luck. And money."

She swallowed. Carl didn't have to spell it out further. They had spent too many evenings massaging the books, trying to make ends meet. Moon Shell Events had to make it. It had to. Her eyes stung. She looked down at her hands, surprised to find them tightly clasped. Carl couldn't understand the implications.

Ronan's betrayal had been uniquely private, and she preferred to keep it that way. She took a muffin and busied herself at her desk. Maybe a miracle would happen. Funny how a practical person could still believe in miracles. But then it was a miracle she had managed to avoid running into Ronan for thirteen years.

She knew he visited his brother and sister-in-law. She had seen him from a distance on a few of those occasions, but by careful strategy, she always managed to avoid actual contact. Until last night. And even that fleeting interaction had been acutely painful – a good lesson in how easy it was to forget the particulars of agony.

Time didn't dull everything. The memory of how it felt to be dependent on the kindness of strangers was as painful as it had been the day she realized she was pregnant. She had never felt so vulnerable in her life.

Back then she was Candy, entitled, desperately needy, vulnerable. She'd had none of the tools she'd needed to survive in the real world on her own. But she was Jessica now. She had built a life for herself and for Liam brick by brick, and she would do whatever she had to in order to protect it. She reached for an invoice, but it slipped from her trembling fingers and wafted to the floor just out of reach.

CHAPTER 3

"I'M SURPRISED YOU agreed to do Lynne Mullin's party."
Clara shoved the heel of her hand into the dough with espe-
cial vigor.

Clara's kitchen always smelled as though something good
was imminent. Which didn't change the twinge of guilt Jessica felt taking advantage of her hospitality at a moment's notice. It wasn't as though she and Liam had nothing to eat at
home. There was a perfectly good leftover casserole lurking
in her refrigerator.

"I'm not dealing with Lynne directly," Jessica said. "Carl
will take care of her event. And I need the business."

"Some business isn't worth the money," Clara retorted.
"And a little pride isn't a sin. That woman is a selfish monster
and she's treated you abominably." The older woman sniffed
and gave the dough another shove.

Jessica couldn't help grinning. Clara reminded her of a
frazzled hen sometimes, especially when she was feeling protective of her chicks.

"What are you smiling at? That soup needs stirring."

Jessica bit her lip to keep from laughing and grabbed a
large spoon on her way to the stove. The cauldron of soup
was rich and nearly ready, filled with carrots, celery and
chunks of chicken.

"It's been over twelve years," she said gently. "I've
learned how to protect myself, and more importantly, I know
how to protect Liam."

"I know, I know." Clara threw her hands in the air, loos-
ing a cloud of flour. "But some people are just poison. And
her husband was no better, may he rest in peace. What kind
of people turn away a pregnant girl, the mother of their only
grandchild? Liam may have your blonde hair but those hazel
eyes and those freckles are straight Mullin. Lynne's a fool."

Jessica stirred, breathing in the fragrant steam. Clara was
incapable of understanding people like Lynne or Jessica's
mother, Cookie, because Clara cared about other people in
ways Lynne and Cookie weren't capable of. Half the soup

would be parceled out to people in need, neighbors, acquaintances, the bagger at the supermarket who had the sniffles. The rest would feed the always generous gathering of guests at Clara's table on Friday night.

"How are my girls?" Hans poked his head into the kitchen.

"I don't have dinner ready yet." Clara waved her arm dismissively. "Come back later." She paused a moment. "Unless you're hungry. Are you hungry?"

Hans grinned at Jessica. "I could eat."

"Me too." Liam trotted into the kitchen and plopped into a chair. Clara tucked the bread dough into a bowl to rise and briskly brushed off her hands.

"There's apple strudel. But only one piece for Hans. He's on a diet."

Hans groaned and the couple fell into good-natured bickering about the nutritional importance of apple strudel. Hans and Clara might have poor opinions of the Mullin family in general, but they adored Liam. So now that he was in hearing range, the topic was closed. Instead, they peppered him with questions about school. Before Jessica could intervene, Liam was telling them about the concert and about the man who had rescued them and pretended to be a chauffeur.

"He said he and his brothers own The Grand. You know, the big old hotel on The Point? And they have a bunch of old cars he said needed exercise and that maybe he could show me how to drive one."

Hans shot Jessica a sharp look from under his bushy gray brows but said nothing. That wouldn't last. Sure enough, the moment Liam had been bundled off to the living room to do his homework, Clara sat down next to her. With Hans on the other side, Jessica was effectively boxed in. She sighed and gave in to the inevitable.

"Was it him?" Clara asked. "Ronan?"

Jessica nodded. Hans reached for another piece of strudel but, at Clara's pointed stare, switched mid-motion to rub his forehead. Clara pulled the platter out of his reach with one hand and patted Jessica's shoulder with the other.

"Now that one was a nice boy. Is he still single?"

Jessica winced. She could see the calculation in Clara's eyes and knew she had to nip it in the bud.

"I have no idea." That wasn't completely true. She had watched his hands on the steering wheel and had definitely not seen a ring. Not that it mattered. "Besides, Clara, even if he were interested in me, which he is not, I'm not interested in him."

Hans rubbed his mustache. Jessica made an effort to look relaxed. It was hard not to squirm when Hans had that thinking look.

"Maybe we should have him over," he said.

"No!" Jessica knew she sounded like a petulant teenager and tried to repair it. "He's only in town for a few days to visit his brother and sister-in-law. I'm sure he'll be busy doing family stuff."

Hans's eyes met Clara's and Jessica knew she was sunk. If she didn't act quickly, Clara would invite the entire Durrell clan to dinner where she could grill them mercilessly under the guise of being a hospitable host. Nothing broke down a person's defenses like Clara's cooking. She opened her mouth to say something, anything on a different topic when Clara spoke. "She's catering an event for Lynne Mullin."

Hans frowned.

"Come on, Hans. It's a business decision. You've said it yourself. If you only did business with people you liked –"

"– I'd never do business with anybody. Ya, ya. How is business?"

She flushed and cleared her throat. "Not great. We had some unexpected cancellations this spring. But I'm hoping we'll catch up this summer."

"You know the planning board just granted the Durrells permission to build an event facility?"

She sighed and despite her desire to appear upbeat realized her shoulders had slumped. "I heard. Carl is worried." She picked up her fork and moved strudel crumbs around on her plate until they were lined up. "I still think we can get the business that's too small for a Durrell facility. But there's no question, any special event packages they offer could eat into our client base."

Hans's calloused hand patted hers. "We have a little money put away. You know we'll help if you need it."

Clara stood to clear the plates. "You just tell us what you need," she said firmly. "Barbara said she would help too."

"I appreciate the offer. But I can't accept it."

"Of course you can," Clara said. "And you should. We want your business to succeed so you can take care of yourself and your son. That's what is most important to us. Right, Hans?"

Hans fumbled for his handkerchief and blew his nose loudly. He muttered something about big business and the little guy and stomped off into the living room. From the rumble of conversation, Jessica guessed he was checking with Liam about the status of homework. The answer must have been encouraging because the television clicked on and the canned laughter of a game show mingled with the clatter of flatware as Clara emptied the dishwasher.

Jessica's eyes stung, and she blinked fiercely to keep the tears from coming. Although Hans owned the only hardware store on the island, lately he had been feeling the pinch from big box stores on the mainland. Summer residents especially had begun purchasing tools and building supplies online to save a penny here and a dollar there. And even locals were coming into the store less than they used to.

In addition, she knew they had been talking about retirement. Well, Clara had been talking about it. Hans had resisted so far, but it was only a matter of time. They would need every penny of their savings if they were to fulfill their dream of buying a condo in Florida where they could live during the winter months.

Barbara, despite her generous offer, had a growing young family of her own and a struggling law practice. After all the kindness she had shown, Jessica wouldn't consider taking advantage of her generosity now. Especially since Jessica had been such a snob about money initially.

When Barbara first introduced Jessica to Hans and Clara, Jessica had considered the family low class. What surprised her was they didn't seem to know it. Their home was cramped compared to the Piers' estate. Barbara wore second hand clothes from designers no one had ever heard of. Worse still, no topic was off the table. International scandals, local politics, neighborhood activities and high school social life were all discussed with the same energetic interest, regardless of the comfort of the discussee. Advice on sex and dating was dispensed with the same ease and liberality as recommendations of good cookbooks or the ideal drill bits for installing a porch rail.

But over time, as irritating as their unasked for advice was, Jessica came to love them for it. Because Hans and Clara were the first adults she had ever met who cared enough about her welfare to be irritating in this way. Her own parents were so absorbed with their lives, they didn't have time to care much about Jessica's, except as it reflected well or poorly on them. So when Barbara had introduced Jessica to her parents, Hans and Clara, Jessica had felt not only awkward, but alarmed.

In general, in Jessica's experience, it was better to be unremarkable except in the sense of being perfect. Or as perfect as she could be. A kind of boring ornament – appropriate without being worthy of comment. So observing Barbara interacting with Hans and Clara had been a revelation.

They all cared so *much* about each other. Enough to risk anger or disapproval without ever fearing the other person would just leave. There was a sense of permanence about Barbara's relationship with her parents, which Jessica struggled with at first. Struggled to believe it and then struggled to accept it. Because Hans and Clara didn't restrict their concern and affection for their daughter. They extended it to all the stragglers she brought home. Nestlings fallen from trees, feral cats, a limping aged dog and, eventually, a pregnant homeless classmate.

At first, she had been so uncomfortable taking advantage of the Ulrich's kindness, she had considered finding another solution. Any solution. So she had applied herself to finding one.

Approaching Lynne for help had turned out to be a waste of effort and mortifying to boot. Chris wasn't an option – he was high pretty much all the time and any money he had went to feeding his habit. And it was the off season for tourist businesses on the island, so the usual job options for high school students weren't available yet.

In the end, she resigned herself to staying with the Ulrichs, at least until high school graduation. Hans offered her an after school job at his hardware store. Barbara's big brother, Zack, was planning to take summer courses at UPenn and insisted she use his old room for as long as she needed it. His only request was that she make sure nothing happened to his collection of baseball cards. So Jessica hid them under the thick wool blanket in the chest at the foot of his bed and tried to ignore the sense she was an interloper. A usurper of love, like a cuckoo child tucked into a nest of robins.

CHAPTER 4

BEAR GRASPED THE bone between her molars and wrapped her paws lovingly around the other end of it. A string of drool hung from her lips, and she rolled her eyes upward toward Ronan.

"Enjoying yourself?" He kept his tone mild lest the Bernese Mountain Dog decide it was her responsibility to share. At one year old, Bear tended to be enthusiastic when it came to disgusting stuff. She was a great dog, but any expectations Ronan had entertained of her guarding his Boston apartment had faded by the first week she had lived with him. The best he could hope for in the event of a burglar was death by licking. Not that there was much risk of that on the island.

He left her happily gnawing in front of Max and Aidy's fireplace and headed out to the Demerest Cove Diner. He hoped the rain cleared up before he had to take the ferry to Boston that afternoon. A sodden Bernese Mountain Dog in a closed ferry cabin was never a fun thing. The cold rain came down in sheets. May in New England didn't count as spring. Sometimes even June didn't. So it was the perfect day to indulge in a nostalgic visit to his old high school haunt. But when he entered the cramped entryway he stopped midstride. It would have been warm and pleasant in the cozy little place if it hadn't been for the chilling glare he was being treated to by Candy Piers. What were the odds?

The aisle was too narrow to squeeze by her, but he refused to step back out into the rain so she could mince past him to leave. Instead he stepped closer and just before he reached her, he slid into a booth. She strode by him without a word and closed the door quietly behind her as she left.

As he settled into his seat, it occurred to him Candy had flinched as he approached. She had made an effort to hide it, but he had seen the flicker of fear in her eyes. Which struck him as odd. If anyone should be flinching it should be him.

He had certainly never given her cause to fear him. The idea she might have had reason to fear men in general chilled him. He would cheerfully forgo ever seeing Candy again, but that didn't mean he wished her harm. Even when he was in the worst pain of heartbreak, he had never wanted to see her suffer. He had just wanted the pain to stop.

And he had managed to accomplish that. Time helped. Other women too. Although there had never been anyone who had touched his heart in quite the same way Candy had. He had made a point of putting his yearning for her behind him by labeling what he had felt for her puppy love. But last night, as he had struggled to get her out of his head, he had wondered whether if perhaps he hadn't been as effective at eradicating her from his heart as he had thought.

She hadn't changed much. The slim, delicate girl he remembered had morphed into a sturdy woman with a steady gaze. The curtain of long blonde hair was gone now, replaced by a blunt shoulder length cut. And there were faint lines at the corners of her brown eyes and her mouth. He liked them. He had always enjoyed looking at her face, but those lines added interest.

Della, the waitress, slapped a menu on the table and gestured with the coffee pot she held in her other hand. Startled, he looked up and nodded. She poured exactly enough to slop over the edge of the cup into the saucer. Della had never forgiven him for the one time he had accidentally spilled a pitcher of pancake syrup on the bench of a booth while trying to impress some high school classmates after late night bowling. As far as he could tell, that particular booth cushion had never been cleaned. So she couldn't have personally spent a lot of time repairing the damage. But she had never gotten over it. Just to annoy her, he ordered pancakes. With extra syrup.

The wind slapped a sheet of rain against the side of the diner. He leaned close to the coffee cup and slurped enough to allow him to lift it without spilling. It was strange being home, or as close to home as he could reasonably expect to get. Life had changed so much since he had been a boy on the island. In some ways, for the better. Certainly, financially. Sanderson Hospitality was in the black, and he and his brothers had put themselves on the payroll. Not that he expected to ever be as wealthy as Candy had been.

He wondered if Candy worked for a living. Not that it mattered. She had a trust fund to fall back on. The sort of cushion people like Ronan could only dream about. For a moment he replayed the ride to her son's school, the worn collar on the boy's shirt, the slightly too short trousers. Candy had been a clotheshorse as a teen. But Ronan didn't know many teens any more. Maybe worn ill-fitting clothing was a style. Either that, or Candy was a negligent parent. But everything he remembered about her argued against it. Or maybe he had misread her about that too. There seemed to be no end to his ability to misread people.

He sighed and picked up his fork. He was halfway through his drenched pancakes when the door behind him opened, letting in a gust of rain-laden wind. Turning at the squelching sound, he repressed a grin. Candy dripped from head to toe and looked equal parts miserable and furious.

"The food's good here. But it's not *that* good," he said.

Her eyes narrowed.

"Shut. Up. I couldn't find my purse so I had to retrace my steps. And I have a meeting in half an hour, so there isn't time to go home and change."

She stomped past him and stared accusingly at the table in the booth in the far corner. A purse slouched next to the sugar packet rack. Turning suddenly, she glared at him.

"Why didn't you tell me my purse was here?"

A number of possible responses flitted through his mind. But none seemed sufficiently deflating. He stood, prepared to give her a piece of his mind, but stopped mid-breath. She had wrapped her arms around herself in a vain attempt to get warm. But her teeth were chattering. Her sodden hair dripped, and he didn't like the blue tinge to her lips.

"Della. A towel and some hot coffee, please."

"I don't need your help." Candy's dismissal was undermined by a great shudder.

Della, who specialized in exceptionally slow service, had either seen the problem for herself or leaped into action at his request. He preferred to think it was the latter. Or maybe she just had a soft spot for Candy. There must be some people who hadn't been burned by Candy Piers.

"Thanks, Della." Candy smiled grimly through her shivers and took the handful of bar towels. "I guess it's wetter out than I thought."

"You want the coffee on your regular table?" Della cast Ronan a suspicious look as she spoke. Okay, then. Still not a favorite with Della.

Candy sighed and gestured at Ronan's booth.

"No. Here's fine. And thanks."

Della plopped the mug onto the table across from Ronan and gave him a hard look before shuffling back to the kitchen.

"I owe you an apology," Candy said. "It's not your fault I forgot my purse. I'm just having a bad week."

She wriggled out of her jacket and draped it over the edge of the booth. Her blouse was damp too, although not so wet that it clung to her. A part of him, the stupid part, was sorry about that. He slid back into his seat, keeping his eyes on her face. But that wasn't much better because she was sipping the coffee and he couldn't help noticing her lips. She had always worn lip gloss but now she didn't. It was a surprisingly vulnerable look for Candy. At least for the Candy he remembered.

She wrapped her hands around the mug with a sigh. Her hands shook and when she sipped, some of the liquid slopped over her fingers onto the table. He shoved a few of his napkins over to her and fingered the pen in his pocket. "How was Liam's concert?"

So she told Ronan about Liam's concert and about how the music teacher had made a point of talking to her about sending Liam to regionals. Ronan laughed at her description of the painful grimaces on the parents' faces when the string section started on the wrong page and the entire orchestra ground to a confused halt. He had forgotten how good she was at telling stories. And how she managed to poke gentle fun at people without being in the least hurtful.

"You're still drawing, I see," she said.

He looked at his hands blankly. It slipped by him, occasionally, this visceral need to draw.

"Just a doodle," he said. He moved to crumple up the napkin, but she plucked it away and cupped it protectively in her hand.

"Don't," she said.

"Why? What do you want it for?"

She shrugged but didn't offer it back to him. "I'll give it to Liam. He thinks you're cool."

That seemed fair since it was a sketch of Liam and his tuba. Although now that she had the napkin, he wanted to take it back to work on it a bit more. There was something not quite right about the background. And the tuba was probably inaccurate.

"What about you?" she asked. "Are you planning anything fun besides visiting family?"

"I'm leaving this morning," he said. "I have to get back to my job."

There was a flicker of something in her eyes, an easing of her shoulders. The idea that she might be relieved to hear he was leaving was irritating in ways he didn't choose to explore at the moment.

"I'll be back in town soon. I'm thinking of doing some fishing. I haven't done that since high school." The lie popped out. He disliked fishing, but it was the first activity that came to mind. He just wanted the satisfaction of seeing the corners of her mouth tighten again. There were a lot of things he hadn't done since high school. Sneaking into the drive-in movie theater, for instance. He used to dream of going there with Candy once he could drive. Hadn't happened then. Wasn't going to happen now. Or ever.

"So. Who are you meeting, once you are dry again?"

She flushed. And he felt like kicking himself. Candy had always enjoyed jewelry. If she had a reason to wear a ring she would wear it, so she wasn't married. Still, given her reaction, it would be a man she was meeting.

He couldn't put himself through this again. He would honor his promise to Liam, but then he would stay far away from Candy Piers. And to be fair, it wouldn't be difficult. She seemed pretty determined to keep him at an arm's length. Which just went to show she hadn't changed.

Candy knew exactly what was good for her. And it wasn't Ronan. As it happened, he agreed with her assessment, which meant he should have no difficulty keeping a polite distance between them. All he had to do was make sure she never caught a glimpse of his heart. Reaching for his wallet, he tucked an ample sum under his mug before slinging his jacket over his shoulders and striding out into the rain. The ferry would leave shortly and he needed to be on it.

CHAPTER 5

RONAN STARED AT the blinking light on the copy machine with a sense of righteous indignation. He had followed every request, lifting and pulling levers and drawers, and he was quite sure he had removed every bit of the offending piece of paper. The display no longer flashed *Misfeed*. This time it read, *Replace Waste Toner Bottle*.

Not fair. He rooted around in the cabinet under the copier, hauling out several boxes of obscure copier related items until he found one labeled Waste Toner Bottle. He glanced at the clock. Fifteen minutes left until the monthly staff meeting. Plenty of time to make copies of the agenda.

He leaned forward and reached far into the machine with both hands to get a better grip on the brimming container of used toner and tugged. It didn't move. Maybe if he was more forceful – experimentally, he gave the thing a little twist. The sense someone was behind him came just a little too late.

"Guess who?" Hands clamped over Ronan's eyes.

"Aaargh!"

Startled, he staggered back, one hand grasping the liberated waste toner bottle as he flailed. The hands over his eyes released, but to his surprise the room remained dark. Or at least some of it did. He jerked around, anger replacing his panic, and his heart sank. Ashleigh. Of course.

Ashleigh's long ringlets and slender physique were complemented by a sweet if somewhat spoiled personality. But from the day Ronan had been introduced to his boss's daughter, she had been completely besotted with him. Ashleigh hovered over his shoulder as he worked, she laughed extra loud at his jokes. Most uncomfortable of all, she had begun touching him in passing. Awkward, to say the least.

She was twenty three, seven years younger than him. With any luck, she would fall in love with someone closer to her own age and would move on. He hoped so. Because he was pretty sure the looks his coworkers had been giving him were more warning than approval. They didn't have to worry.

The last thing he needed was to lose his first job because the boss's daughter didn't know how to take no for an answer.

So he tried to walk a careful line between cordial and distant. But now he had covered Ashleigh's outfit, hair and every available inch of her skin with a fine layer of black inky dust. Someone had left a box of tissues on a table next to the copier. He grabbed a handful and headed toward Ashleigh, but she shook her head, her mouth opening and closing silently as she backed away. Tears streaked white through the inky mess on her cheeks and dripped onto the once pale pink fabric of her dress.

They spoke at the same time.

"It's my fault."

"I'm sorry."

She fled. A thin cloud of ink dust settled in her wake. It was her fault, but that didn't matter. Ronan still could end up losing his job over her behavior. All it would take would be one word of complaint to her father and the job would be gone. A weird sense of relief whispered at the thought. He tamped it down firmly.

A position at MacAllen Design was the ultimate prize for a new graduate with a master's in architecture. But any illusions Ronan had about supportive coworkers were scuttled on his first day at work when he had found his new desk barren except for the cardboard backing of an exhausted sketch tablet, an eraser-less pencil and a broken pair of scissors.

Ronan's inquiries about how he might access a computer were met with vague shrugs. And no one seemed to know where the key to the supply cabinet was. And then there was the cautionary email at the end of his first week, reminding him he had missed a staff meeting. Since no one had put him on the invitation list, that one was hardly his fault. Still, it had made him look sloppy.

Finally, Keisha had taken pity on him and had "found" the supply cupboard key. Terrance had rolled his eyes but had still helped Ronan load the firm's proprietary software onto his laptop. And in a gesture of not welcome exactly, but a kind of resignation, Phil had removed a portfolio from an adjacent chair one day, allowing Ronan to sit next to him at a weekly staff meeting when it became clear all the rest of the seats were taken.

So Ronan supposed things were going as well as could be expected. Or at least as well as he should be expecting them to go. He had been stupid to have thought the excitement of getting the job would necessarily translate into excitement of *doing* the job. And now, of course, he would be showing up late for the staff meeting. Again. Without proper copies. Again. And this time with ink dust tickling his neck as it slid from his hair down the nape of his neck onto his shirt collar.

Considering how much of the toner had settled on Ashleigh, he guessed there was some remaining on the back of his shirt as well. Maybe he could keep his back to the wall, and no one would notice him. Although it occurred to him he shouldn't lean on the wall because he would leave a silhouette, and people would remember it had been him after he left the room.

To his relief no one seemed to notice his belated arrival to the conference room. Instead, there was a flutter of excitement he had not seen before. Terrance was setting up a projector. Ronan guessed the strangers mingling with the coworkers he knew were from the New York branch of the company. Which meant MacAllen himself would be likely to attend. And that they didn't need copies of the agenda after all. Keisha brushed by him to place a red folder on each seat and gave him a sharp glance.

"Your new look sucks."

"I spilled toner."

"Well, whatever you do, if it's on fabric, don't get it wet. You'll never get the stain out. And don't vacuum it with a regular vacuum – it'll ignite. There's a special vacuum for toner in the closet next to the fax machine. Phil!"

Phil jerked erect at her tone, grabbing at his sketch pad before it slid off his lap.

"Get the toner vacuum and take care of – what's your name, kid?"

"Ronan."

He was pretty sure Phil didn't remember who he was either, but at least the guy winked at him. Ronan trotted after him, remembering what being sent to the principal's office had felt like once, when Emily Pound had tripped him and he had accidentally spilled goldfish water on Mrs. Goldthwaite's shoes in first grade. That hadn't been his fault either. Phil pulled a black case from the cupboard and had the thing assembled with an ease and speed that spoke of long practice.

"Happens pretty often," he said happily.

Ronan nodded gently, trying to dislodge as little of the remaining dust as possible from his scalp.

"The copy machine has problems?"

Phil edged a bookcase away from the wall to reach an outlet. "Hates new people. Shirt's not too bad. It's mostly in your hair."

To give Phil credit, he was thorough and surprisingly gentle. Which went a little way toward making up for the fact that Ronan's head was being vacuumed when Ian MacAllen strode by on his way to the conference room. At least the process didn't take long and if the back of Ronan's shirt was ruined, most of the damage could be covered by his blazer.

The meeting room was cramped and warm, but Ronan squeezed against the wall behind the last row of chairs and kept his jacket on. When the meeting finally dragged to a close, he purposely mingled with a group of designers filing toward the door. He was a few steps away from freedom when he heard Ashleigh. She stood near her father, inkless and resplendent in a white dress. The only reminder of the incident was her hair, slightly damp and bearing a slight bluish tinge. Maybe she had used the showers in the fitness center.

"That's him, Daddy. Ronan Durrell."

Ian MacAllen turned his head slowly, his eyes piercing under shaggy gray brows. Ronan froze. He was aware of his coworkers in that moment, their faces curious, envious, a little malicious. This could go several ways, he thought. None of them good.

"Humph," MacAllen grunted.

Ronan automatically shook MacAllen's outstretched hand. MacAllen pulled back and stared at his own now inky hand for a moment, shook his head and pulled out a large handkerchief from his pocket.

"Ashleigh says you're brilliant." MacAllen finished scrubbing at his hand. "But your portfolio is skimpy and surprisingly unimaginative."

"Daddy!"

Ronan opened his mouth and shut it again. MacAllen gave him a long look and sighed.

"Fine. Come out to the house on Saturday. We're having a little get-together. You know the address."

Ronan swallowed. This was really happening.

"I do, sir. That is, I can find – thank you."

Ashleigh gave a little hop of excitement and wrapped her arm around her father's.

"I knew you'd like him, Daddy."

"If he works out, I'll like him." He shot a menacing look at Ronan.

"Wear a real suit," he added. "Not that thing."

Ronan sagged in relief and slipped into the men's room to scrub his hands, avoiding the now openly envious gazes of his coworkers. He was tempted to text message his brothers but slid his phone back into his pocket. He might never be able to compensate fully for the way Jock and Max had stepped into a semi-parental role for him when their parents had died, but he was on the verge of being able to pay them back in a small way. He wanted to savor the knowledge in private for a while.

Succeeding at MacAllen would make a real difference financially. But more importantly, it would finally earn Ronan adult status in the family. So maybe he would just wait and see how things worked out with Ian MacAllen before he spread the news around. Because like it or not, Ashleigh was a factor in the equation. Things could go south fast if a guy thought you were fooling with his daughter. Even if you weren't.

CHAPTER 6

RONAN HAD WORRIED his wool suit would be too hot for an outdoor garden party in late May. But as it turned out, men's formal wear was great for hiding in brambles. Less overall damage to the skin. Although it remained to be seen if the same could be said about the suit.

He peered through the brambles and relaxed a fraction. Ashleigh, resplendent in a lacy white party frock, stood far across the great lawn, engaged in animated conversation. At least she wasn't likely to ambush him again. He twitched at the memory and hissed as a thorn scratched his hand.

He considered his options. He had already shaken hands with a bunch of the upper management folks. He had received a cordial if impersonal slap on the back from Ian MacAllen and a nod from the great man's wife. Hiding in the brambles had only become a necessity when he saw Ashleigh heading toward him across the great lawn with a look of determination in her eyes.

He had never properly appreciated the benefit of large urns as garden décor until that moment. They were great for ducking behind. The brambles had come in handy too, despite their thorns. All he had to do now was get to his car without being seen. Slowly, he began backing deeper into the woods, listening with half an ear to the party noises.

Odd.

The party had kicked off with a bagpipe troupe marching through the throng, presumably in honor of the MacAllen's Scottish heritage. Ronan was pretty sure the pipers had packed up once the procession was over, but maybe they had decided to stay for an encore. Because, over the cheerful chatter and the clink of dishes, he now heard a distinct buzzing hum.

He puzzled over that as he worked his way backwards through the thorns. The bagpipes were growing louder now and were surprisingly out of tune. Maybe it was feedback from a speaker system? If he followed the woods along the edge of the great lawn, he should be able to make his way to the parking lot without being seen.

He batted at a particularly aggressive wasp but no sooner had one left than it was replaced by two more. Then another four. Then a group. He turned with the kind of gluey slowness he associated with nightmares, raising his head by degrees until he could see the vast paper globe, teeming with wasps, hanging on a bough far above him.

For a moment it occurred to him this might be some sort of cosmic joke. But there was no question the wasps were unhappy to meet him and growing unhappier by the second. Without pause, he scrambled out of the bramble patch and raced toward the parking lot, skidding between trees and slapping away the pursuing insects as he fled. But stumbling over roots was costing him time and giving the wasps an unfair advantage. He glanced toward the lawn as he ran but decided to keep to the woods.

The wasps seemed to be slowing down, and he thought his weaving through the trees might be confusing them. Until he took what was clearly a wrong turn. Either he had stumbled upon a second nest, or the first one was more populous and organized than he had realized. There was really no choice.

In a burst of speed he tore across the open green space. Ronan had been the slowest on the track team despite Coach Rossi's lectures about motivation. Well, he was motivated now. One glance back told him the wasps had brought reinforcements. The vast in-ground pool lay ahead, its blue waters shimmering and moving slightly in the breeze. He leaped for it and felt the water close over his head with a depth of gratitude he hadn't felt in years.

The water seeped through his trousers and more slowly through the thick wool of the jacket. The shoes would be a dead loss too. He had always hated the tie, which was some consolation. With his last bit of oxygen, Ronan swam into the shadow under the diving board and surfaced cautiously.

The wasps were gone. His relief was tangible. He swam to the edge of the pool and hauled himself up. It occurred to him, it might be difficult to explain why he had jumped in the pool. But when he looked around to do just that, there was no one there.

The great multi-paned windows of the house that faced the lawn were closed, but he could see crowds of partygoers within. The story of their hurried flight from the swarm was marked by a trail of detritus on the once pristine grass — crumpled napkins, an overturned whisky glass, a lone high heeled shoe.

He staggered toward the house. As he climbed the shallow steps to the patio, Ian MacAllen rounded the corner and strode toward him. Ronan felt a wave of relief. MacAllen might be gruff, but he was clearly a caring individual. After all, he loved his daughter.

The big man stopped several yards away, as though to avoid any droplets should Ronan decide to shake himself off like a dog. The game smile Ronan had forced to his lips froze in position.

"You're Durrell, right?"

Ronan nodded stiffly.

"Durrell, you're fired."

CHAPTER 7

JESSICA'S HABIT OF being early for appointments had its down side, especially when it was an appointment she wasn't looking forward to. Now she had fifteen minutes with nothing to do except get more nervous. What if Max hadn't meant the offer of employment to be more than a polite gesture? Or what if Carl had misunderstood altogether?

At least she didn't have to worry about seeing Ronan. Despite his taunt in the diner, there was no way he would be around more than an occasional visit. He had moved on from small time small town Demerest Cove. Last she heard he was working for a big shot architectural firm in Boston. She hadn't noticed a ring, but some people didn't wear them. For all she knew, he was married. Maybe he and his wife had children. Her heart thudded dully at the thought. Irritated, she reached for a magazine but couldn't sink into the avid descriptions of movie stars and their travails.

She closed it and glanced around the great lobby. The Grand had been thoroughly renovated when the Durrell brothers took ownership, but the lobby had been preserved and restored to its original glory with a few modern but necessary touches. As a result, while guests felt at ease in the space, there was an air of past elegance that pervaded the room. She closed her eyes and could almost feel the nerves of debutantes from the 1800's, hear a riff of ragtime from some long ago wedding reception.

She glanced toward the reception desk and caught Jeannine's eye. Jeannine looked away deliberately, first focusing on some paperwork, and then turning away to speak into a phone. The elderly receptionist was a force to be reckoned with, which made the tinge of sympathy in her glance even more worrisome. Jessica rubbed her palms against her slacks.

Maybe there was no point to this exercise, she thought suddenly. She had a list a mile long of things to do before the weekend. The chair rental for Thursday was not going to magically order itself. And Party Harty had dropped its tent installation service as of next month, which meant she would have to find a new supplier. She could hardly expect Carl to put up tents too. She would just reschedule her meeting with Max. She pushed off the couch, revitalized at the thought. And there were receipts and calendar changes to process. Even bookkeeping sounded palatable.

"Ms. Piers." Jeannine's tone had the same no-nonsense impossible to ignore tone Jessica associated with grade school teachers. "Mr. Durrell will see you now."

Jessica swallowed and followed Jeannine's gesture toward a hallway marked Private – Staff Only. It felt as though she were being sent to see the principal. For a moment, she had the ludicrous idea she might simply walk into a broom closet and stay there until Max went home for the day. But the thought of being found in hiding and having to explain herself was mortifying. Not to mention ridiculous.

She was a grown woman with a business of her own. She was here for a business meeting with a peer, or at least a business associate. She should act like it, she decided. She had been in charge of her own life for over a decade now, and she refused to let an old wound make her forget that. There was just something about this meeting that had her hackles up, and despite that she couldn't justify it, she had to admit the feeling was real.

Max stepped into the hall from an open doorway at the end and waved. At least he was smiling. Maybe he would tell her he had been kidding about the idea of working together, and they could both have a good laugh about it. Then she should go home and prepare for a financial meltdown. Which, in fact, she could handle. She certainly had before. It was telling Carl that would be painful. And letting go of her office, which she had been so proud to open.

"Welcome."

Max held the door wider and ushered her into a bright sunny room. His desk faced the bank of windows overlooking the sea, and there was a comfortable seating area nearby.

"Tea?"

"Sorry?"

"Would you like some tea?"

She nodded carefully. He looked related to Ronan in a general way, the jawline and the way one ear stuck out just a little. But now she wondered if he shared any of Ronan's personality traits as well. When she had been close to Ronan, both Jock and Max had been in college and were rarely around. Even when they did come home for holidays and vacations, it wouldn't have occurred to her to spend time with them. College students might be the object of distant admiration but didn't figure into a high school social dynamic. So except for recognizing him well enough to nod to when she passed him on the street, she barely knew the man. Since Max had returned to Demerest Cove, her overall impression had been that he was implacable.

The historical society had been reluctant to permit renovation on The Grand. The Board of Selectman insisted on an environmental impact study before the Durrells and their company, Sanderson Hospitality, could break ground on the Retreat Center. Still, the Retreat Center had opened right on schedule. Even the Department of Public Safety had weighed in, expressing concern about the impact floods of tourists might have on the crime statistics of the island. But no matter the obstacle, Max remained on target and, as far as she could tell, on time with whatever schedule he had set.

It probably didn't hurt that he had settled on the island and married another local, Aidy Jones. Although there too, there had been muttering. Aidy's parents had sold The Grand to Sanderson Hospitality and some of the islanders implied Max was trying to buy his way into what passed for high society on Demerest Cove. Rumors like this didn't seem to bother him, however. Unless they bothered Aidy. Which in itself demonstrated the rumors were untrue.

Jessica had seen Max and Aidy at the annual Business Association fundraiser for the Emergency Fund. She had watched the way Max curved his arm around Aidy as they wandered through the crowded room. Not possessively, protectively. If there was one thing Jessica was certain of it was that Max Durrell was thoroughly and utterly in love with his wife.

But he was also unquestionably a tough and battle tested businessman. So there was no real need for him to be polite. Moon Shell Events was no competition for Sanderson Hospitality, not even in the same league. He could have easily steamrolled right over her, and Carl and no one would have thought badly of him for it. It would have simply been the natural course of business.

She looked up at him. He was frowning.

"You look familiar but I'm not sure why." He snapped his fingers. "You were a friend of Ronan's. In high school."

She nodded, hoping she looked casual, sure those dark intelligent eyes would see through her. But he headed toward the seating area as though it meant nothing. She breathed and wondered whether she was obligated to clarify. It was hard to know sometimes how much truth a person needed to hear. Besides, it wasn't exactly a lie. She and Ronan had been friends. They just hadn't ended that way.

"I made cookies." Max nudged a platter of chocolate cookies toward her. She took a bite and nearly moaned. The crispy outer shell gave way to a chewy center.

"They're amazing!"

"My grandmother's recipe. Aidy was having a hard time keeping food down at the beginning of her pregnancy, and these were one of the few things she could stomach. Now she's hooked."

"Understandably."

Jessica eyed the platter and wondered if taking another would appear unprofessional. She sighed internally as she decided it would.

"I appreciate your taking the time to meet with me," she began. "I'm guessing you're pretty busy with your new venture. Are you having any push back from the town?"

"I think the event space will come together on schedule. And when it does, I expect bookings to ramp up quickly. That's why I hope you'll consider being head of the team running the new facility. You and Carl have exactly what we need in terms of experience and connections. And I expect to make it worth your while."

Jessica felt numb as he outlined a salary package with benefits. It was more than she had anticipated. Moon Shell Events was in the black occasionally, but the income depended on the time of year and on the economy. If she took Max's offer she would be able to set aside money for a college fund. Maybe even send Liam to music camp. Liam hadn't asked, of course – he knew the tuition was out of reach. But she knew from the well-thumbed pamphlet she had found under his pillow, he yearned to go.

She cleared her throat. "Moon Shell Events has committed to running events through the summer. How soon would you need me to start?"

"I'm actually hoping you both could begin Wednesday. I can assign a couple employees from The Grand to work under Carl until Moon Shell Events' commitments have been met. The proceeds of those events will be yours and his, naturally. But I will need you and your input in our offices at the Retreat Center as soon as possible."

She reached for her tea and took a sip, her mind racing. Carl would go for it. Liam would be thrilled. She felt as though she were standing at the edge of something wonderful. Something she probably didn't deserve and would end up paying for later. But just for the moment, the sense of anticipation was delicious.

"Okay. Yes."

"Excellent." Max clapped his hands together and rose. He strode to his desk and selected a file. "Forms for you and Carl. The sooner you get them back to Jeannine, the sooner you'll be on payroll."

She took the file and leafed through it to cover her discomfort. He had been awfully sure she would say yes. He hadn't been playing her, exactly. But it was odd to have been so expertly maneuvered.

"How did you know I'd say yes?" she blurted it out despite herself.

"I didn't." He grinned. "But I'd hoped you would. Most of business, I find, is being prepared to take a good opportunity when it presents itself."

"So this was a kind of test. You wanted to see if I would bite. And I did."

"Nope. I saw an opportunity and I took it. You have exactly the skill set I'm looking for."

She felt a rush of joy. Respect was a rare pleasure these days.

CHAPTER 8

"**DON'T GET ME** wrong," Max said, kicking a stick off the path. "I'm always glad to see you and you know you're always welcome to visit. But why are you here?"

It was a good question and one Ronan wasn't willing to examine too closely. There was the having gotten fired thing, of course. And maybe that was the most obvious reason. But that wasn't what Max was asking. Because where Ronan should have been was back in Boston, filling out job applications and going to interviews.

He hoped he wasn't having some kind of crisis of faith about what he wanted to do with his career. He had friends who had changed their minds mid-stride, but he couldn't afford the luxury. He was in debt up to his nose with student loans. Maybe it was more of an existential angst sort of thing. He couldn't very well tell Max he was at sea about where he fit into the universe. Max was never at sea about anything. And their older brother Jock always seemed certain when it came to major life decisions.

"I needed some time to decompress. Being fired kind of took the wind out of me. I think between finishing school and dealing with the new job, my brain got fried. Plus I missed you and Aidy."

Max gave him a sharp look but didn't probe. "It's unfortunate for MacAllen he fired you. His loss. The company is missing out on something extraordinary. But as it happens we could use your skills this month," he said.

"Oh?" Ronan didn't want to sound too eager. After all he had just complained about being mentally exhausted. But his heart hummed at the thought of a new project. A project all his own. Which in and of itself was a kind of relief. He had wondered, given how much he had disliked working at MacAllen Design, whether he had made a terrible mistake pursuing architecture. The combination of guilt and embarrassment had been weighing on him.

But if he could throw himself into an architectural project that was meaningful and important to him, he would be able to bury that nagging sense of incompleteness. That persistent whisper he must not listen to. Because when Ronan had read the story of Jason and the Argonauts in his classics course in college, he had understood exactly why the song of the Sirens had been so dangerous.

It wasn't because the Sirens were so beautiful. Nor even because their voices were so alluring. It was because they sang to each man of his own heart's desire. So even though Jason in the myth had made his men tie him to the mast as his ship neared the Sirens, while prudently making sure the crew blocked their own ears so they could not hear, the song itself drove him nearly mad. Because once he had understood what he truly desired, needed, all the gold in the world would not be enough. Ronan shook his head and forced himself to pay attention to his brother.

"Arno Gunderson, the designer you recommended for the event space and healing garden project bowed out last month," Max said. "So we've put the whole project on hold temporarily. But the town permits are time limited, and I'm concerned about pushing the window on them. It's always a challenge getting support from the Board of Selectman, and any delay allows naysayers to come up with more arguments against. But now you're here and available, we may be able to meet our deadline after all."

"Do you have the blueprints?"

"Arno never completed them. And to be honest, I wasn't crazy about the initial sketches, anyway."

Ronan knew about the project of course. The weekly conference call Jock had instituted when the three brothers had first started Sanderson Hospitality had become an unbreakable ritual. This way each brother could report in, and they could all benefit from the ideas that sometimes sprang up when the three of them were shooting the breeze.

Normally, Jock was in charge of legal stuff, property management and the Boston end of things, Max handled The Grand and the Retreat Center on Demerest Cove and Ronan drew up and implemented whatever architectural design was required in either location. But this year, with the challenges of the new job at MacAllen Design, he had felt too stretched to do the event space project justice. Which explained Arno. Until Arno shifted to half-time and moved across the country.

The relief was almost palpable. There was the usual pleasure of being given his head on a large project. But there was also something alluring about having a reason to stay on the island – a thought he didn't want to explore too deeply. Except for Max and Aidy, there wasn't anything holding him here. The few friends he had been close to in school had moved away years ago. Except Candy, of course. But she didn't count.

"I'll start tomorrow. Want me to check in with Barney about his requirements?"

Barney, the longtime chef at The Grand, would oversee the catering end of the operation at the event space. His input would be critical in planning the food service aspect of the venue.

"No. Barney won't be around forever. He's already making noises about retiring. So while you may want to ask for his input about food service areas in the building, I want to keep his focus on our needs at the main hotel dining room as long as possible."

Ronan nodded. "So what's the plan?"

"I've just hired a coordinator for the new venue," Max continued. "You know Jessica Piers – you were friends with her in High School. She runs a small party planning business downtown called Moon Shell Events. She's been subsisting off the townspeople who can't afford to hire The Grand for their receptions and parties. She's bright and dedicated, and I think she'll bring a lot to the job."

Ronan racked his brain. The only Jessica he could recall from High School had been a quiet kid in chemistry class – Jessica Pearson. Not exactly a friend, but a friendly acquaintance. Her grandparents and his had been friends, so she always attended his grandparents' annual Christmas party. She seemed an unlikely bet for a party planner but who knew. He shrugged.

"If you give me her phone number I can call to ask about what sort of office she wants before I start sketching."

"She can give it to you herself. She's starting tomorrow. I want you to work closely with her in designing the entire event space. Jessica has years of experience – her insights would be invaluable."

They strolled on briefly in silence, watching Bear explore the thick undergrowth until the woods gave way to hillocks of grass. The meadow was bounded by a natural outcropping of boulders that marked the edge of the bluff. Beyond it was the sea.

"Nice." Ronan took a moment to inhale the view. It was more than nice. It was a phenomenal location. The only issue would be putting in plumbing since the island's fertile topsoil was often a pleasant cover for thick rock shelving. But he had found ways around that problem for the Retreat Center, and he would find a solution here too.

Ronan closed his eyes and breathed. The mingled scent of sea spray, meadow grass and spring growth was enticing. For a moment he wondered why anyone would ever want to live away from it and its implicit promise. But he lived in the outskirts of Boston now, he reminded himself. And there were lots of advantages to that too. Although, as he took another intoxicating breath, none of them sprang to mind.

"Aidy was thinking the healing garden with a bower here and the event space on the other end of the clearing. But she's not set on it." Max gestured as he spoke.

"Good," Ronan responded quickly. "Because it needs to be the other way around."

Max's lips twitched.

"What?"

Max shook his head gently. "Just the way you said it. As though the land was telling you what to do. Arno wasn't like that, you know."

"Probably not. But maybe he's the smarter one. I can only afford to think this way because you're my brother. In the real world, the client dictates and the architect implements."

"That can't be pleasant." Max stuck his hands in his pockets and frowned at Ronan. "Is that the real reason you're back on the island?"

Ronan shrugged and nudged one of the little grass hillocks with the toe of his sneaker. He had forgotten how incisive Max could be.

"Maybe. But I can't afford to be particular if I want to make a living."

Max stared at the water for a while. "I ever tell you about Sycamore Ridge?"

"No."

"I worked there briefly during graduate school. We had just launched Sanderson Hospitality. You remember — we stretched every dollar so thin you could practically see through it."

Ronan did remember. He and Max had slept on the floor in Jock's living room and had worked two jobs each. His memories of that summer were thick with sadness. Their father had died in May. They had no family left except each other and precious little to live on. Ronan had worked as a supermarket stocker by day, which had given him access to dented boxes and cans to round out their meager pantry, and at night he had waited tables. His brothers had similar schedules.

"The business school had a career center of its own," Max said, "and I snagged a job at this woodworking company in Athol. Hell of a drive, but the pay was good. It was a family run business, and I was only there as a temp, but I ended up meeting most all of the family members one way or another. Meanest bunch of people I ever met."

He shook his head.

"Every one of them worked for the company their whole life, and not one of them had chosen it. Instead, they let their father, the founder of the company, make the choice for them. They had money, but they were miserable to the core, and it showed in everything they did. It was a good lesson for me. I didn't want that, and neither should you."

Ronan blinked and stared at the ocean too. Max wasn't much into displays of emotion, so sniveling was definitely out.

"I see your point," Ronan said finally. "I just don't see how it's possible to do what I want, whatever that is, and still manage to fit into the regular working world."

"Welcome to adulthood," Max said, slapping him on the shoulder. "Turns out no one knows what they're doing. We're all just bumbling along trying to keep our heads above water. So you might as well find out what you want to do and do it. Because there isn't any extra security in doing what you don't love."

Fine for him to say, Ronan thought sourly. And it would be different if that was how Max had lived his own life. But in fact, both Jock and Max had walked away from their dreams to meet family responsibilities. It was what a Durrell did. And now it was his turn. That was, if they let him do it.

CHAPTER 9

JESSICA DITHERED BETWEEN outfits, finally settling on a black pantsuit and an ivory blouse. It wasn't exactly a fashion statement, but she wasn't exactly sure what this new position called for. And besides, the suit was a little like armor. Especially when she added a short string of pearls. It was cloudy but rain wasn't forecast until that night. This was good since her raincoat was embarrassingly shabby. But as she drove toward The Grand, fat raindrops began plopping on her windshield. Figured.

She had assumed she would be working out of the old hotel until the event space was ready for business. But Thomas, the doorman, handed her an umbrella and directed her toward a wooded path he said would lead her to the Retreat Center.

The paved walkway had probably once been a footpath. It wound around thickets and between trees until all she could hear was the drip of raindrops on new leaves above and on the thick matting of old leaves below. She stopped a moment and closed her eyes so she could concentrate properly on the damp spicy smell.

"Bear!"

Her eyes sprang open too late to process what she was seeing. A small bear hurtled determinedly toward her. Jessica staggered backwards and stumbled off the path just as the bear's head intersected with her stomach.

In the moment it took to catch her breath, Jessica realized three things. She was staring up at the leafy canopy. Her entire back was cold and wet. The animal straddling her wasn't a bear. The dog looked down at her face with interest and leaned forward to lap at it with its broad tongue. She pushed at its broad shoulders and managed to shove the dog off her, but the big animal seemed to feel this was an invitation to play and lunged forward again, knocking Jessica back into the mud.

"Bear! Off!"

Immediately, if reluctantly, the dog backed off and sat neatly on the path, wagging its mighty tail proudly.

"I'm so sorry. Are you hurt?"

She looked up at the concerned blue eyes and thought she might die. Now. It would be preferable to speaking with him, to letting him haul her up from the mud with his out-stretched hand. She turned away and scrambled to her feet, keeping as much distance between them as she could manage.

"Candy."

He said it flatly with an air of resignation that so nearly mirrored her own reaction, she almost laughed. At least they could agree on mutual distaste. She took a futile swipe at her mud-encrusted clothing before giving up. The umbrella was a mangled mess.

"Ronan. What are you doing here?"

"I could ask the same thing."

"I'm here to work. Or at least I was. I'm not going to make much of an impression on the first day of my new job looking like this."

"Job? Max and Aidy didn't tell me you work here." He scowled and yanked a leash from his pocket, clipping it to the dog's collar.

She gritted her teeth. "I didn't work here until today. What part of *first day* do you not understand?"

He shook his head irritably. "What is it you do exactly?"

"I'm the coordinator for the new event space."

"No you aren't."

A chill crept up her spine. He sounded quite sure. Worse, he looked it. Ronan had worn that determined expression when he'd wanted to take an art class in sophomore year. Budget cuts meant art wasn't offered after freshman year. But Ronan had pulled out the big guns, writing letters to the school board and even pleading with the school superinten-dent until he got his way. He had no power then, but still, he had managed to bend the world to his needs.

She stepped closer. "Didn't Max tell you he hired me?"

"He told me he hired Jessica Pearson from High School." There was a grimness to his tone that suggested he would be broaching the topic with Max the moment the opportunity arose. She let go the breath she had been holding. "He meant me. Jessica Piers. I go by my middle name now. When I started my event planning business my name got in the way. I kept getting calls from people who assumed Moon Shell Events was selling escort services or at the very least spicy party entertainment."

He snorted. "Awkward."

"No kidding. Carl thought it was hilarious. Me, not so much."

"You should have told me."

"Why? I figured, well, I hoped, I wouldn't see you again. So what would be the point?"

"You kept your last name."

She shrugged. "It's not as though I had a reason to change it. I never married. You?"

"No. But I'm surprised you didn't. I assumed you would be Mrs. Chris Mullin by now."

"No."

"And Carl is?"

"My employee. Or at least he was until Max hired him."

An odd look crossed his face. Almost like relief. Which made no sense at all. She shivered. He rolled his eyes and pulled off his jacket, wrapping it roughly around her shoulders.

"Come on." He grumbled as he stomped off toward the Retreat Center, Bear frolicking by his side. She glared at his back but tugged the jacket over her arms before trotting after him. It was warm from the heat of his body, and she was grateful for it. She wasn't proud that she was equally pleased at the knowledge the mud dripping down her outfit was now also coating the lining of his jacket. Not nice to be vindictive, she chided herself.

"What are you doing on the island, Ronan? I had the impression you were working in Boston. Are you on vacation?"

"No."

"Oh." She forced her shoulders to relax. She could do this. She could make small talk, at least until she could get away from Ronan. If there was one thing her mother had taught her, it was how to focus a conversation on insignificant things. It was the only kind of talk Cookie engaged in. She pretended to concentrate on avoiding low hanging branches as she thought frantically. It was none of her business, but she had to know. "So are you living here on the island now?"

Her heart sank at the thought. But there was a little tremor of hope too. Which was a problem. Wanting Ronan was destructive and dangerous. And it was unfair of him to re-enter the safe predictable world she had managed to fashion after he left the first time. The least he could do was stay away.

"Not a chance," he growled. "I'm just here to design the new garden and event space. I thought I would stay through the construction phase too. But if you're involved, I'll leave just as soon as I have the designs finalized."

She breathed out her relief silently. She could cope with a limited amount of Ronan if that was the price she had to pay to keep her new job. Because she wasn't going to let her past interfere with Liam's future any more than it already had. And Ronan was definitely in the past.

CANDY HAD THAT supercilious look again, that "someone smells and it isn't me" wrinkle to her nose. Ronan wondered whether he should just tell Max he would phone it in. He already had the measurements for the garden and the building sites and could come up with a reasonable blueprint back home in Boston while he looked for a new job. But as he strode under the dripping branches, his conscience twinged.

He didn't owe Candy anything, but he hadn't come to the island to destroy her either. He remembered the quiet terror he had felt in the beginning days of Sanderson Hospitality. There had been no safety net for him and his brothers. Candy was in no danger of a straight ramen diet, but still.

He didn't want to imply to Max she didn't play well with others. She for sure didn't play well with Ronan, but Ronan was free to leave the island once he met his obligations to Max and Aidy. If he pushed it, maybe he could even complete the blueprints in a week and a half. Ten days. He could do ten days with the ice queen.

He glanced back at her under the guise of checking Bear for a burr. Mud streaked her face and caked her hair. If that was what she looked like from the front, he could only imagine what she looked like from the back. If he didn't dislike her so much, and for good reason, he reminded himself grimly, he would have felt sorry for her. She trotted along gamely, a determined set to her jaw. It was hard not to admire her for that.

He stopped at the clearing. He always allowed himself to do so just for a moment. The Retreat Center and the cabins that surrounded the great meadow were all his design. He looked back at Candy over his shoulder and then moved to the side. He thought she would simply walk past but she stopped next to him.

"Wow."

"Thanks."

"I meant *Wow, what a beautiful building.*"

"And again. Thanks."

"That was you?" There was surprise there and maybe a little grudging respect. "You designed it?"

"Yep. And Max and Aidy's house too."

She nodded. "You got your dream. I'm glad," she added. "You worked hard for it."

"I'm surprised you remember."

She shot a sharp look at him. "Of course I remember. You never went anywhere without those little pencil stubs in your pockets. No piece of paper, no matter how humble, was safe."

"Definitely a misfit." He shoved his hands in his pockets.

She shook her head. "Not a misfit. Brilliant. Everyone knew it too."

"Not so brilliant now," he said lightly. "A person with real brains wouldn't be standing out here in the rain."

"Want your coat back?"

He looked pointedly at a smear of clay on the lapel. "Nope."

She threw her hands up in exasperation and clomped off toward the main building. If the back of her pants were any measure, his jacket was probably a dead loss. On the other hand, watching her as she marched away almost made it worth it. Only Candy could make her backside look as annoyed as her front. He had forgotten how much fun it had been to tick her off. Maybe the next few days wouldn't be so bad after all. He followed her, feeling slightly cheered.

CHAPTER 10

IF CANDY HADN'T still sported a tiny smudge of mud on her forehead, Ronan would have thought he had imagined the entire incident. Her hair, freshly combed, curled at the edges from its drenching, and she had replaced her destroyed outfit with a dress borrowed from Aidy's closet. The frock probably had been in style in the forties. The cut looked surprisingly good on her. Edgy but flattering. Very Lauren Bacall.

Ronan turned his focus back to Bear who required more toweling before she could qualify as muddy. He rose slowly and rubbed his hands on his trousers, conscious of his damp, probably rumpled shirt.

"You look like the girl who always spells trouble for the noir detective she visits."

Candy gave him a withering look but didn't respond. Ronan snapped his fingers for Bear and gestured for Candy to accompany him down the hall.

"I've set us up in temporary digs in the conference room. It has a big table and I had a couple desks moved in there too. Obviously, once construction is done, your office will be in the new building."

"Us?" Her eyes narrowed. "Why would we be working together?"

"Because I am designing the facility and gardens you will be functioning out of. Max feels it would be better if you have input in the planning from the ground up."

He tried to keep his tone even, but he couldn't avoid the little spike of resentment. Not at Max. Max couldn't have known there was a conflict because Ronan hadn't been aware of the issue until this morning. But fate had something to answer for. Ronan needed this opportunity to spread his wings one more time before he started applying for more real life jobs and the strictures they included. And it seemed remarkably unfair that he would have to curb this final experience of freedom based on the whims of an entitled, self-centered ex-friend. It wasn't as though she needed the money.

"You don't agree with Max." The challenge was implicit.

"Ours is not to reason why."

"Why not be honest, Ronan? Don't you think you at least owe me that?"

"You want honesty? Fine. I think it's ridiculous." He opened a drawer looking for his pencils and was irritated to find they weren't where he had left them.

"Because?" Her tone was cool, but he noticed her fist was clenched.

Because every time I look at you, I remember. Because I hate the way I react to you. Because I still remember how it felt to run my thumb across your cheek bone and around the curve of your ear. And how you shivered when I did. He slammed the drawer shut and pulled open the next one. Pencils. Someone must have moved them – no, he remembered – he had put them there.

"Because you may have fooled Max into thinking you are a good candidate for this position. But you don't fool me. Max needs employees with a strong work ethic and impeccable honesty. Integrity wouldn't hurt, either, Candy."

"Jessica. I'm not Candy anymore."

He threw his hands up. "No kidding. You're not sweet either. I don't know why I keep making the error."

She stared. "I can't work with you."

He raised a brow. "What's your problem? Am I still too lowbrow for your taste?"

"Of course not," she snapped.

"Then why?"

"Because you hate me."

She stared at him defiantly, daring him to deny it. And for one contrary moment he was tempted to agree with her. But behind the flash of anger in her eyes there was a fleeting moment of fear. He was sorry about that. It would have been easier, simpler, to meet her anger with his own. He tapped a tattoo on the corner of the desk top with a pair of pencils.

"Maybe a little," he admitted.

She puffed a breath out disbelievingly. "Liar. You hate me a lot."

"Don't flatter yourself. I save hating a lot for important things like disease or war. You're not in that league, darling."

"Fine. Then maybe you think of me more like you think of green Jell-O."

He shuddered. He couldn't believe she remembered how much he disliked Jell-O, most particularly the green kind. The way it wriggled on the spoon as if it were alive and slithered down the throat leaving a slug trail of slime in its wake. Even the memory of it was making him queasy.

"Maybe not as much as green Jell-O either," he said. "You're more of a general irritant. Like poison ivy."

"You just can't stand being around a polite person."

"If polite means snobbish, you're right."

"Ucchh. You're impossible. I get the desk near the window."

"No way. Blueprints require lots of space. You get the small, cramped desk."

She rolled her eyes and huffed as she sank into the swivel chair opposite his.

"If I weren't so polite, I'd call you a pig," she muttered.

He leaned closer and sang softly, "Poison Iveeeee, Poison Iveeeee."

JESSICA RUBBED HER eyes and logged out of the computer. It was only her second day at the Retreat Center but the strain of working two jobs was already taking a toll on her. Carl had taken on the bulk of the daytime events, but she couldn't expect him to work around the clock. The Freedman's engagement party last night had lasted at least two hours longer than scheduled.

"You look exhausted," Ronan said.

He was observant. She had forgotten how much so. Maintaining an energetic façade couldn't make up for the shadows under her eyes.

She sat a little straighter and tried to look awake. "I'm sorry. I had a late night."

"Hard to have a nightlife on the island. But I guess if anyone could find one, it would be you."

Jerk. She waited a beat to make sure she hadn't actually said it. "I won't just abandon my clients. They trusted me to run their events and I'm keeping that promise."

"I thought Max was making sure Carl had extra help during the transition."

"He is. He did. And I can't thank him enough. But extra help is still inexperienced help. I still need to coordinate and make sure everything runs smoothly."

"You should have told me." Ronan frowned. "I would have sent you home at noon. You should take time off if you are working nights."

"Not necessary. Really. I'll be fine." She watched him warily.

Ronan fiddled with his pen for a moment and then raised his gaze to hers. He studied her for a moment before speaking. "What's your problem?"

She wasn't prepared for the wave of fury that washed over her. Without thinking, she rose to her feet, fists clenched. "You really want to know what my problem is? You. I should never have accepted Max's offer, and I wouldn't have if I had known I would be working with you. But once I did know, I should have backed out."

"Is this about how I hate you again? Because I have to admit, some of that has faded into a dull distaste."

She didn't smile. "As Liam would say, not everything is about you. It's not simply that we don't get along. It's that I need this job. I hate needing it, but I do."

He gave her a puzzled look. "And you'll succeed at it. You're good at what you do. Max is lucky he hired you."

"As long as he continues to feel that way, I have income. But he is your brother. And his allegiance is to you." She stopped talking, her pulse drumming in her ears as she watched him follow the idea to its natural conclusion.

Ronan glared at her. "You can't be serious. I don't know whether to be more offended for myself or for Max. You think if I complain about you to Max, he'll fire you. And if you complain about me to Max, he'll also fire you. Is that why you've been so disagreeable this afternoon?"

"Disagreeable? I think I've been downright charming considering I'm likely to be fired. And it'll be your fault."

"That's ridiculous," he snapped. "Max says you have the skills we need. So my personal feelings about you have nothing to do with it."

She raised her hands in a placating gesture. "You asked."

"And you answered," he ground out. "Don't you think there is an element of farce here? If anyone is at risk of being cast away without a second thought, it's me. Remember?"

"That's not how I remember it," she shot back.

"Maybe not. But that's how it was. You were happy to take everything I had to give until you decided I wasn't good enough for you. Need coaching for the history exam? Ronan will do it. Need a backup date for the junior prom just in case your first three options don't work out? Ronan will provide that too. Someone to practice kissing with before the real deal? Ronan's your man. But when it comes to pleasing Mom and Dad, Chris Mullin, head of the football team is the only one who will do."

The memory of his lips brushing hers that one time, tentative, almost apologetic was so clear, so immediate, her lips tingled. She caught herself reaching up to touch the tips of her fingers to them and instead gripped the edges of her chair, digging her nails into the cushion until her knuckles ached. It was better than remembering.

"I'm not like you, Candy, or Jessica, or whatever you want to call yourself now. Maybe you don't remember that about me. You used me until it was no longer convenient. But I don't just throw people away when I move up in the world. Sure you were young. I was too. But I would never have done that to you."

He was standing now and she was too, her fists clenched by her side as she glared up at him.

"No," she snapped. "Of course not. You were Mr. Integrity. You would just wait until your best friend was hanging over the edge of a cliff by her hands and then you would stomp on her fingers before you left. Because that's what you did, Ronan."

She raised her hand to prevent him interrupting.

"And I get it. High school wasn't your forte, but you were going to be a shining star in college. And now I was slated to be the loser who dropped out of academic life to have an unexpected unwanted baby. I wasn't surprised you didn't want to associate with me socially. But I was surprised you left town right after graduation instead of waiting one more month until Liam was born. Especially after I begged you to stay.

"I wasn't asking you to give up all your big plans – I just wanted a little moral support. And that was a reasonable expectation. Because maybe I wasn't your girl friend, but I thought we were friends, at least. I was pregnant, Ronan. At seventeen. My life was falling apart. I was terrified of everything, suddenly. And unlike you, I had no one reliable to turn to."

Ronan blinked. "What about your parents?"

"My parents told me I'd be on my own if I kept the baby. They wanted nothing to do with the embarrassment I was carrying in my womb. They said they would pay for an abortion. Or arrange for an adoption off the island. But I couldn't do it. It wasn't that I had religious scruples. But for the first time in my life I had something more important than myself to fight for. And believe me, I fought. It wasn't easy, but it was worth it."

Ronan sat down heavily. "That's Liam. Chris' son."

She nodded.

He cleared his throat and leaned forward. "I'm not interested in participating in a Whose Life Sucks More contest. You would probably win, primarily because that's your goal. And you have always driven to meet your goals. However –"

He raised a finger.

"Maybe you thought you were being charitable to the new kid. I was a perfect charity project. Motherless. Suddenly poor. A little weird, what with the incessant drawing. I'm surprised you didn't use me later for a college application essay to demonstrate your humanitarian values. Or maybe you just liked having a pet. In either case, you didn't do me any favors by letting me think you were my friend."

The second finger popped up.

"When I found out you were going out with Chris, you told me you had never been in love with me. That you never would be. Because I don't have – what did you call it?" His lips curled. "That mysterious something that made your heart sing."

She cringed at the memory of how his face had frozen when she had said those words and prayed he would stop. But the third finger rose as he continued. She hated the cool calm of his tone.

"Then you had the arrogance to expect me to hang around while you gave birth to Chris Mullin's baby. I don't know, in retrospect, whether it was because you thought I was stupid or a sucker."

The fury that had powered her through the story seemed to have bled away, leaving her feeling oddly empty.

"I didn't think that." Her throat hurt as the words scraped out. "None of it. And I'm sorry I hurt you. But I've never been more lonely in my life than the day I heard you had taken the ferry to Boston."

CHAPTER 11

JESSICA TOOK A bite of her peanut butter sandwich supper and waited for the traffic light to change. Evelyn Gordon's party was scheduled for eight. Because it was a Thursday night, the party wasn't likely to go much beyond eleven. Besides, the birthday girl was turning ninety. This was exactly the sort of event Moon Shell excelled at – intimate and a little funky. And the best part was she would be too busy to think about Ronan. After the past two days, especially after their conversation this afternoon, she needed the break.

Carl had been working overtime since she had started her new job, so she had told him to leave early tonight. Jessica could do the take down at the end of the party without worrying about Liam's homework getting done because Liam was staying at Hans and Clara's house for the evening. Her son was pretty good about school assignments, but he was still human. And he absolutely hated book reports. She smiled at the thought.

Maybe the party would end early and she would be able to bring Liam home for the night after all. Hans and Clara called Liam their bonus grandson and always reminded her he could stay the night if it was more convenient, but she hesitated to take them up on it too often. Partly because she felt guilty imposing, but also because the cottage was lonely without Liam. She would have to adjust when he was away at music camp, she realized uneasily.

She pulled into the small lot on the back side of the big brick building. The car juddered as she twisted the key to turn off the engine. She sat for a moment glaring at the dashboard before pulling out a box of supplies from the trunk. Shoving the driver door shut with her hip, she climbed the cement stairs to the utility door, pausing to beep the car with her remote. Although if someone stole the car, it might be a good thing. She smiled at the thought until it occurred to her a thief might just as easily bring the blasted thing back.

She hadn't been to this particular entry at night before. Whoever had installed the motion sensor light over the door must have made a wiring error because the moment she reached the landing, the bulb went out. She felt for the handle, but it was locked. Of course. Her arms were full of box, so she kicked at the metal door. Another reason for wearing sturdy shoes to work. Not sexy but easier on the feet. It was too early for the band to be here, so Carl should be able to hear her thumping. Unless he was playing the oldies rock and roll he favored. He tended to blast it when he was doing set up.

No luck. Carl should have left the door wedged open. That was their normal procedure. She shifted the box so it was balanced on the rail that surrounded the landing and held it level with one hand while she used the other to pound on the door. There was a scuffling sound on the other side and the door swung open suddenly.

"I've got you now, you little rat."

The determined tone was offset by a weird squalling sound, a muffled thump and a loud "Ouch!"

"Ronan? What on earth are you doing here?"

He was framed by the light pouring out the door. She gaped. A snug T-shirt and well worn jeans accentuated his muscular build. His arms were outstretched, his fingers gripping a squirming yowling tabby cat. Several long scratches on his bare forearms demonstrated the depth of the cat's disapproval.

Ronan scowled. "I hope you have antibiotic ointment in that box. I'm going to need it."

"Sorry. It's just another balloon tank and some back-up balloons. But Carl should have our first aid kit with him. We always bring it just in case. Although cat related injuries aren't as common as burns or splinters. How on earth did this happen?"

She held the door open as he stomped down the stairs and put the cat down near a hedge. For a moment the cat appeared to be considering another run toward the door but to Jessica's relief, it changed its mind.

"Carl insisted on keeping the door wedged open for set up. He said you always do it too. It's a stupid idea."

"Are you saying that's how the cat got in? That's a first."

"As far as you know," he responded darkly.

She snorted and pulled the box into her arms again, holding the door open with her back as she watched him climb the stairs toward her. "You're such a baby."

"That's right, laugh at the wounded guy," he said. But his injured tone was belied by the twitch at the corner of his lips.

"What are you doing here, anyway?"

"Apparently, saving you from feral cats. You're welcome."

She grunted. He looked irritatingly smug. She tucked the box next to the tidy pile of supplies Carl had set up behind the folding screen in the corner and reached for the red emergency knapsack. It was good she had restocked it recently. Maybe the antiseptic was the stinging kind. She unzipped the bulging bag and began rummaging through the contents.

"I was thinking a couple alcohol wipes and a couple bandages. I didn't realize you had an entire survival kit at your disposal."

"This was Liam's idea," she said. "And I've been surprised at how often it has come in handy."

"What's in it?" Ronan stood next to her watching with interest as she rooted around in the bag. She gave up trying to find the first aid kit by feel and starting taking items out of the knapsack, naming them as she did.

"Chef's jacket. It makes you look fresh and clean and it fits over everything," she explained at his mystified expression. "Batteries. Inevitably someone needs one. Flashlight. Nitrile gloves. Because one time – well, you don't want to know."

"I do, actually."

She glanced up at him and her breath caught. He was too close, she thought hazily. Close enough she could feel the puff of his breath on her hair, smell the tang of his sweat. And his lips. She remembered how they would feel, tenderly brushing hers. Across the room, Carl dropped a wineglass. She turned away hastily and reached deeper into the bag.

"It, um, it involved a summer cottage, a July fourth party, and a refrigerator that had been left unplugged but not empty since the previous summer. And, drum roll, please –"

She pulled out the first aid kit but paused mid-motion. Ronan couldn't exactly dress the scratches one handed. If it had been anyone else, she wouldn't have hesitated. But she felt a wave of warmth at the thought of touching his bare forearms. They were muscular, more from frequent use than from a gym. The urge to trace her fingers down the lines of tendons and veins was discomfiting.

"I should probably wash up first," he said.

"Good idea."

She watched him leave the room and sagged with relief. She wasn't sure what was wrong with her these days. Jessica had dated sporadically over the years but pickings on the island were limited. And adding a young son to the mix – well, it complicated things. Most men wanted to start a family fresh, untrammeled by the constant presence of a child they hadn't fathered. She understood the issue in principle. But the application of that principle was hurtful to say the least. Jessica didn't want a relationship with a man who saw Liam as a necessary hurdle.

Liam would grow up and move out. Maybe even marry and have a family of his own someday. And she would not. Because Liam wasn't the only argument for staying single. She had seen firsthand what happened when a parent had divided loyalties. Sometimes in life you had to choose. And she had made her choice.

Leaving the first aid kit on the table, she trotted across the room to let the band members in, reminding them to watch for the cat as they hauled in their equipment. When Evelyn had asked for band music, Jessica had assumed she meant a big band type of sound. Evelyn had been polite but firm. She wanted hardcore punk. It would have been an edgy choice for most people, but for the spitfire ninety year old retired history teacher it somehow felt right.

RONAN HADN'T INTENDED to come to the high school tonight. But he had driven by on his way to Augie's Bistro and had seen Carl yanking open the big windows that lined the cafeteria. Stopping had been fortuitous since Carl was short handed. The extra help Max assigned had called in sick and the tables hadn't even been set up yet. At least the caterer had shown up, but even that had created problems. The open windows were necessary because a pan of hors d'oeuvres had nearly caught fire. And then there had been the cat.

But that was not why he had stopped. He had wanted to see more of Jessica. Apparently it wasn't enough that she irritated him all day long. That in itself was worrisome, since she had done nothing to earn his irritation. She was professional, knowledgeable, polite. If she had been anyone other than Jessica he would have considered her a joy to work with.

He stood in the doorway and watched her. Jessica had always excelled in school, but she hadn't seemed to work too hard at it. There were no excess motions now either, just a kind of grace. Although that seemed to be more a matter of intent and long practice than the sense of entitlement he remembered. She shifted from setting up the band, to solving a catering issue, to catching spots on silverware without pause. It was like watching a shepherdess directing a herd of elephants and somehow managing to get them where she wanted.

Twenty minutes until they opened the doors to guests. He thought he might slip away rather than interfere with her rhythm, but she must have seen him out of the corner of her eye. She stiffened and headed toward him, first aid kit in hand, her expression maddeningly polite. It wasn't fair she was unfazed by him. Because he was certainly aware of her. All the time.

She reached for his arm and for a moment he allowed himself to imagine how it would feel if things were different. If she wanted him. If her touch meant more than the simple, slightly rushed consideration a school nurse would have offered.

"Jessica, we're short on vases."

She froze and turned to look over her shoulder. "Nothing you can use in the kitchen, Carl?"

Carl shrugged and shook his head.

She thought for a moment before saying, "Do that thing we did for the Donnelly reception."

Ronan's gratitude to Carl for having broken his train of thought washed over him like a wave. It was okay to be a fool once. Everyone did that. But he refused to be a fool twice. He kept his tone casual. "What did you do for the Donnelly reception?"

She used her teeth to tear off the top of an antibiotic pouch and grabbed his wrist.

"Put a flower on each plate. Hold still."

"Very efficient."

"Yeah, it's amazing how work-arounds sometimes look like inspiration."

"Isn't most inspiration a work-around?"

"I guess." She smoothed the last bandage into place and crumpled the paper wrappers into a ball. "Kind of puts Michelangelo into perspective, doesn't it?"

He grinned. He had missed this – the quick banter that morphed from funny to serious and back again without a hitch. The impatient way she tucked wayward strands of hair behind her left ear. The flicker of challenge in her eyes.

And despite that challenge there was a kind of restfulness in knowing she was only interested, if she was interested at all, in trading words with him. Because there had been no intent in her touch except to fix a problem. Her fingers had been brisk and light in their task without lingering.

"I think you should be all set now. And I really appreciate your helping Carl."

Anyone who didn't know Jessica as well as he did would have said she was being courteous. He knew this was a dismissal and it pissed him off. He had been planning on leaving. There was a burger calling his name at Augie's. And despite the earlier snafus, preparations for the party seemed to be well in hand now. He frowned. "You're understaffed. You'll need help with serving and clean up."

He watched her carefully now. She stood still, like a forest animal taken by surprise. A deer, maybe. Wondering whether it was safe to graze or whether she should flee. Breathing out slowly, she studied the emergency kit in her hands. When she looked up again, the mask was back – that polite distancing he had once admired until he had learned to hate it.

"I'd appreciate that, Ronan."

CHAPTER 12

JESSICA NODDED TO herself quickly and headed toward the stage. The band was testing the sound system, and they were looking for an extension. She refused to look back at Ronan. He looked irritated. Good. Maybe he would leave. She needed him to.

Spending all day with him in the office was do-able. Mainly their conversation was centered on blueprints and building plans. And if, accidentally, she lost focus and found herself noticing the way his shoulders moved when he leaned over to alter a sketch, at least she managed to keep it to herself.

"Fifteen minutes," Carl called out.

She scanned the room carefully. Guests to parties often arrived early, so a fifteen minute warning was actually a five minute warning. But at least on the surface everything looked ready. The caterer peeped out from the kitchen and gave her a thumbs up.

She could do this. She just had to avoid Ronan, which would be easy since he was probably going to stay away from her too. That should have made her feel better, but there was a lump in her throat she couldn't explain.

The next two hours were a blur of wrangling guests, serving dinner, clearing and setting out a dessert bar. She caught glimpses of Ronan, snapshots. He wove between chairs balancing a tray laden with loaded plates with an expertise he could only have developed working as a waiter. If conversation was flagging at a table, his quick wit and brilliant smile was enough to spark laughter again. He even managed to get people dancing by escorting Evelyn to the dance floor for an energetic bout of flailing to the band's take on the Sex Pistols' "Anarchy in the UK."

By ten thirty the last guest had drifted off and the band had nearly finished packing up. The caterer was long gone, having promised to drop off the remaining food to Evelyn's house in the morning. Despite his perfunctory protest, Carl was gone too. They always split duties and he had done most of the set up so it was only fair she should do the take down. It shouldn't have been a problem, and it wouldn't have been if Max's two extras hadn't come down with the flu.

She should have known better than to schedule an event of this size on a Thursday. High school would be in session first thing in the morning and the cafeteria would have to be ready for use by then. Of course, at the time she had accepted the booking, Moon Shell Events had been her only job.

Ronan was nowhere to be seen, which was hardly his fault – she had gone out of her way to make him feel unwelcome. And that had been unfair of her. Ungrateful, really. She looked at the mess and her eyes prickled with tears. Stupid emotional jags. She was tired was all.

She reached for the nearest kitchen trolley and yanked it closer. One of the wheels was out of line so she dragged more than wheeled it to the nearest table. Most of the dishes were already air drying in the kitchen, but there were wineglasses to be dealt with along with a few remaining lone pieces of china and cutlery. And the linens, of course.

She had cleared three tables when she heard static. Carl's boom box was still tucked into the corner near the screen, and Ronan was crouched in front of it. He fiddled with it for a moment, settling on a country and western classics station. Then he rose and walked toward her.

"I thought you had left." Hastily she placed her handful of cutlery onto the cart and rubbed her hands against the worn fabric of her jeans.

"I said I would stay," he said, stepping closer.

"Why?" she whispered. Her throat was tight.

"Because you drive me crazy. And maybe because I miss being your friend."

He was too close. She moved her feet inch by inch backward but found herself blocked by a table.

"And because of this." He reached toward her face and rubbed his thumb gently against the tears that had spilled over onto her cheeks. "Don't cry."

She flinched reflexively as he pulled her close but, to her relief, he didn't try to kiss her. Instead he wrapped his arms around her and swayed to the music. It was a ballad, something about a doomed bandit named Pancho. It shouldn't have been soothing, but it was.

"Why are country songs so sad?"

"They're not all 'My Mom Stole My Truck And Ran Over My Dog,' but I know what you mean." He turned her out and then in again.

"Maybe it's an opposites thing. Like drinking hot tea in summer because you think it will cool you down."

"Or maybe songwriters are just good at putting feelings into words. Why are you sad?"

"I'm not."

"Liar."

The song ended and it was a perfect opportunity for her to step away, to gently remove his hand from her back, to make it clear he had caught her in a moment of unaccustomed weakness that would not recur. That was exactly what she should do. And she would have, she assured herself, if the next song hadn't begun. He grinned and pulled her close, quickening his pace.

They stomped and turned, sashaying across the littered dance floor until she called a halt, leaning over to pant. She twisted to look up at him and was relieved to see he was equally red faced and out of breath. At least she wasn't the only one who was out of shape when it came to dancing.

She stood straight again and paused at the unfamiliar sensation. It took a moment to identify it, which in itself was disturbing. It had been so long since she'd had fun, she hadn't even recognized the feeling. She couldn't remember the last time she had been out of breath and enjoyed it. Probably high school.

"Pretty fancy moves, Ronan. Mr. Chin would be proud."

"Whatever happened to him? He's not still teaching ballroom dance classes to reluctant middle school kids, is he?"

"You bet. Seventh graders all take it. Liam already had an introductory class Mr. Chin gives the sixth grade."

"What's he – seventy?"

"Seventy-three. And he still doesn't take any crap from the kids."

"Can I tell you a secret?"

She smiled up at him. "Go for it. Who am I going to tell?"

"I was terrified of him."

She chortled. "He was shorter than I was. I probably could have taken him in a fair fight."

"Yeah, but he was fearsome."

Ronan was grinning down at her now, his eyes twinkling as much, she thought, from the fact that she was laughing as from his own joke. They weren't dancing now so much as swaying. But it didn't matter because the music had faded into some chatter about upcoming events on the monthly events calendar.

She reached up to trace the line on Ronan's cheek. It bracketed his smile and gave him a kindly look. He was kind.

Something in his eyes changed and his smile faded as her fingers left his face. He released her slowly, but with intent, and stepped back.

"We'd better finish cleaning up," he said. "I hear the coworker at your day job is ridiculously demanding."

She rubbed her thumb against her fingertips, not so much to erase the lingering feel of his warm skin as to embed it into the lines of her own. She couldn't have him, she reminded herself fiercely. He wasn't hers. He never had been and he never would be. She had made a stupid decision that ensured it. The fact that her decision had been based on flawed reasoning was no excuse.

"I never asked – how are your parents?"

She rolled her eyes and kept her voice light. "Dad's in California with wife number three. Maybe. Could be number four by now. We're not in touch much. And Mom's in Florida most of the time."

The moment the words were out, she wished she could take them back and edit them. She didn't need pity, didn't want it, especially from Ronan. Mostly her parents and her lack of a meaningful relationship with them was just something she accepted. And normally, when someone asked after them, she reverted to her carefully created, witty version of her family life, delivered in a brittle, dismissive tone. But Ronan's question had caught her off guard. She hoped he hadn't registered the pain that had surged when she spoke of her mother.

"So – that gives you some great vacation destinations, right?"

"Sure." She grabbed a push broom and shoved it savagely across the floor, avoiding his gaze. "It's great."

Ronan stood still watching her for a moment before silently heading toward the step ladder. Carl had gone above and beyond in festooning the walls with streamers and balloons and now they all needed to be taken down. Jessica hated ladder work, but she couldn't bring herself to be glad Ronan was there to do it. Because his being there, his being on the island, was complicating things. She shoved the broom harder, taking out her feelings on the steadily growing pile of refuse.

Life hadn't been easy for him either. But Ronan always seemed to have it together in ways she had never been able to manage. Even when he was angry, it was a clear kind of anger. Not the murky, roiling depths of blackness that infused her when she realized she had to choose between her family and her heart's desire.

Ronan had been her best friend. The one she had invited to join her trick or treating group on the first day he walked into school in sixth grade, shy and nervous at being the only new kid. He helped her see the point of World History in eighth grade. She helped him survive algebra in high school. He had braved the girls' room to hold her hair back when she was vomiting because she had just watched her parents break up. Again. This time, maybe, for good. It had been the kind of friendship everyone hoped for. Full of laughter, shared secrets and caring. Until Ronan walked out on her when she needed him most.

Ronan had been justifiably furious when she had left him for Chris. To some degree, that righteous indignation had been a useful tool for him. She hadn't had the same benefit. But the howling pain she felt when she decided to deprive herself of him had probably been worse than his.

Even now, the agony she had felt when she realized he was truly gone clawed at her. And that same pain fueled her anger. Because had the tables been turned, she would have stayed. That was what real friends did. They stuck with you when your world came tumbling in around you. They stood up for you when you were surrounded by people who only wanted to hurt you. And definitely, definitely, a friend stayed near when you found out you were pregnant at seventeen.

"Maybe after you finish beating that trash pile to death, you can murder some balloons."

She looked up, startled. He stood before her, his arms filled with streamers, a bundle of balloon ribbons clenched in his fist. He was the Ronan she once knew, but he was also a new Ronan. An adult with mysteries she did not know, probably never would. Because he had moved on, built a life and a career for himself. Grown from a boy to a man.

She flushed. "You're going to think I'm ridiculous."

"You still don't pop balloons?" The intimacy in his tone surprised her, warmed her. Even more the fact that he remembered, touched her.

"I let them go," she admitted.

He dropped the mass of streamers into the trash barrel and headed toward the door. She followed him into the cool darkness, past the parking lot and into the football field. Crickets chirped and the smell of newly mown grass perfumed the air. The full moon silhouetted the balloons against the starry sky.

"Make a wish." Ronan's voice was soft and deep. He reached for her and pulled her to his side, wrapping his arm around her shoulders. It was unwise of her to squander a wish on something that was simply impossible. But in that moment when the balloons slipped from his grasp and tumbled toward the sky, she did.

CHAPTER 13

RONAN LOOKED AT the cardigan on the seat next to him. Jessica must have dropped it on the way to the parking lot as she left the Retreat Center. Bringing it to her had seemed only sensible, so he had looked up her address in the old-fashioned phone book in Max's office. The more he thought about it the better a plan it seemed. It was Friday afternoon and she might need it over the weekend.

Dancing with Jessica last night had been a mistake. Last time he had made that error, she had given him a pity dance at the junior prom. But he was an adult now. Falling hopelessly in love with a woman who was unreachable was something he could manage to ward off before the damage was permanent. Didn't mean it wouldn't hurt.

Ronan pulled the Bentley to a stop in front of the tiny cottage and parked. He considered pressing on the horn but decided that was a coward's way out. He ducked as he opened the little gate and passed under a trellis into the front yard. Someone had a green thumb, he noticed absently. Probably the landlord, since the Jessica he remembered had an aversion to dirt.

On the other hand, the Jessica he remembered would not have chosen to rent a dilapidated cottage. The modest working class neighborhood was not her style either. A vague image of the Piers' mansion flashed unbidden into his mind, pillars, a portico over a circular drive. Rooms filled with elegant furnishings. And throughout an overwhelming sense of isolation. It was nothing like the home his grandparents had welcomed Ronan, his brothers and their father to after Ronan's mother died. Gran and Gramps had been wealthy then too, maybe more so than Austin Piers even. But their home had a kind of old wealth ease. And it was warm, worn and livable. He wondered whether Jessica took after her parents or whether she had found her own version of home.

She shouldn't leave the door ajar. Even on the island, safe as it generally was, there was crime. He peered through the screen door and raised his hand to knock just as Liam tore into the cottage through the back screen door and hurt-led through the living room toward him.

"Oh. Hi, Mr. Durrell." He halted long enough to open the door and beckon Ronan in. "Excuse me for a moment. I just have to – Mom's out back hanging the laundry. She said I can go to the carnival."

Ronan stepped inside and latched the screen door before peeping around the bedroom door frame. Liam was bent over his bottom bureau drawer, yanking out sweaters and what looked like an ancient blanket. Once the drawer was empty, he pulled it out completely from the bureau and rummaged in the cavity below.

"What are you looking for?"

"I just need – oh, here it is." Liam pulled out a worn wallet and waved it triumphantly. "I saved my birthday money."

"Not much of a piggy bank guy, huh?"

"I had a piggy bank once," Liam said, "but we had a break-in and it got stolen. So now I hide anything important here."

He opened his wallet and looked inside as though to re-assure himself the few bills were all there.

"There would be more but I bought a present for Mom for her birthday," he said.

Ronan blinked. A collection of poems. Hardcover, bur-gundy with gold lettering. He had known his mother liked poetry and it had seemed the sort of gift a twelve year old should give a mother who was surprisingly tired. She had been sick already, but he hadn't truly understood the implications. He understood about cancer, of course. But everyone reassured him that even though chemo was hard on the body, it was even harder on a tumor. So he had assumed she would survive. Until she hadn't. And his world fell apart.

The night his father came home with her death written on his face, Ronan stole into his parents' bedroom and snatched the book, slipping it inside his sweatshirt. He slept with it tucked inside his pillowcase, with his hand pressed against the raised gold letters. After the first year, all that re-mained of the letters were gold flecked ghosts.

He had read the book often over the years that followed, untangling unfamiliar vocabulary and struggling with obscure references. He liked the feeling that his fingers were brushing against the same pages hers had. One page was dog-eared. He hadn't been sure which of the two poems she had intended to mark or whether she had simply put the book down when she was tired. So he had memorized both Henley's "Invictus," and Donne's "Death Be Not Proud."

He cleared his throat. "What did you get her?"

Liam held up a hand and tiptoed to the door to ensure his mother was out of earshot. "I got her a briefcase for her new job. Want to see it?" He reached under his bed and pulled out a worn leather satchel.

"I got it at a yard sale," he said. "It was a really good deal. And Clara said it probably just needs some shoe polish and a bit of elbow grease. And Hans said he could fix the handle. So I'm bringing it with me next time I go to visit them."

The back screen door bumped shut again, and Liam shoved the satchel back under his bed.

"Liam?" Jessica sounded tired. "Oh. Hi, Ronan. I didn't know you were here."

Ronan took the basket of folded laundry from her and set it on the couch next to a towering pile of more tablecloths and napkins. It occurred to him that the thunking, grinding sound coming from the basement must be a washing machine. If so, it was breathing its last.

"You know we have commercial laundry machines at The Grand. You could do all of these in a couple of hours. I'll speak to Max and Aidy –"

"Nah. It's okay."

He frowned. "Doing this much laundry in a home machine is inefficient. It's no wonder you look tired."

Her eyebrows arched. "Gee, thanks."

"It's reasonable to take some time off occasionally." He kept his tone mild. "You can't expect to feel rested if you never rest."

"It works for me." Her tone was light, but she was digging her heels in. He could see it in the set of her jaw.

"But Mom," Liam protested. "If you got all the linens done in a couple hours, you would have more time to –"

"I said no, Liam."

Liam shrugged and headed out of the house, settling on the porch steps, his shoulders hunched. Jessica looked stricken.

"I'm sorry," Ronan said quietly. "I didn't mean to press on a sore point. Or to get between you and Liam."

"I don't like being ganged up on," she hissed. "Liam thinks you're a hero. I'm sure he'll get disillusioned eventually, but until then, I'd appreciate it if you would support my decisions instead of undercutting them."

He wasn't surprised by her temper. It was the jagged edge of fear in her voice that concerned him. He turned toward her and was surprised to see tears glistening in her eyes. This was something bigger than an argument about laundry – he just had no idea what it was about. He eyed her cautiously.

"Of course I support your decisions. I'm amazed at what you have done – raised a truly admirable young man, built a business. You've surmounted incredible hurdles. And more important than my acknowledging that – Liam appears to know it."

"I know he does." She sank into the couch next to the tablecloths. One of the towers of linens swayed perilously but did not fall. "And I know you are just being kind. I didn't mean to snap at either of you. It's just –"

She broke off and studied him for a long moment before continuing. "I can't depend on other people to be there when I need any little thing. Because dependence breeds weakness. And I can't afford to be weak."

He shot her an incredulous look. "And using industrial washing machines would be a mark of weakness?"

"Not a mark of weakness. An actual weakness. You know how muscles get flabby when you are on bed rest? Self reliance is a muscle too." She glared at him, her jaw set.

Over her shoulder he could see the worn upholstery on the couch where a colorful shawl had slipped out of place. This was wrong. Because Jessica, when she had been Candy, would never have suffered worn furniture. Once, he remembered, she had thrown away a brand new binder on the first day of school because she discovered a tiny imperfection inside near the rings. He had fished it out of the trashcan and used it at home. It was one of the expensive ones rich kids carried.

He knew shabby chic was in. But this couch was simply worn. He glanced at the coffee table. A corner of the thick wood top had been broken off once, probably by a previous owner, and the rough edge was fringed with fibers torn from the clothing of unsuspecting passersby. Candy Piers would never have put up with it.

"No offense intended." He kept his tone mild. "But if you change your mind, the offer still holds." He gestured toward the coffee table. "I could sand that down for you if you want."

With a bewildered look, she stared at the napkin twisted in her hands. Carefully, she straightened it and pressed it against her knees in a vain attempt to flatten it again. A tear splotched onto it, then another.

Liam had crossed the street and was demonstrating the finer points of shooting hoops to some younger children. Ronan reached for Jessica's hand and pulled her up from the couch.

"Come on," he said, tugging her toward the door.

"What are you doing?"

He didn't respond directly. Instead he pulled her out onto the porch. "Liam?"

"Yeah?"

"I think your mom needs some cotton candy therapy. Want to head over to the carnival?"

Jessica tugged her hand free. "No, Ronan. I'm just dropping Liam off and picking him up later."

"There might be a pie eating contest."

"Ronan, if I don't get the chores done today, I'll be behind all weekend."

She was weakening. He could feel it. "Hot dogs with chili. Fried dough."

"Not fair."

"Shaved ice. Candy apples."

"Aargh!"

"I'll even spring for a ride on the Ferris wheel, little lady. You know you always wanted to go to the top and see the whole town."

"Right, Grandpa." She gave him a withering look. "Because the carousel would be too much excitement."

"Roller coaster it is. Or are you saying you want to go into the Tunnel of Love? That's considered pretty exciting."

"I'll stay on the ground, thank you very much."

"Chicken."

THE ANNUAL CARNIVAL had been held in the town park for as long as Ronan could remember. Not much about it had changed – colored lights winked, the smell of burnt sugar pervaded the air as did the shrill cries of excited children. The carnival seemed to have shrunk in scale since the last time he had tried the rides, but it still retained the whiff of magic it had always had. As though anything was possible.

Liam ran ahead with a shout and disappeared into the milling crowd. Jessica had changed from her jeans to a sundress and cardigan. He stole the opportunity to look at her as she watched Liam run from the parking lot. She had always been beautiful. So logically it should not have surprised him that she still was. But it did – every time he saw her. She stole his breath away.

He stepped closer and reached for her hand. "I bet I can win a huge ugly stuffed animal for you."

She looked at her hand in his with a slight air of surprise but did not pull away. "No one wins the huge ugly stuffed animal. All carnival games are rigged."

"That may be true, but I can still beat them."

"How much money did you waste on this carnival when we were kids?"

"Money spent on learning a valuable skill is never a waste," he said in a lofty tone. "I consider it tuition."

She snorted and swung their clasped hands as they walked.

"You think that's an empty boast, right?"

"I know it is."

"How sure are you? Sure enough to place a bet?"

"Not for money."

"Okay. How about this." He stopped in his tracks and turned to face her. The crowd flowed gently around them, a stream embracing a small island. "If I win you the huge ugly stuffed animal, you go on a ride with me. Ferris wheel or Tunnel of Love. Your choice."

"And if you don't, which is one thousand times more likely – what then?"

"Not an issue. But assuming my losing this bet was even a possibility, what would you like?"

"Take Liam out for the driving session you promised. He hasn't stopped talking about it."

"I would have done that anyway. Choose something for you."

She shrugged her shoulders helplessly. "I don't need anything. I have enough to keep us fed, clothed and housed. With this new job I'll even be able to have a savings account."

"I wasn't talking about needs. More about wants. If you could have anything in the world, without regard for practicality, what would it be?"

She stood stock still, her face pale in the dusk. "I can't tell you that."

"Can't or won't?"

"Won't."

She looked so lost, he wanted to fold her into his arms. Instead, he folded his hand around hers and pulled her toward the midway. "Prepare to pay up," he said.

CHAPTER 14

JESSICA WONDERED IF anyone saw their linked hands. It was such a childish concern, she nearly dismissed it. But, on second thought, it did matter. For one thing, she didn't want any of Liam's friends drawing inappropriate conclusions. In addition, it might be awkward explaining herself to Max and Aidy. Not that her private life was any of their business, but it did involve family. A concept she still wasn't entirely sure she understood. But she imagined Max loved Ronan as fiercely as she loved Liam. Gently, she removed her hand and covered the withdrawal by fussing with the buttons on her sweater.

As a child she had been fascinated by Jane Goodall. The idea of embedding oneself into a society one wasn't naturally a part of, one with distinct rules, patterns of behavior and language, was seductive. Goodall crouched behind a screen of vegetation, observing the social structure of chimpanzees and taking notes on a small pad of paper. Jessica didn't take written notes, but going to slumber parties had provided ample opportunities to study how other people's families worked. And that had been a revelation.

People like Ronan had an intimate experience with family social dynamics Jessica could not begin to replicate the kind of visceral understanding a person picked up by spending a lifetime in a supportive loving family group. The Durrell's had suffered losses, but their essential core of trust, love and support for each member had remained strong. But that had been a foreign language to Jessica, at least until she learned the rudiments of it from Hans and Clara.

She sneaked a glance at Ronan. His physical presence walking beside her took her breath away. It wasn't just that he was handsome, although Lordy, Lordy, he certainly was. But the fact that he was here, next to her – she hadn't dared hope for that.

Dusk was falling rapidly, which meant people were less likely to identify her. Liam was nowhere to be seen. And maybe Max and Aidy weren't coming to the carnival. Surreptitiously, she edged closer to Ronan, so their arms brushed against each other. Trying to make it seem casual, she slipped her fingers back into his hand. He squeezed her hand gently, a private acknowledgment.

The wave of pleasure that flooded her was so potent, she nearly skipped with the joy of it. Strolling with Ronan toward the concession stands, as though they were any other normal couple out for the evening felt too good to be true. Not in an ominous way, but more like an unexpected and extraordinary birthday gift. The kind you were too in awe of to unwrap right away.

He had asked her what she wanted. What her secret desire was. And she hadn't been able to choke out the words. It was critical he never learn how deeply she wanted him, yearned for him, missed him. Revealing that would be misleading, self indulgent and ultimately hurtful. But as long as she hid that deep below, as long as she remembered that protecting him from the mess that was her was the ultimate goal, maybe it would be safe enough to pretend he could be hers for a night. Just one night. The idea was intoxicating. She squeezed his hand back and when he turned to her with a smile, she grinned back.

"What do you want to do first?" he asked.

Anything. Anything at all. As long as her hand could keep nestled in the warmth of his. And then he turned his palm and interlaced his fingers with hers. She was so focused on the sensation of his skin against hers, she forgot the question for a moment.

"Fried dough," she said. She liked shaved ice better, but fried dough required two hands. And it occurred to her now that it might be a good plan to let go of his hand. The idea was for her to pretend they were a couple, not for her to be fooled into thinking they actually were.

There was a flicker of something in his eyes, compassion she thought. But that couldn't be right. She didn't need his pity. The idea that he thought she did annoyed her. As did the lump in her throat. Because when he handed her the plate brimming over with the steaming confection, her appetite disappeared.

"Let's sit down at a picnic table and wait for it to cool," she suggested.

"Best to be cautious," he agreed. "Did you know forty percent of all carnival injuries are directly attributed to fried dough? Plus, fried dough accidents impact the world economy as a whole." He sat at a picnic table and looked up at her expectantly.

"Okay." She slid onto the bench across from him. "How?"

"Taste testers," he said solemnly. "Think of all the taste testers who have to take time off after burning their upper palates on fried dough."

"But that's kind of an occupational hazard, don't you think?"

And just like that, the lump in her throat was gone and they were back to light banter. She reached out her index finger to touch the glistening surface of the dough. It seemed cooler now, but when she pressed through the brittle skin, a burst of steam escaped and she pulled her finger away, cooling it in her mouth. The air between them seemed to crackle with electricity as Ronan stared at her finger, her lips. She pulled her hand down and laced her fingers together on her lap, alarmed.

In the distance, she caught a glimpse of Liam. She waved enthusiastically, knowing it was the coward's way out. To Ronan's credit, he didn't seem in the least put out by the interruption. If she had been going on a date with him for real, this would have ratcheted him up to the level of serious contender. Luckily neither of them was going there.

"Hey Liam, having fun?"

"You bet. Woh, fried dough."

She reached for the plate again and this time found the pastry cool enough to break. She handed Ronan and Liam each a large chunk and took the smaller remaining piece for herself. The first bite, a mixture of crunchy and chewy, piled high with confectioner's sugar, was heaven.

"See any good rides, Liam?" Ronan asked casually.

"Usually I do the roller coaster," Liam said. "But this year they have a new ride called Plummet of Doom that's pretty cool. I haven't decided which one to go on yet."

"Plummet of Doom, huh?" Ronan said. "They don't hold back on description."

"Wanna go on it with me? It's two people at a time," Liam said.

Jessica grinned at Ronan's expression. "Go for it, Ronan. You said you wanted to try the rides," she teased.

He shook his finger at her. "You're in deep trouble, little lady."

She burst into laughter, but there was a tinge of panic there too. Because as she watched him walk ahead toward the rides, his arm draped loosely around her son's shoulder, she knew he was right. She shivered, hugged her cardigan close and hurried to catch up.

The sun had nearly set. The rosy fire that had formed a backdrop for the skeletal metalwork of the rides had faded and the colored lights took on a new significance as they sketched the paths of the roller coaster and Ferris wheel. She was so distracted by the light show, she nearly slammed into Ronan and Liam as they gaped up at the Plummet of Doom. She could see how it had earned its name. What she couldn't figure out was why anyone with an ounce of sanity would want to ride it.

Three benches each equipped with two passengers rose slowly like elevators to the top of a four story tower. At the summit the benches stopped so the hapless victims could have an opportunity to fully appreciate the impossible height. Then, with a sudden jerk, the benches plummeted toward the ground at horrifying speed. The screams of terror were contagious – a lot of the observers from the ground joined in with the panicked riders. But about ten yards from the ground, the benches slowed to a halt, allowing the shaken passengers to stagger off to the cheers of the crowd.

She glanced up at Ronan and her heart stuttered. How could she have forgotten his fear of open heights? As a teen, he had hidden it from everyone except his family and her. And she had only found out by accident when she had teased him into picnicking on the bluffs. But she had assumed he had found a work around to the fear in order to function as an architect. Surely there were plenty of open heights on job sites. But as she gazed at his face, she knew even if he had developed coping mechanisms for work, this was a different situation. Even a person who was not afraid of heights would be frightened of the Plummet of Doom.

"Isn't it cool, Mr. Durrell?" Liam breathed.

"It sure is, bud." Ronan looked queasy.

"Wanna get in line for tickets? It might take awhile, and then there's a line to actually get on the ride, but it looks like it's worth it."

Ronan swallowed, his face pale in the shadows. "Okay. That sounds great."

Any hope she had that the ride would be sold out was dashed once they had inched their way to the ticket booth. Jessica looked around the crowd frantically hoping for a solution. But none of Liam's classmates were nearby, or if they were, she couldn't see them. The line moved slowly but inexorably toward the loading platform. She slipped her hand into Ronan's. His palm was cold and damp. She couldn't bear it anymore. This was just cruel. She tapped Liam's shoulder. "Honey, I know you were hoping Ronan would ride with you, but would it be okay if I take his place?"

Liam looked at her in surprise. "Okay. I mean sure. If Ronan doesn't mind."

Ronan's expression of gratitude mingling with terror on her behalf would have been funny if she hadn't been so scared herself. The line snaked forward slowly. It was a mystery to Jessica why so many people were willing to pay money to terrify themselves. She scanned the crowd again hoping none of her customers were there to watch her vomit up the fried dough she had just eaten. Not exactly good publicity for Moon Shell Events. Not that it mattered in the long run.

"Liam?" A pretty red haired girl stood outside the rope that separated the line of riders from the crowd.

"Hi, Stephanie." Liam's face turned bright red.

"I can't believe you're going on the Plummet of Doom. I wanted to go, but my friend Julie wimped out and I don't want to go with someone I don't know."

Liam nodded, clearly at a loss for words.

Jessica breathed in the first full breath she had taken since volunteering to plunge to her death and turned to her son. "Liam, maybe you should invite Stephanie to go on the ride with you."

His look of delight was immediately tempered by his sense of responsibility. It was charming and she appreciated it generally, but for once she wished he wasn't so altruistic. Because if he didn't catch on more quickly, she was going to have to do something she dreaded even more than riding the Plummet of Death.

"But you said you wanted to –"

She flinched but accepted her fate. "I know. And I'm embarrassed to say it, but I'm not feeling well. I think the fried dough didn't agree with me."

Ronan gave her an inquiring look. She felt like kicking him.

"Should we go home?" Liam asked.

Her heart twinged at his conflicted expression. "No, no. I'm sure if I stroll around a bit I'll be just fine. I know Ronan had a hankering to go on some of the old-fashioned rides, like the carousel."

"Okay." Liam nodded. "Kind of a nostalgia thing?"

"Exactly." She made a point of avoiding Ronan's eyes. "So, Stephanie, if you're up to it, you're welcome to my ticket."

The sense of relief as she released the little stub of cardboard into Stephanie's hand was almost tangible. And ducking under the ropes so she and Ronan could escape into the crowd was even better. She felt giddy as they wove between cheerful groups of teens, families pulled along by overexcited children and the occasional older couple.

"Where are we going?" She gasped.

He didn't answer, just pulled her along even faster until they were sheltered beneath a great maple tree on the outskirts of the carnival. The dark was thicker there and his face was simply a darker shadow among the silhouetted branches. His arms were tight around her now, his body pressed to hers. And as he lowered his lips to hers, she could hear the carousel's calliope begin its selection.

"Boys and girls together," Ronan whispered hoarsely, his breath against her lips. "Me and Mamie O'Rourke. We tripped the light fantastic on the sidewalks of New York."

And then there was only the touch of Ronan's lips on hers and the gentle sway and turn of a long lost dance.

CHAPTER 15

WASHING THE KITCHEN floor before Max and Aidy were up was the least Ronan could do for them since Bear tracked in a significant amount of garden mud. There was something meditative about the whole process. Swirling the mop in the warm sudsy water. Wringing it out. The path of damp cleanliness stood in sharp contrast to the remaining dry. It would be nice if life could be like that. Clear cut.

Maybe there was something about becoming an adult that ruined one's capacity for painful honesty. Ronan hadn't asked Jessica flat out if she were in a relationship. She hadn't volunteered. And he wasn't entirely sure he wanted to know. So he was in the awkward place of avoiding being lied to. Although in high school she had been blunt when he had finally gotten up the nerve to ask her to junior prom.

"I think we should stop hanging out together," she had said. "I'm going to junior prom with Chris Mullin."

The words were seared into his psyche. Her cold, distant delivery. Clinical, almost. As though she had been dithering between two different colors of spiral bound notebook and had finally shrugged and made her decision. He had no trouble summoning compassion for the girl he had once loved so desperately. She had been a kid, not much older than Liam was now. He didn't expect a teenager to think like an adult. So it wasn't about forgiveness.

But he couldn't forget her behavior either. Because it would be stupid to ignore the past. People grew, but in his experience, they didn't change much. Jessica might not love Chris any more – maybe she never had. But love or the lack of it didn't seem to influence her decisions about who she chose to relate to. And if Chris ever returned to the island it would only complicate matters.

Because Jessica would choose her path based on what she thought would be best for Liam. And Liam, understandably, probably wanted his birth father to be part of his life. So it was a no-brainer. Which made Ronan an idiot. It was very, very lucky he hadn't slept with Jessica. Their kiss last night under the maple tree could have been a precursor to much, much more. Probably would have been if circumstances had been different.

Instead, they had strolled back to the midway. He had won her the ugliest hugest neon pink teddy bear he had ever seen. She had agreed to join him in the Tunnel of Love on condition the stuffed animal sat between them. Which, after that blistering kiss, was probably wise. It was only the wistful part of him that wished he could have followed through on his desires.

It wasn't a fair wish, he knew. Nor wise. Because a memory like that could only bring pain in the end. What was it in human beings that made them want things that were obviously bad for them? Some people, like Chris, fell into the drug trap. But Ronan knew he himself could be just as susceptible to the right lure. Battling his yearning to fritter away his time on art was a daily challenge. And now he had the additional problem of wanting Jessica. The worst part was he didn't just want to sleep with her.

At least Liam had found his heart's desire at the carnival. The look of joy on his face when they had caught up with him had been transcendent. A part of Ronan had wanted to tell the boy, "Don't. Don't look like that. Don't be so vulnerable." But he knew there was no point. Because when you were in the middle of love, you never believed it could go so horribly wrong.

He opened the door to the garden and stepped onto the stoop, bucket in hand. Spring had finally settled in. The sun, newly risen, warmed his face, birds chattered busily as they went about their housekeeping and the smell of mown hay puffed in the breeze. He looked across the great meadow to the Retreat Center. The great room was probably full of ministers, or nuns, or rabbis, or imams, or whatever. He wasn't exactly sure which denomination was on the calendar for this weekend, not that it mattered. The schedule was always the same. Prayers or classes after breakfast each morning. Lunch followed by contemplation. Or, in the case of some attendees, naps. Communal dinner followed by music.

But perhaps today's game plan was different. The long windows were open like wings and he could hear singing wafting across the meadow. Plainsong, maybe. Clear tones and determined sinewy melodies. Considering its ethereal floating quality, it impressed him as particularly muscular music.

That was the thing about love. It seemed so innocuously pleasant at first. Like ivy. It might be cute when you brought it home in a little pot and planted it in the shade. But if you let it grow unchecked, it could choke the life out of the tree that sheltered it.

He walked a few steps away from the stoop. Max grumbled that the biodegradable cleaning solutions Aidy insisted on didn't actually clean anything. But it meant Ronan could slosh the contents of the bucket onto the grass without hurting the plant life. And the floor was cleaner than when he had started, which he guessed counted for something.

He liked listening to Max and Aidy's friendly squabbling. It felt like home. Love. The good side of it, anyway. But he wasn't fooled. You couldn't have that warmth without accepting the unyielding steel core at its center. Not that he resented it exactly. There was no point in resenting a law of nature. You could resent gravity all you wanted, apples would still fall.

He had loved Jessica once. He had come perilously close to doing so again last night. But he couldn't have her. So it would be best to cut himself off now, before the desire became need. He took the bucket back into the house.

Two hours later, he had sent out three applications to architectural firms in Boston. Less prestigious ones than MacAllen, but then he had avoided mentioning MacAllen on his resume. His degree was still fairly recent, so he could probably get away with it. To be on the safe side, he had also sent his resume to a couple firms in Western Massachusetts. Competition for those positions might be a little less fierce.

There were forty nine other states, of course. Okay, forty eight. He drew the line at Florida. He had been there once on vacation and hadn't liked it. But ideally he would stay in Massachusetts. His brothers were here. And he liked hanging out with his niece, Jock and Charlotte's little one. Plus there would be a new niece or nephew coming. Aidy had suffered a miscarriage in the first year of her marriage with Max, but there was cheery air in the house that made him feel this pregnancy was going to stick. So there was that.

His determination to stay in Massachusetts had nothing to do with Jessica. Obviously. Because she was not interested in a relationship with him beyond friendship. And he knew better than to convince himself otherwise. To demonstrate his own open-mindedness to himself, he had sent one additional application to Domain Architects, a small firm in New York City.

There would be tons of applicants for the position at Domain Architects because in addition to being under much admired architect Kobi Ellis, it offered a generous salary. Nonetheless, in a gesture of defiance, he had attached the images from his portfolio he had been careful not to share with MacAllen. The wild ones, Escher-like structures. And the ones his teachers had called lush and curvaceous. Fantastical confections, all. And his most loved creations, the caravans. Wheeled dwellings intended for the homeless. Foldable, relatively light, durable. And nonetheless endowed with a generosity of spirit he felt ought to be implicit in any human being's living environment.

There was no way he would be considered for the position, of course. But at least someone would see the work he cared most about. The sensation of sleeping on Jock's living room floor after their father had died was seared into his memory. Not the discomfort, per se, but the vulnerability of rootlessness. And the fear. It had been safe enough in Jock's apartment, although Jock's then fiancée had been less than welcoming. But for Ronan, the knowledge that the safe journey into adulthood he had relied on had been yanked out from under him had provided frequent nightmares he could not tell anyone about.

It had given him a unique perspective on the needs of the suddenly poor. And a determination never to be one of their number again. Which meant he could never risk following his heart when it came to earning a living. No question he yearned for the pure art he had once wanted to focus his life on. Every day. Every minute, if he were honest. Sometimes so much it was hard to breathe. But art didn't pay bills. And hearts didn't have the capacity for rational thought. Which was why you couldn't trust them.

CHAPTER 16

RONAN WAITED FOR the traffic light to change and considered turning around and going back to Max's house. He would just text Jessica and tell her something had come up. But when he had the opportunity to pull a U-turn, he couldn't bring himself to take it. Liam seemed like a person who had a great deal of practice forgiving the adults in his life. Which made it all the more difficult to purposely disappoint him.

The porch floor of Jessica's cottage sagged alarmingly as Ronan crossed to the doorbell. And the doorbell itself didn't work. He rapped on the door with his knuckles and waited until the hum of the vacuum cleaner subsided and Liam stood in the doorway. The boy's eyes widened.

"You came."

"I said I would." He kept his tone light, although the mingled disbelief and reserve in the boy's expression bothered him.

"Mom's working."

Which was why Ronan had chosen Saturday morning to keep his promise to Liam.

"I thought, if you have time that is, you might like to come for a ride."

"I have time," Liam assured him quickly. "My chores are done and my homework is too. Well, except for algebra and Mom said she'd help me with that."

"Math was always her strong suit. I wouldn't have made it through ninth grade without your mother."

"Really?"

"Really. Grab a jacket. We might want to ride with the roof down."

Ronan grinned at Liam's awed expression. He had intended to keep his promise, of course, but he hadn't anticipated enjoying the boy's company. It was hard to beat hero worship.

"Okay."

Liam almost closed the door in Ronan's face but stopped mid-motion as though suddenly remembering some long ago hosting instructions. He swung the door wide again. "Want to come in?" He ushered Ronan into the living room and gestured solicitously toward a sagging couch. "Please make yourself comfortable. Would you like something to drink?"

Ronan didn't smile although he wanted to. Liam had a sweet earnestness to his manner that made Ronan wonder what he must have looked like as a little boy. Serious, Ronan thought. "No, thank you. But I appreciate the offer."

Liam glanced around the room quickly and cast a guilty glance at the ancient vacuum cleaner he had abandoned when Ronan appeared.

"I didn't mean to interrupt you," Ronan said. "Do you need to finish vacuuming?"

"I guess not." Liam scanned the carpet. "I don't think it's picking anything up anyway. I tried to change the bag, but – Mom got this vacuum cleaner at a yard sale last week because the last one died, and I can't figure out how to open it." He shrugged eloquently.

Privately Ronan thought it was just as well. The carpet was too threadbare to withstand much more punishment. In fact, most of the furnishings seemed aged without the charm of being antiques. They were just old and worn.

Still the space was not depressing, which was an accomplishment. Richly colored scarves covered the worst of the wear on the couch and armchairs. Someone, Jessica he guessed, had painted the bureau that served as a buffet buttercup yellow. The plates stacked on it were a joyfully mismatched collection of stoneware. Overall there was a sense of care and love. A breath of spring breeze puffed in the open window bringing the scent of the garden into the house.

A gray ceramic pitcher on the tiny kitchen table was filled with a generous bouquet of daisies. Ronan wondered if the flowers were a gift, perhaps from a friend, perhaps from someone closer than a friend. It was pointless to dwell on it. And it wasn't as if he had any right or even any reason to know the answer. He wasn't staying on the island any longer than he had to. But now the question lingered, and he couldn't get it out of his head. Jessica was a beautiful woman, maybe even more beautiful now than she had been in her teens. Crazy to think she was available.

Liam had disappeared into his bedroom, looking for a jacket. Ronan meandered over to the vacuum cleaner. A vacuum bag in its original packaging lay on the trunk nearby. Like the rest of the cottage, the machine was dated, but Ronan's grandmother had had one like it, and he had a vague memory of changing the bag on hers. He tugged at the latches on the sides of the canister until they gave way.

"Did you get it?" Liam was shoving an arm into a jacket as he rushed from his bedroom.

"It was just rusted in position," Ronan said. "See?"

He tipped the ends of the latches away from the canister and pressed on the hose connecter to open the top. The ancient rubber gasket rim was stuck too. Figured. He gripped the edges of the top but couldn't loosen it.

"I can pull the top if you pull the bottom," Liam offered. "My fingers are pretty strong."

They changed places, and braced themselves.

"One. Two. Three."

For a moment it seemed the vacuum cleaner would win, but then Liam gave a cry of triumph and the top loosened its grip. The bag, as old as the vacuum itself, gave way to the ravages of time spraying its contents all over the carpet and floor.

"Cool!" Liam looked at the open vacuum cleaner with satisfaction. Ronan gave him a disbelieving look, but Liam was clearly delighted at the result. He definitely liked this kid.

Between them, they got the bulk of the dust swept up. Then Liam with an air of proud ownership loaded a brand new old bag into the canister and demonstrated how effectively the vacuum cleaner worked now. Not terribly well, Ronan thought. But Liam was thrilled, which he guessed was all that mattered. The boy's delighted expression as he clambered into the passenger seat of the Bentley made Ronan wonder how many broken promises the boy had experienced in his twelve years.

Not from Jessica, he guessed. The few bits of information about her private life he had managed to wring from her told him she was a ferociously protective mother. But even so, life had a way of interfering with keeping promises even with the best of intentions. And the cottage, no matter how lovingly cared for, was a clear signal that Jessica was no longer the privileged woman he remembered.

"I moved to the island when I was about your age to live with my grandparents," he said. "It's a special relationship."

Liam nodded politely.

"I remember your grandparents too," Ronan added, keeping his tone carefully casual.

"What were they like?" Liam asked.

Ronan contained his surprise at the question. Surely Jessica wouldn't have deprived Liam of the chance to relate to his grandparents. Although now he thought about it, he couldn't think of much good to say about Cookie and Austin. They had given their daughter all the material goods a girl could have wanted and none of the emotional support a child needed. But he couldn't exactly say that to their only grandson.

"Did you never meet them?"

"Nope. They moved away before I was born."

That was weird. "All of them?"

"Yep. Well, I don't know much about my dad's family. And I'm not sure I would want to meet Mom's folks even if I could." Liam spoke quietly as he stared out the windshield. There was a determined set to his shoulders, but Ronan could hear a whisper of longing in his voice. He shot Ronan a defiant look.

"She doesn't really talk about her parents much. She used to tell me they loved me. But then once when I was six, I was being a brat and I asked her why they never call me for my birthday or Christmas or anything and she cried. Mom never cries, at least not in front of me. So I don't ask anymore."

"I don't think you were being bratty."

"Yeah, I was. I just wanted more presents. But I didn't realize how lucky I was. Hans and Clara Ulrich call me their honorary grandson, and they care for me a lot more than my real grandparents do."

"The Ulrichs? They had a daughter my age I think. Barbara, maybe?"

Liam nodded. "She's Mom's best friend. But Barbara lives off the island now. She's married to Salim. They have two kids. Ethan is three and he's kind of a pain because he likes to bite people. And they just had a baby, who's pretty cute. For a baby. But Barbara's brother Zack is cool. He taught me to skateboard. Well, he tried. I'm still not any good at it."

Ronan pulled into the empty parking lot and put the car in park. He was hardly in position to argue, but he remembered Barbara as a quiet kindly girl with an unfortunate acne problem and a heavy build. Not the sort of girl a queen bee like Jessica would have considered best friend material. "Want to change places?"

Liam's face lit up. "Seriously?"

As an answer, Ronan opened his door and got out of the Bentley. Liam nearly fell over his feet in his hurry to get around the car. Once buckled into the driver's seat, he looked at Ronan uncertainly. "What if I crash it? I'm pretty clumsy."

"You won't," Ronan said firmly. "If you can play a tuba, you can do this. Plus it's an automatic transmission, so it'll be easy."

An hour later, Liam was flushed, his eyes shining. "I did it. I can't believe I drove a car. Thanks, Mr. Durrell."

Ronan winced. "Call me Ronan."

"Really? Mom says I should always call adults by Mister or Mizz."

"Sure, that's a good policy." Ronan kept a straight face with effort. "But I think your mom might make an exception in this case. After all, two guys who fix vacuums and drive Bentleys together have a certain amount in common."

"Yeah." Liam was nearly bouncing in his seat. "I'll ask her."

"Are you hungry?"

"A little. If we go home, I can make sandwiches. I'm good at grilled cheese."

"Do you like hot dogs?"

"Sure. I don't think we have any though. Mom hasn't had a lot of time to go grocery shopping recently."

"I was thinking about Walt's. I haven't been there since I was a kid. Are they still in business?"

The boy's eyes widened. "Yes, but –"

"You're not vegetarian, are you?"

"No, but I don't know if Mom –"

A look of unease crossed Liam's face. Ronan rummaged in his pocket and pulled out his cell phone. He scrolled through his contacts and accepted the whisper of anticipation as he touched her name.

"Ronan, what's up?" Polite but brief. Almost dismissive. He grinned.

"Liam did great driving the Bentley, but he thought we should check in before I took him to Walt's for hot dogs."

He handed the phone to Liam and walked away to give the boy some privacy. He remembered being twelve in a flash of unexpected clarity, that sensation of being on the cusp of something both thrilling and terrifying. He savored the memory, tasting the sweetness of it. He rarely remembered anything good from that year. Most of it was a blur of pain and loss.

"Mister – I mean, Ronan. Mom says – hey, are you okay?"

Ronan shook off the tang of sorrow and smiled. Liam was a little too perceptive for his own good. Useful tool, Ronan knew to his own cost, but also exquisitely painful at times.

"You bet. Ready for Walt's?"

"Sure am!"

It had been years since Ronan had considered dogs and fries a treat, but Liam's enthusiasm was contagious. Everything was worthy of comment and enjoyment, from the picnic tables on the gravel lot, to the red oval plastic baskets lined with red checked tissue paper, to the can of soda Liam said his mother rarely allowed.

"Mom says it's bad for my teeth, which is probably true," he said earnestly. "But I think it's okay once in while."

"Everything in moderation." Ronan forked up strands of sauerkraut that were overflowing the bun. "Except maybe chocolate and roses."

"That's what Mom says." Liam nodded. "I think girls like them especially."

"Do you have a girlfriend, Liam?"

"Not exactly. You?"

"Same."

"Mom doesn't have a boyfriend either. She used to go out sometimes, but not anymore. She says she's happy the way she is."

The invisible band that had tightened around Ronan's rib cage loosened slowly. He was pretty sure Jessica wouldn't be pleased about the direction the conversation was taking. On the other hand, he had reached a kind of détente with her by the end of last night. Unfortunately it wasn't the sort of truce that involved open honest conversation. All their daily talk at work revolved around, well, work, and while normally Ronan found building plans fascinating, he was beginning to feel he and Jessica were dancing around something crucial.

Increasingly, getting to what mattered in Jessica's life, mattered to him. It shouldn't have. He would leave in a few weeks while her life continued on the island without him. But the strands of their old friendship were weaving themselves into something new. She seemed determined to ignore that, deny it. But he couldn't help watching this new fabric emerge, even if he did so with a horrified fascination.

"You don't need a boyfriend or girlfriend to be happy."

"No duh." Liam gave him a withering look.

Ronan felt a jolt of pleasure. Liam's careful politeness up to now had been appropriate, Ronan supposed, but still a bit wearing. He might not be making progress with Jessica, but at least Liam liked him enough to be frank.

CHAPTER 17

JESSICA FELT A pang when she thought about how excited Liam had sounded to be going out to lunch at Walt's. It was kind of Ronan to offer. It had been kind of him to help her out at Evelyn's party too. A part of her wished he hadn't been so thoughtful. She resented it, actually. It would have been easier to deal with Ronan if he was a jerk. She could have dismissed a jerk.

She tapped at the screen of her phone and put it to her ear with a sigh.

"Hi Mom!"

"Wow. You sound happy."

"Yup."

She waited for Liam to elaborate but he seemed uncharacteristically content to keep the reason for his good cheer to himself. Which made her mom antennae twitch. "Okay. So. I'll be home soon."

"Great. See you when you get here." There was clanking and a loud thump and moan in the background.

"Liam, what's going on?"

"Nothing, Mom. I gotta go."

She looked at her phone numbly. Maybe Walt was putting something extra in his pickle relish. Whatever it was, she didn't trust it. She had intended to stop at the grocery store on the way, but she decided to skip it. They could get along without eggs until tomorrow. It was more important to find out what Liam was up to. She hoped it wasn't an extra credit science project he had forgotten to tell her about. Again. The last one had involved a minor explosion.

She had pulled into the driveway and locked the car before she noticed Bear.

"Woof!"

What was the big black dog doing dancing around happily on her porch?

"Mom." Liam looked as if he would burst. "Ronan said we could go on a picnic to the bluffs. I said we already ate but he said I was probably hungry again and I was. Plus, he said you probably hadn't eaten so we —"

He stopped mid-sentence at her expression. "I mean, if you want to. I made sandwiches. And Ronan bought dessert."

She couldn't unsee the yearning on Liam's face. Ronan stood halfway into the kitchen, his hands in his pockets. Watchful. He was big in the cramped space, his hair tousled and his shirt rumpled with a dusty smudge on the front left. A little of her melted. She couldn't remember the last time she had attended a picnic she hadn't organized.

"I don't know," she stalled. "What kind of dessert?"

"Chocolates and green Jell-O," Liam announced.

She shot a startled look at Ronan. He gave an embarrassed shrug.

"Liam said green Jell-O was his favorite."

A wave of fury shot through her.

"Liam, I'd like to speak to Ronan privately for a moment. Would you take Bear out to the backyard?"

She smiled at Liam in what she hoped was a reassuring way. He looked at her uncertainly but nodded.

"Sure. Come on, Bear. Wanna play catch?"

She waited until the door was closed before turning to Ronan. "I won't let you hurt Liam."

Ronan raised his brows. "Hurt Liam? He seems fine to me. Happy, even."

"Sure. Now. Driving the Bentley. Going out for lunch. Special treats. It's all terrific until you walk away and the party's over. Then I'm the one picking up the pieces. Again."

Ronan looked stunned. "You think I would do that?"

"I know you would do that."

"You're wrong," he bit the words and spat them out. "I didn't walk away from you, Jessica. You did the walking, right into Chris Mullin's arms. And when you did, you ever so casually broke my heart."

She felt the blood drain from her face. "What are you talking about? We were friends."

"I loved you. I worshipped the ground you walked on. And don't tell me you didn't know it."

He looked savage. She raised a shaking hand to her forehead and covered her eyes. She refused to cry. It would be horribly unfair to ask him to comfort her for breaking his heart. And there was no question she had done so intentionally. He hadn't deserved to be sacrificed on the altar of her family's dysfunction. The fact that her own heart had been broken too was irrelevant. She, at least, had been granted a choice.

"Loved. Past tense. You don't anymore." It scraped her throat coming out.

"Of course not," he snapped. "I learned my lesson."

"Okay," she whispered. "Okay."

It was more of a plea than a response. It was one thing to guess it. It was another thing to hear him say it. She swallowed. "It was complicated."

"No. It was simple," he retorted. "I loved you and you didn't love me. But as you say, we had been friends. Minimally you owed me an explanation instead of just tossing me aside like a used sandwich wrapper."

She stared at her interlaced fingers without seeing them. "You must have hated me. After."

"Some." He fiddled with a stray teaspoon and shrugged. "I probably hated Chris more. But he was too much of an idiot to waste energy on."

"It wasn't Chris's fault anyway. It was mine."

And it had been. She had pursued Chris with single-minded ferocity. Not because she loved him, or even wanted him. No. This had been about protecting her family, her home, her life. And in the end, the whole endeavor had been pointless. Well, not Liam, of course. Never Liam. But her attempt to stop the inevitable had been hopeless from the start.

She studied Ronan's face. Some of his anger had dissipated now. She felt the tension in her shoulders release a fraction.

"I hated hurting you. You were my best friend." She was proud her voice didn't quiver.

"Then why did you do it?"

"Mom and Dad were on the verge of breaking up. I thought maybe if I was perfect – if I dressed just right, if I had the best grade point average, if I went out with my mother's best friend's son. I thought maybe they would love me enough to stay together."

"But their relationship had nothing to do with your behavior."

"Sure. As an adult, I know that. But I was a kid, Ronan. Dad hated you, probably because you made me happy. Mom kept urging me to go out with Chris. She wanted to join the country club, and she thought Lynne was the way in. And then I got pregnant and Mom and Dad broke up anyway. And I had lost – I know I hurt you, Ronan. I truly apologize for that. And I understand if you can't find it in your heart to forgive me. But the thing is, I can't let Liam get hurt."

He gave her a long look. "Liam will get hurt. Probably badly. But it won't be by me."

"No. I guess not," she admitted. She watched her toe rub against the rug. "You wouldn't do that."

"No. And as far as forgiveness goes, I think it probably runs both ways. I could have given you the benefit of the doubt too. But, as you say, that's the advantage of being older and having more experience with relationships."

He sighed. "Jessica, I could use a friend without complications while I'm here. From the sound of it, you could too. Why don't we just pretend we don't have a past and start fresh? Liam seems to feel you could use a male buddy."

She rolled her eyes. "Liam's a romantic. At least he's not gullible. Some guys think if they're nice to Liam, they'll make points with me."

Ronan snorted. "You don't have to worry about that in my case. I'm more likely to be nice to you to make points with Liam. I admire him."

She should have been relieved at his response. And she was. Absolutely. Because Liam's welfare was what mattered here. And now they had set the record straight, she could relax knowing Ronan had absolutely no ulterior motive.

And the twinge of pain at how definitively he had put her in the past was manageable. All she had to do was push it down underneath the surface, the same place the other pains lived. Under the ice. She had always been a good skater. Not Olympic quality, but competent. And it turned out that was all you needed to make it through life. To concentrate on gliding carefully forward and to never look down.

"Me too," she said quietly. "And thank you."

Ronan pulled several bulging plastic carry bags from the refrigerator and placed them on the kitchen table next to a cooler. "See if you still say that after you try the sandwiches. We had to get inventive given the state of your larder."

"I know. There hasn't been a lot of time for grocery shopping this week. I meant to stop on the way home, but – I'm babbling."

"Understandably. It's not every day a girl has the opportunity to feast al fresco with two eligible bachelors. Luckily I found some aged lemonade powder on an upper shelf. It's the suggested beverage to accompany peanut butter pimento cheese sandwiches. Your heart must be all aflutter."

He was uncomfortably close to the truth – her pulse beat thick and slow, intentful. Her skin felt tight, as though it were waiting for something she didn't want to examine too closely. Excusing herself to change out of her work clothes, she fled into her bedroom and leaned against the closed door to catch her breath. Ronan ought to come with a surgeon general's warning. He wasn't even trying to attract her. He had made that embarrassingly clear.

She scrambled to her closet, frantically eliminating options. Too formal. Too flattering. Too revealing. She wondered irritably why she had never considered stocking an outfit for this sort of occasion, clothing that was presentable but made it plain she too was unavailable.

She settled on worn paint stained jeans and an old pregnancy sweatshirt she had held onto for grubbier household chores. A pair of scuffed torn sneakers completed the ensemble. She pulled her hair back and in a final burst of inspiration jammed on a baseball cap and tugged the ponytail through it.

"Mom, are you ready?"

She opened the door. "You bet."

Liam and Bear tumbled out onto the porch. Ronan eyed her and smirked as he passed the last bulging tote bag to Liam to load into the car.

"Shut up," she muttered.

"I didn't say anything." He grinned and leaned against the door frame, looking her up and down in a leisurely fashion.

She put her fists on her hips and glared at him. "What's so funny?"

"You. Thinking that wearing scruffy clothes will make you less attractive."

"Don't flatter yourself," she said stiffly. "I like being comfortable."

He was still grinning like an idiot, she noted irritably as she climbed into the passenger seat. She sat quietly, listening to Ronan and Liam chat and watching the lines on the road disappear under the long hood of the Bentley. It was surprisingly soothing.

She let her forehead rest against the cool window glass. She had always liked that about Ronan – that she could push and he would push back and in the end, it would still be easy between them. The chance to fight without permanent damage mattered because she knew it was rare. Or at least rare in her experience.

Her parents sure hadn't managed it. As far back as Jessica could remember, Cookie and Austin had fought – vicious screaming bouts that might not have resulted in actual blood, but still scarred. She had often wondered why her parents had married at all. There was certainly no love left in their relationship, if there had ever been any to start with.

Nonetheless, the fear that they might divorce had permeated her childhood. Social stigma was part of it, probably. But more, she had known in a dark corner of her heart that her parents stayed together not for her sake but because they were addicted to the fighting. That if their marriage broke up there would be no reason for her existence.

She pulled her mind back to the present as the car bumped over the pitted gravel parking lot. She hadn't been to the bluffs for years but apparently not much had changed. The path down to the narrow rocky beach was still littered with detritus dropped by teenagers. Beer cans, empty cigarette packs. She hoped Liam hadn't seen the used condom. Or maybe, since he was entering adolescence, she should hope he had.

The beach itself was sparsely populated. A group of teens huddled in the sand watched them curiously from a distance. Closer, a pair of seagulls eyed the cooler and bags speculatively. Jessica reached for one of the bags but Ronan clicked his tongue reprovingly.

"Man's work. Right, Liam?"

Liam grinned and lunged for the edge of the sheet Ronan tossed him. Jessica raised her hands in a gesture of surrender and shambled toward the water's edge. The few clouds hung solid and low, puffy white and defined against an unnecessarily blue sky. She had lived in Demerest Cove so long, she often forgot to look past the litter on the path. On the other hand, litter was more reliable than a horizon. Horizons dangled rewards that did not in fact exist and then, in the epitome of meanness, snatched them away again.

CHAPTER 18

A SALTY BREEZE played with the corner of the sheet, and Ronan leaned back to prop his elbow on the flapping fabric. The sandwiches had been a hit. Or at least, not awful. Liam had eaten all the green Jell-O with a delight that almost made up for having to watch him do it.

Liam and Bear were far down the beach now, Liam scouting for interesting stones to share with his earth science teacher and Bear searching for disgusting things to roll in. Jessica sat facing the water, her knees hugged close so she could rest her chin on them.

"What are you thinking about?" he asked.

"Families."

"What about them?"

"Just how every family is different."

She was fobbing him off and he didn't like it. "That's true," he said. "I loved spending time with my grandparents. Sounds like you haven't given Liam the same opportunity. Even if you can't afford to travel, there's Skype."

Her shoulders hunched. He rolled toward her and propped his head on his hand. "You're allowed to tell me to shut up and mind my own business. Even if I did provide a deluxe box of chocolates and a fabulous surprise package of cheese curls."

They listened to wavelets lap the shore. A gull sidled closer and tilted its head to better assess a bottle cap. Jessica puffed out a breath and looked at Ronan.

"I hate talking about this. I hate it. You have no idea how lucky you and your brothers were."

Ronan stared at her in disbelief. "My mother died when I was twelve," he said. "My grandparents died when I was in college. My father died three months later."

"I *know* all that. And it's awful. But at least while you had them, they loved you. I bet you never doubted that for one minute. And if you had done something socially improper, something your parents or grandparents might find embarrassing, they would still have loved you. Right?"

"Sure."

She shook her head. "It's not a sure thing. When it comes to parents, you get what you get. And what I got was Cookie and Austin."

He sat up next to her. "Right, but even if parents don't get along with their kids, grandchildren are a whole different matter."

"That's what I thought. Mom and Dad were mortified by my decision to keep Liam. But once he was born, I was sure they would come around. I mean who can resist a little baby, right? I actually begged them for help, just until I could find a job. And you know what they said?"

He shook his head mutely.

"Dad explained he was marrying his secretary and just wanted to move on. And I should do the same. Mom –"

Her voice wobbled. Without thinking, he draped his arm around her shoulder and tugged her close.

"Mom said she would never be able to look at Liam without remembering he was a little bastard. And that Lynne Mullin had already scuttled Mom's chances of membership in The Pines. And it was all my fault because I wouldn't marry Chris.

"And then there was Lynne. She pulled me aside one day and explained there wasn't any point in ruining both our lives. Chris's trajectory was all planned out. Undergrad. Medical school. Internship at Mass General."

"But Chris offered to marry you." He could hear the flat tone in his voice, but he couldn't manage to modulate it out. Freakin' Chris Mullin. Chris, football team captain, had been as close to royalty in Demerest Cove High School as possible. Rich, and coddled, with a heavy dose of entitlement.

"He did. But when I refused, he looked as though the weight of the world had been lifted from his shoulders. But he didn't need to worry. I wouldn't let my son be raised by an addict. Chris got hooked on painkillers after a sports injury senior year. His mother never saw it. As far as I know, she still refuses to see it. She can't even admit he fathered a child.

She tells everyone she talks to that I was the class round heels. That Liam's dad could be anyone."

Ronan's breath hissed through his teeth.

She shook her head impatiently. "Lynne and Chris are beside the point. I've been lucky. Remember Barbara Ulrich?"

"Barely."

"I get that. I'm embarrassed to say, I also barely noticed her until spring of senior year. Mom put the house on the market and told me she was moving to Florida. Alone. She said if I was old enough to ruin her social life, I could just live with the consequences.

"I was too mortified to tell anyone at school about the pregnancy, and now I knew I was going to be homeless as soon as the house sold. Barbara happened to be in the girls' room when I had a bad bout of morning sickness and somehow she guessed. She made me come home with her that afternoon and taught me what real friends do. What real families can be.

"The thing is, once I knew, really understood what parental love looked like, I had to give that kind of love to Liam. How could I not? Cookie and Austin avoided having to parent me by giving me stuff. It took me a while to figure out that love can sometimes mean depriving Liam of something he thinks he wants. Particularly if the thing he wants isn't healthy for him."

Ronan glanced toward Liam who had managed to enlist the high school kids in his treasure hunt. One of the boys obligingly threw sticks into the shallows for Bear to leap after.

"So Liam doesn't spend time with Chris at all? What about child support?"

She pushed her heels into the sand and shook his arm off her shoulder. "I don't want Chris's money. And I definitely don't want him spending lots of time with Liam."

Ronan sank back onto his elbows, uneasy. She was protective. He got that – admired it too. The image of her struggling with such a heavy responsibility when she had been no older than the carefree teens frolicking with Liam and Bear was painful.

So he understood her rationale, but he also remembered how much he had needed his own father at Liam's age. Part of that dependence was because he had lost his mother, certainly. But not all. He had leaned on his father and on his grandfather too for advice. He used them as models, not only for their values and ethical beliefs but also for more visceral cues – how to behave, how to think. How to love.

Belatedly he glanced down the beach. Liam, returning, cradled a collection of stones. Bear loped ahead of him, proudly shaking her find, a tree limb festooned with seaweed. Her pace quickened as she neared, and he could see water streaming from her sodden coat as her trot became a gallop. There was no time to warn Jessica, only to act. Her limbs flailed as he yanked her back, curling her under him and pulling the sandy sheet around them like a cocoon.

"What are you doing," she hissed. "Let me go."

"Right away. Just as soon as – ow!"

She poked him hard with her elbow. Maybe chivalry was overrated. He rolled away again but kept his end of the sheet wrapped around himself. Jessica scrambled into a sitting position and glared at him. She looked ready to scold him but she didn't have the opportunity.

True to form, Bear skidded to a halt, dropped the limb at Ronan's side and braced herself to shake.

"Oh, yuck," Jessica sputtered. Ronan took one look at her and dissolved into laughter. She was soaked.

"Shut up." Jessica tried to keep a straight face, but it was a losing battle. Bear lost interest in her stick and flopped down between them. Promptly rolling onto her back, she squirmed energetically, rubbing her wet fur against Ronan and Jessica in turn. There was an industrious quality to her attempts to dry herself that made them laugh harder, even as they scrambled to get out of the way.

Liam, clearly mystified at their hilarity, dumped his rocks into the cooler and began gathering the bags together.

"Hans and Clara said I could stay over tonight, remember? Clara said there would be fried chicken for dinner."

Only a twelve year old boy would be thinking about dinner after two lunches. Ronan shook his head, amused.

"I don't think we'll make it back in time," Jessica said. "I can't show up in public looking like this. I have to change first. Besides, we need to go home to get our car."

She had a point, Ronan decided. The sheet had protected him from most of Bear's fur drying attempts, but Jessica's clothing was covered with damp sandy blotches and streaks of something he couldn't identify and probably didn't want to. Tar, maybe. Liam looked crestfallen. Clara Ulrich's fried chicken must be pretty amazing.

"Jessica, you could stay in the car when we drop Liam off. Then I can bring you back to your house and you can get cleaned up without feeling rushed."

"Yes! Thanks, Ronan." Liam pumped his fist and lost his grip on the cooler.

Jessica rolled her eyes at him and mouthed a "Thank you" to Ronan.

"Does Moon Shell Events have a catering gig tonight?"

"We did," she responded over her shoulder as she reached down for the sandy sheet. "But the party's been postponed. It was supposed to be a baby shower, but the guest of honor is on bed rest."

"Wow. Leisure. How are you going to cope with that?"

"Probably wash the kitchen floor. And the freezer needs defrosting. So."

THE THING ABOUT dogs being loyal was obviously a crock. Bear had been delighted to desert Ronan in favor of a game of catch with Liam and her new best friend, the Ulrich's dachshund pup. Which meant Ronan was alone with Jessica. He had been alone with her after the party of course, but there had been the ghosts of years of students and teachers lingering in that room. Despite the elegant dining Jessica had provided, the walls of the cafeteria were steeped in the daily scent of tater tots.

This moment, as she pulled the car door closed behind her and reached for her seatbelt, felt different, weighted. He wondered whether a storm was coming. He associated this tingling sensation with the moments before thunderstorms. There was no calm before storms, just anticipation – a kind of dreadful, wondrous waiting. But the sun shone bright and the few clouds were small and white. He put the car in drive and pulled away from the curb.

Fifteen minutes and he would drop her off at her cottage. He would drive back to Max and Aidy's house. Probably forage for dinner. Watch a movie from their small collection. Go to bed. Tomorrow, Sunday, would be sunny. Maybe he could get a head start on measuring out the healing garden. He sighed and parked in front of Jessica's house.

"Do you have a date tonight?"

She sounded friendly and interested, but not overly so. The way a longtime friend should sound. Which was exactly what Jessica was, he reminded himself. At least she was handling the situation like a mature adult. He sure wasn't. All he could think about right now was what it would feel like to kiss her.

"My date cancelled on me," he said.

Her brow puckered. "When did that happen?"

"When she met Liam and his friend the dachshund and decided they would be more fun to hang out with tonight. That's okay. Our relationship was getting kind of predictable anyway. Eat dinner. Go for a walk. Hang out on the rug together chewing bones. Fall asleep watching television."

She stared. He could see the moment the information clicked.

"So you're on the rebound from a bad break up," she said.

He laughed delightedly. He had missed this. The quickness of her mind, her sharp wit. The way she never gave him an inch. It was like the smell of rain, after a long drought, so sweet and sharp, the need to breathe it was urgent. But their friendship, relationship, whatever you called this thing they had, couldn't go further. At least, he couldn't let it go further. There was Liam to consider.

"Yep. I'm going to go back to Max and Aidy's house and drown my sorrows with whatever they have in their refrigerator."

She waited a beat, one hand on the door handle, the other cradling Liam's bag of rocks.

"You could stay for dinner at my place. That is, if you want. I'm sure I can rustle up something."

She sounded hesitant, which made no sense. After all, she wasn't likely to make a fool of herself. He, on the other hand, was feeling perilously close to doing just that. Dropping her off and leaving would be the prudent thing. Yes. He would make an excuse and would drive toward town. But his hand refused to change gears and he heard himself blathering inanely. "I'd like that. Something is actually my favorite meal."

When he saw relief flood her face, there was no going back.

CHAPTER 19

JESSICA LEFT RONAN in the living room and fled to take a shower. Smelling like a wet dog might work for Bear, but she was pretty sure it was a turn off for humans. Not that she was trying to turn Ronan on, exactly. Which made choosing what to wear a challenge. Again.

She studied her face in the mirror and sighed. She was proud of what she had accomplished in the last twelve years, but there was no denying the hardships on the way had taken their toll. Caring for Liam meant she had neither time nor energy to pay much attention to her looks. Now she wondered if that had been a mistake. Shrugging, she turned toward her closet. There wasn't much she could do now. Besides, it wasn't as if Ronan was interested in her that way. Looking nice was more a matter of personal pride than practicality tonight. She pulled on a soft pair of slacks and a scoop necked T-shirt and padded barefoot into the kitchen.

Ronan stared at the selection of canned and frozen goods he had arranged on the counter.

"I'm thinking Stella's," he said. "Unless a brick of frost-bitten casserole with a side of canned spinach is what appeals to you."

"Canned spinach? Ick. And I'm not sure when that casserole happened or what's in it."

She pulled open the refrigerator door and looked at the sparse selection.

"Okay. Stella's," she said "But only if I'm buying. I invited you to dinner, remember?"

Men who paid for dates sometimes drew the wrong conclusions. Not that this was a date, of course. Just two old friends sharing a pizza.

She had forgotten how crowded Stella's got on Saturday nights. The portions were generous, the prices reasonable, and Stella made the best pizza in town. Maybe anywhere. By the time a table was open, Jessica was pretty sure everyone in the place had noticed she was with Ronan. She did a mental eye roll. The sensation of being watched, however subtly, was like a scratchy tag on the neckline of an otherwise comfortable shirt. Ronan seemed oblivious, however. He ushered her into the booth, his hand on the small of her back. The warmth of his touch lingered as she sank into the cushioned bench, suddenly ravenous.

"Stella's hasn't changed much," he remarked once they were settled with menus. "Vincenzo and Maria still own the place?"

"He died a couple years ago and their daughter Stella took over the business."

"That was a couple I admired."

"Why?" She put her menu aside.

"They enjoyed being with each other, and they didn't try to hide it. Mortifying for Stella, probably, but I liked it."

"I think most kids are romantics at heart. I was. Liam too. They groan when Prince Charming kisses Sleeping Beauty, but they still peek between their fingers. Childhood is probably the only time human beings can afford to believe in love."

They squabbled in a friendly fashion about pizza toppings and appetizers before settling on mushrooms and peppers and Stella's famous tomato crostini. Ronan flicked the slice of lemon into his glass of ice tea and stirred it around with his straw for a moment before speaking.

"What did you mean by that – about only believing in love when you are a child?"

She shrugged. "There is no happily ever after. You're faced with options. And sometimes the choices you make mean your story can't end happily."

He folded his forearms on the table. "So you're saying life is like those *Choose Your Own Adventure* books."

"Kind of."

"But those books were designed to limit options. Life is broader than that."

She leaned her elbows on the tabletop and cupped her chin in her hands. "Maybe. For some people. But life, my life anyway, is just like those books. I'm boxed in by choices I made."

She broke off as the waitress slid a generous platter onto the table. The scent of roasted tomatoes, garlic, and olive oil coated crusty bread was so heady, Jessica's mouth watered. She was ravenous. When all that remained on the platter were crumbs and a lone cube of tomato, she shifted uncomfortably.

"It's not that I regret all my choices. Keeping Liam was the best choice I ever made."

"I agree." Ronan nodded.

"And I have a good job now, thanks to your brother."

Ronan handed the platter to the waitress in exchange for steaming pizza and clean plates.

"Plus I have friends. The Ulrichs have been wonderful to me."

He served them each a slice of pizza without comment.

"And I even had a chance to repair things with you. I always hoped I would be able to do that."

"So why do you sound so sad?" he said, finally.

"I do not." She meant to sound offended, but it came out a forlorn protest and she wondered if crawling under the table was an option.

"Do too. Are you going to eat your pizza?"

She reached for her fork and then put it down because this for sure wasn't a date and she had no one to impress. Picking up the slice, she shot a defiant look at Ronan.

He smirked. "Only you could turn eating your own slice of pizza into an act of aggression."

"Yeah, well. I'm afraid if I throw my ice tea at you they'll make me leave. And I won't get my pizza. You're incredibly annoying."

"So I've been told. But I've learned to live with it. You have some sauce. There."

He gestured toward her face. She licked her lip and missed. Or maybe not. He stopped breathing for a moment and his gaze sharpened as he watched the tip of her tongue search for the sauce.

"Did I get it all?"

He snatched a napkin and leaned over the table to rub at her cheek. The contact was fleeting but it was enough to make her skin tingle. She had believed she had grown accustomed to lack of physical contact, but clearly she had been wrong. Because the yearning to feel his touch again was intense. When she could focus, she reached for a second slice, hoping he wouldn't notice her hands were trembling. Maybe it wasn't lust, she thought hopefully. Maybe it was a twenty four hour bug of some sort. Surreptitiously she brushed her hand against her forehead. No. No fever.

"How long are you planning to stay on the island, Ronan?"

"A week more. Assuming everything goes according to plan."

A week. She avoided his gaze and put her slice of pizza carefully back on her plate. She didn't feel hungry now. A few days ago she would have been delighted to know he was leaving. Now, she wasn't so sure.

"So, what's next for you?"

"I'll look for a job." He shrugged. "There's bound to be some firm that wants to hire a disgraced disgruntled architectural intern."

"I DON'T UNDERSTAND." She frowned at him as though he had made a joke in poor taste.

"I was fired."

Her eyes widened and he felt a jolt of irritation. "It's complicated."

She leaned back in her seat. "You're talking to the queen of complicated. You might as well spill it. I'm not going to stop pestering you until you do."

So he tried to keep it light. Amusing. But when he finished, she wasn't smiling.

"If you were a woman and Ashleigh was a guy, I would tell you to file a lawsuit. Maybe you should do so anyway. What they did to you was disgusting."

Her eyes flashed. He had teasingly called her princess as a teen, mostly to get a rise out of her. But secretly he had delighted in her seemingly effortless elegance. She had reminded him then of a Disney heroine – flawless, charming, beautiful. Having Jessica as a friend had felt like a dream.

But now she was more of a warrior princess, scars and all. The sort of woman who fought to protect her citadel, leading her troops into battle. She looked ready to take on an army on his behalf and it humbled him.

She yanked her purse onto her lap and slapped a handful of dollars onto the little tray the waitress had left on the table. "People like that make me so angry I could spit."

He followed her out of the restaurant, weaving between the crowded tables. She strode, her shoulders back. Her hair practically twitched.

He caught up with her on the sidewalk and grabbed her arm. "Slow down, tiger."

She rounded on him. "And you? You're not much better. You had a chance at your dream. Are you just going to let it go?"

He dropped his hand, stunned.

"I said I'm applying for other jobs."

"Sure. As an architect. But you never wanted to be an architect. You wanted to be an artist."

"Yeah. Well, I grew up." Seemingly of their own volition, his hands had balled into fists.

"And you shouldn't confuse my life with yours. Mathematics with a minor in education, wasn't it? You were going to change the way children were taught math. Or was your true dream to manage parties for demanding snobs?"

The moment it was out, he realized it had been a mistake. Her face was white and she stepped back slowly, one hand out in a vain effort to halt the words after they had been said.

"Jessica, I'm sorry."

It seemed important to move slowly, to speak gently. As though one off-rhythm breath might destroy whatever this was they had built between them. Friendship, maybe. Certainly a kind of bridge.

"I know." Her voice was low, almost inaudible.

He saw she would lose her balance before it happened, but he couldn't move fast enough to prevent it. Her heel caught on a crack in the pavement and she stumbled, grabbing at the parked car behind her for balance.

"Whoop! Whoop! Whoop!" The car shrieked. "Alert! Alert! I have been tampered with!" a mechanized voice announced in urgent tones.

He pulled her to him. Shaking, she buried her head against his chest. His heart hurt at the thought his angry remarks could have caused that. Gently, he pulled away, crouching slightly so he could look up at her face. She was laughing. His knees nearly gave way at the relief of it.

"Whoop! Whoop! Whoop!" she gasped.

"I have been tampered with!" he wheezed.

They clung to each other helplessly as they laughed. Eventually, their hilarity subsided into hiccups on her part and silent tears on his. It helped that the car subsided into silence at about the same time.

"Don't look at me," he said. "You'll set us off again."

"You think so?"

Slowly she turned toward him, her eyes still merry. Remnants of laughter lingered on her lips. She looked vital, strong. Less brittle than she had a moment ago but still with that fine bone china delicacy that was her hallmark. She rested the her hand on his chest. Her palm radiated heat and yet he shivered.

"It would be a terrible idea to invite you to stay the night with me."

"It would be a terrible idea for me to accept an invitation like that," he replied hoarsely.

They stared at each other silently.

"Want to?"

"Yes" seemed too paltry a word, but in the moment, he was having trouble coming up with a more clever one. Silently they climbed into the Bentley, and he concentrated on driving because if he didn't he would run off the road. He glanced at her.

"It's okay if you change your mind," he said.

She shook her head calmly. "Are you having second thoughts?" she asked.

"No, it's just —" He gestured toward her laced fingers.

"Oh, that. I just think we're more likely to get home safely if I keep my hands to myself."

His heart beat slow, steady, determined. Spending the night with Jessica was a terrible idea, but that was irrelevant. Because if he didn't take this one opportunity he would regret it for the rest of his miserable life. And life as he expected it to go would be miserable.

Not that there was anything wrong with architecture — he loved certain aspects of the field in the abstract. The lines, the use of hard materials to create something ethereal, the idea of creating a vast sculpture that served as a living artwork for the humans who interacted with it.

It was a field he ought to like. A practical way to support his family. So he no longer bought paint. Or canvas. Or charcoal pencils. He avoided art stores because he couldn't bear the earthy scent of clay. And under no circumstances did he set foot in either the Institute of Contemporary Art or the Museum of Fine Art. Killing a dream required discipline.

But he couldn't live with the loss of every dream. The one remaining parking spot on the silent street waited in the pool of darkness under a broken streetlamp. He pulled the car to the curb and turned off the ignition. In the silence, he could hear the tick of the engine cooling. A lone cricket chirping in the grass. And his pulse, beating hard and steady.

CHAPTER 20

FOR A MOMENT, Jessica wasn't sure. But he had an uncertain look to him, an expression so alien to his usual easy manner that a wave of tenderness swept over her. So she took his hand in hers and tugged him gently toward the porch.

The house felt oddly unfamiliar. Maybe it was the sound of Ronan's heavier footsteps or the scent of him, ocean with a side of pizza. She closed the door and walked toward the bedroom, heavy and slow. Either he would follow her or he wouldn't. She hoped he would.

Her shoulders eased a fraction when she heard him behind her. His breath rattled hoarsely and she wondered if he heard hers hitch at the sound. When she neared the bed, she turned to face him. She watched him carefully. Even now, he might leave. And she would understand if he did. It couldn't be easy taking the risk of being rejected twice by the same woman. She didn't kid herself that he loved her anymore, but that didn't mean he couldn't be hurt.

She didn't want to think about how it would feel when he walked away from her as he surely would do. But the agony would be worth it. Because, she needed something to hold close when the loneliness got to be too much. She had friends, of course. But the need for Ronan, and Ronan alone, was a specific loneliness none of them could ease.

He wasn't smiling but the corners of his mouth twitched, and she let out the breath she had been holding. At least she had cleaned up the bedroom recently, so the usual pile of laundry was gone and the bed had clean sheets. But as a space for seduction, it left a lot to be desired – drab wall to wall carpeting with stains no amount of shampooing could remove, the spider like crack in the corner of the ceiling that dripped during rainstorms.

"Changed your mind? We don't have to do this. I'd settle for a cup of tea and a session of knock knock jokes on the front porch."

And that was exactly what appealed to her about Ronan. Because even though she could hear the strain in his voice in his attempt to sound casual, she knew he meant it. He simply enjoyed spending time with her. She stepped forward until she stood toe to toe with him, reaching up for his shoulders. "If we're going to kiss, you're going to have to lean forward. That is, if *you* haven't changed your mind."

His lips were gentle at first, tender. As though paying homage to the young man who had longed so hopelessly to kiss her. But she kissed him too and then it was no longer a matter of gentleness but of need, hunger.

She had always considered clothing an enhancement, but now her garments, his, were barriers to closeness. And the need for that closeness was urgent. She reached for the buttons on his shirt and halted, stricken.

"I didn't even think to put on nice underwear."

"What's wrong with it?"

"It's boring and sensible."

"Champagne tastes good in any glass."

He was looking down at her now and the hunger in his eyes warmed her. She put her hand on his chest to feel the steady thumping of his heart. She could hear his sudden intake of breath at her touch, and it made her feel bolder. Maybe the underwear didn't matter so much after all.

On the other hand, clothing covered a lot of flaws. She had a sudden image of the way she had once looked. The woman she caught a glimpse of in the mirror on her bureau was saggy by comparison. Her breasts drooped now, and there were stretch marks on her no longer toned belly. The contrast was unavoidable, and she didn't want to see acknowledgment of that shock and disappointment in his face. Nor did she want his pity. It would be better to cut her losses now because she couldn't bear to be a charity case.

"Jessica." He sounded hesitant. "What's wrong?"

"It's not the same. *I'm* not the same as I was when you loved me."

"Of course not. Neither am I."

"Physically, I mean." She dropped her hand. This was not going to work.

"Jess."

The sharpness in his tone arrested her mid-motion.

"I'd rather have honesty. If I have bad breath or you can't stand my taste in jokes, say so. But polite fictions about how badly you've aged are an insult to my intelligence."

"Fine!" She threw her hands in the air and glared at him. "Can you honestly tell me a caesarian scar and stretch marks are a turn on? My breasts droop. My neck is sagging."

He looked dumbfounded. "Seriously? You think that's what matters to me? I don't know whether to laugh or be offended."

She folded her arms. "You're beautiful," she muttered. "You could be a freakin' model. The best you can say for me now is that I'm ordinary."

"Okay," he said. "I guess I am offended after all."

They stood silently staring at each other for the better part of a minute. She wondered if her scowl mirrored his. She was so absorbed in the thought it took her a moment to register the rattling sound. Springing backwards, she held a finger to her lips with one hand as she reached for the door knob with the other.

"It's Liam," she hissed. "Stay here and don't make a sound."

Heart in her throat, she slipped out of her bedroom, yanking the bedroom door shut behind her.

"Liam, honey? Everything okay?"

"Sure. Hans said he wanted to learn how to play video games so we came back to get some."

"Great." She tried to invest as much enthusiasm as she could into her response, but the curious look Liam gave her told her she hadn't quite succeeded. He tucked the game system into a worn tote bag and snatched a handful of games to go with it before pausing.

"Is it still okay if I go? You don't mind, right?"

"Of course it's okay, ba —" She caught herself before she completed the sentence. He hated when she called him baby.

"Great!"

And he was gone, screen door slamming behind him. She turned back to the bedroom with a sigh. There wasn't any point in kidding herself. She and Ronan couldn't roll back time and it was pointless to try. She turned the knob on her bedroom door three times before she realized there was something wrong. "Ronan?"

"Still here."

"Very funny. Can you open the door?"

The knob jiggled, gently at first then more vigorously.

"Nope. It seems to be stuck. Is there a key?"

"There's no lock. But the knob sticks. That's why I don't usually close the door."

She rested her forehead against the door frame. She had expected to politely usher Ronan out of the house at this point. Because their rendezvous sure wasn't going anywhere. And Liam's brief reappearance had served as a much needed reminder of her responsibilities. She sank to the floor, her back against the door, her eyes stinging.

"You still there?" Ronan sounded amused.

"It's not funny," she said finally. "I don't think I can break the door down like they do on those action dramas on TV. Plus the landlord will be furious if I do."

He snorted. "I'll be furious if you do. You'd probably break your shoulder."

"Foot," she said absently. "I was thinking about kicking it in. How about a screw?"

"I'm game. But how do you plan to accomplish that through a door?"

"Not that kind of screw, idiot. Is there a screw on your side of the door knob?"

"There is. Do you keep a Philips-head screwdriver in your bedroom? I knew you were a planner, but I had no idea you were that organized."

"No. It's in the kitchen. But maybe I can pass it to you underneath."

The bedroom door had been cut high which meant she had no real privacy, but now she was grateful for the large gap. Breathing a silent prayer, she gently slid the screwdriver under the door. The knob rattled one last time and fell to the floor. The door swung open and he was close. Too close, she thought dizzily. She closed her eyes for a moment as she inhaled the scent of him.

"Jessica?"

"Mmm?" She opened her eyes and looked up at him, conscious that she should step back now. Put a polite distance between them. But she couldn't bring herself to do so just yet.

"Could we start again?"

"I don't think —"

He traced his fingertips along the curve of her ear and cupped her cheek.

"If you just want to keep things light, I'm fine with that. I respect your sense of responsibility to Liam, and I'd like to think I'd make the same decision if the situation were reversed. But I want you to understand I think you are beautiful. Not just —"

He slid his fingers into her hair and watched as the strands slipped between them.

"Not just physically. Although definitely that. But because people are like art, their essence shines through the cracks in the paint. And your essence was what always drew me in. Even the years I hated you, I couldn't help wanting you, missing you.

"We both have scars. They add a kind of interest and depth we didn't have when we were younger. It's the difference between pretty and beautiful. I always thought you were pretty. Now I think you are beautiful."

She searched his face. But the teasing light she expected was not present in his level gaze. Gently, she rested the palm of her hand over his heart. His eyes widened but he made no other acknowledgment. He was waiting for her to make the next move. For the first time in years, she felt powerful. "Remarks like that will get you in trouble, Mr. Durrell."

"I don't see how that's possible, Ms. Piers. Benjamin Franklin said 'Honesty is the best policy.' You wouldn't want to go up against Ben Franklin, would you?" He smiled down at her and her shoulders eased.

"Absolutely not," she said. "And because I have so much respect for the guy, I need to be honest with you too."

His smile faded slowly. He was bracing himself for rejection, she realized. Her heart hurt at the thought, but there was no way to avoid the conversation now. It had been irresponsible of her to let things go this far. Self indulgent.

"I can't do this. I thought I could. But I can't." It burst from her, leaving the taste of acid in her throat, instead of the sense of relief she expected.

"Too fast?"

"Maybe. I'm sorry. I just think it's a bad idea."

"No need to apologize. We only just got past the wanting to kill each other stage. It might be a little early to leap into bed."

"Well, yes. But what I meant was I'm sorry to lose the opportunity. I wish my life was different, sometimes. That it was the kind of life that allowed for –" she gestured helplessly.

"Life changing sexual epiphanies?"

She snorted. "What makes you think you have anything new to show me? I'm extremely experienced at this point. It's been over twelve years."

His grin broadened. The fact that he was irritating and attractive at the same time was in itself annoying.

"What?"

He shrugged. "If you're so knowledgeable maybe you can teach me a thing or two. I'm a big fan of adult education."

Great. Now he thought she was a lot more experienced than she was. And there was no way she could live up to that expectation. Except for a few fumbles in cars at the end of dates, she hadn't come close to the act since Chris Mullin. And making love with Chris that one time hadn't exactly been earthshaking either. Which was hardly his fault. Neither of them had known more than the physical requirements and whatever they had seen in movies. Plus they had both been drunk, a regular occurrence for him and a first and only experience for her. It had occurred to her since then there must be more to it.

"What are you thinking, Jess?"

She looked up at his face and drank in the smile line on his cheek, the way his eyebrow was a little crooked on the right side, letting those images sink deep. Once Liam had brought her an apple from a field trip to a local orchard. The farmer taped paper heart cutouts to the apples when they were green and the heart shape stayed green as the apple skins reddened. Maybe she couldn't have Ronan, but surely she could imprint this moment in her heart. The moment when the possibility had been offered. When for a split second anything had been possible.

"I think you should probably go."

CHAPTER 21

JESSICA GROANED AND slapped her bedside table until she managed to locate her vibrating cell phone. She squinted at the screen. Fifteen minutes to midnight. It hadn't been easy to fall asleep with the memory of Ronan's kiss burnt into her psyche. And now her adrenalin was pumping again. Because a late night call was never good news. Flicking the switch on her bedside lamp, she scooched into a sitting position and stared at the lit screen.

Mom.

She felt the familiar pull. The unwavering childish hope this time it would be different. This time her mother would love her the way other mothers loved their daughters. And even better, it would turn out Jessica had made a foolish mistake. Her mother had actually loved her that way always.

She glanced at the corner of a business card that peeped over the edge of the little bowl on the bureau and stiffened her resolve. Clara Ulrich had recognized the signs of postpartum depression in Jessica after Liam was born and had insisted Jessica see a therapist. But Dr. Eisenberg had done more than walk Jessica through the months after Liam was born. Jessica hadn't had an appointment with the therapist for several years now, but after this conversation she'd probably need one.

She held her forefinger over the red icon and reminded herself she was allowed to decline the call. Cookie would leave a message. But the thought of Cookie's message waiting in her inbox with its promise of disappointment was unappealing. Better to deal with it now. She pressed the green icon.

"Mom."

"Candy, honey. It's so good to hear your voice. I miss you. It's been such a long time."

Jessica sighed silently. The awful thing was she wanted to hear her mother's voice too. She could feel her treacherous heart ease for a moment at the familiar sound of her mother's breathing. But it wasn't fair. Because that familiarity came with an unacceptable trade off. And every time she heard her mother, she had to remind herself of that. "Mom, what do you want?"

"Can't I just call my daughter to say hello?" Cookie sounded injured and Jessica tightened her grip on the cell phone.

"Sure you can." Although it was unlikely.

Since Cookie had moved away from the island, their contact had been sporadic to put it generously. At first, in an attempt to give Liam a connection with his grandparents, Jessica sent birthday cards signed by herself and Liam. Her father, Austin, never responded – probably so busy with his new family he didn't see the point. And while Cookie sent cards in return on Jessica's birthday, she never sent any to Liam. It was as if she believed ignoring Liam would make him disappear.

For a while Jessica had tried to call her mother regularly in a vain hope their relationship would turn into something more palatable. But Cookie's primary interests were fashionable clothing and social status. Since Jessica's financial status allowed for neither and since Cookie had no interest in Liam, there wasn't much to talk about once they got past the weather.

"I'm coming back to Demerest Cove for a visit," Cookie announced.

In the sudden silence, Jessica could hear the whoosh of her own pulse in her ears. It was as though the world around her with its comforting clatter had gone silent.

"That would be, I mean, Liam would –" she stammered.

"Lynne invited me to her garden party next week. But you and I can get together for coffee, just the two of us. It could be like old times. I'll let you know when and where."

"Oh. Okay. I guess –"

"And wear something nice. Dior always suited you."

"I'm not in that bracket anymore, Mom."

"Oh, pooh. A cute little dress won't set you back much, and it can have a big effect on the rest of your life. You never know who might walk by that day."

Jessica rolled her eyes as much at her mother's foolishness as at the fact that twelve years ago she herself would have thought the same thing. But raising Liam and making sure he was fed and clothed had changed her priorities in ways Cookie obviously couldn't conceive of. The choice between a little black Dior and a month's worth of groceries was a no-brainer.

"Mom," she said finally. "I'm not looking to impress anyone."

"That's ridiculous. You can't expect to get a wealthy man if you dress like a slob."

Jessica covered her eyes with her free hand and concentrated on breathing.

"Are you still there, Candy?"

"Yep. Still here."

"Don't pout. Sulking is only cute when you're young. And you aren't a spring chicken anymore. At your age, you have to make an effort."

"Thanks, Mom."

"Oh, don't be silly, Candy. It's the least I can do. If you can't hear the truth from your own mother who can you hear it from? So. I'll let you know where and when for coffee."

"I do work, Mom, so it would be best if we plan in advance."

"Oh, right. Your little catering thing. Self employed isn't exactly the same as working, dear. It's not as though your boss is going to fire you, is it?"

Jessica didn't enlighten her. She had a visceral desire to keep her connection to the Durrell family private as long as she could in the same way she never mentioned the Ulrichs to her mother. And she absolutely couldn't tell Cookie about Ronan. If Cookie knew there was some sort of friendship thing happening, she would ruin it without even intending to. It was what Cookie did.

COOKIE'S CALL MIGHT have been disconcerting, but at least it had brought on a surge of housecleaning. Jessica sat back on her heels to survey her progress. The oven hadn't been cleaned in – well – too long. She had already stripped the beds and she planned to tackle the refrigerator next. So maybe she should thank Cookie next time she saw her. She shuddered. Maybe her mother would cancel.

"Liam, could you bring up the sheets from the washing machine? If you leave them in the basket by the back door, I'll hang them outside. Also, since you're headed down to the basement anyway, could you bring the tablecloths from yesterday down with you and start them on permanent press?"

"Sure," Liam said.

Jessica was nearly done with the oven before she realized Liam had been in the basement for an unusually long time. The basement was too damp to use as a storage space, and the only furnishings were the washer and the dryer that stood under a hanging bulb. Puzzled, she put down the washcloth and shoved the dishpan to the side.

"Liam?" she called.

When he didn't respond she headed down the stairs but stopped short at the sight of him. Wet sheets were piled on the dryer and part of a tablecloth spilled out of the washing machine. But Liam stood silent, a pair of envelopes in one hand and what looked like a handwritten letter in the other. Slowly he raised his eyes to hers.

"What is it, honey?"

His voice was hoarse. "It's my dad."

The basement suddenly felt unbearably chilly. She walked down the stairs cautiously, as though a sudden motion might startle him. As she reached the last step, she held out her hand slowly. He hesitated for a moment and something inside her died a little.

Dear Liam,

I'm writing to you to try to make amends for the years I wasn't present as your dad. I should have been there for you. I am sorry I wasn't.

Because I made the bad decision to use drugs, I made lots of other bad decisions too. One of those bad decisions was letting your mom send me away when she was pregnant with you.

But now I have been clean and sober for two years, three months and seventeen days. As the new youth minister for Days of Joy Church in Demerest Cove, I will have the opportunity to be a dad to you and a guide for your mother.

I look forward to meeting you soon.

Love,

Your Dad, Chris Mullin

She looked up from the page, dazed. Liam's face was flushed, his eyes wide.

"Is it true, Mom?"

"Liam, where did you get this?"

"It was wrapped in the bunch of tablecloths. Is what he says true?"

Jessica had a sudden recollection of bundling the pile of dirty tablecloths from the Friedman's anniversary party in one arm yesterday afternoon and collecting the mail in the other. It had been a sheaf of circulars, she remembered now, with dull certainty. And there had been letters in the sheaf. And without thinking she had folded the whole mass together into the basket by the door. She held out her hand for the closed envelope.

"Mom?"

She rubbed her forehead and shook her head.

"I can't – yes. Sort of. Part of it is true."

"You sent my dad away?" He spoke in a strained whisper as though the thought was too painful to say aloud. "You told me he left. That you had no idea where he had gone. But you *sent* him away. How could you do that to me?"

She tried to speak but the words wouldn't come. He snatched his letter from her hand, tossed the unopened envelope onto the washing machine and ran for the stairs. She looked at the envelope and looked away again, barely registering the thud of his feet as he fled. Her lips tingled. She grabbed a cold damp pillowcase from the pile on the dryer and held it against the back of her neck. She refused to faint. The envelope squatted, malignant. Waiting. Well it could just frickin' wait until she had hung the sheets.

She pinned the last sheet to the line and took an extra minute to make sure all of them were hanging straight before she was ready. It was probably just an apology letter like the one Liam had received. She had read that Alcoholics Anonymous encouraged their members to make amends. She guessed whatever addiction support program Chris was a part of did the same.

It wasn't a matter of forgiveness. She had forgiven Chris a long time ago. But good intentions could sometimes lead to disaster, as she had reason to know. She sank onto the back stoop and pulled the envelope from her back pocket. She considered leaving it unopened. Or throwing it away. But worse than the fear of being unfair or unkind to Chris was the underlying menace of the thing. She had to know what was in it.

Dear Candy,

Thirteen years ago, when I learned you were pregnant with our son, I made a terrible mistake. When you told me you didn't want to marry me, and that you didn't want my help with the baby, I was only too eager to believe you. So I left the island.

My faith, along with the help of Narcotics Anonymous has helped me turn my life around. I live one day at a time, but my goal is to become a pastor. Over the next two years, while I earn a Master of Divinity online, I'll be serving as youth minister at Days of Joy Church on Demerest Cove.

Raising Liam alone required courage and struggle on your part, Candy, but I am here now to share that burden. And, as a father should, I will be a male role model to Liam as he enters the rocky shoals of his teens.

Part of that responsibility includes protecting Liam from bad influences. My mother tells me you are still unmarried, and I worry about the impact of your single lifestyle on an impressionable boy.

Marrying you would require sacrifice on my part, since I had hoped to wed a devout woman with deep connections to the church. But it is a sacrifice I would gladly make in service of my Lord and of the greater good.

Under the circumstances, I think you will agree quick action is needed. I hope, after some rational thought, you will act in Liam's best interest.

Yours in Christ,
Chris

The sounds of the wind soughing through the neighboring trees and the vigorous bird calls faded away. All she could hear was the sound of her heart slamming against her rib cage and the rasp of her breath. Slowly, deliberately, she refolded the pages and forced them into the envelope. Her hands were shaking as she jammed the papers into her pocket.

"No." The harsh guttural tone sounded as if it had come from someone else. She had a swift mental image of a cave woman, crouched low, sharpened stone blade in hand, long stringy hair swaying as she readied to strike. That was the true Jessica. The one who would do anything it took to protect her son, even if Liam hated her for it.

CHAPTER 22

SHE YANKED HER phone out of her pocket and dialed automatically before she wished she hadn't. Barbara's busy legal practice rarely allowed for time off.

"Jess, what's wrong?"

"Nothing that won't keep. I forgot it was Sunday morning."

"No, no, no – don't you dare hang up. Salim took the kids out to the playground and the last thing I want to do with a precious thirty minutes of me time is to sleep. Besides, we haven't talked in forever. Are you okay? You sounded off kilter for a minute. And how's Liam?"

"Not great. Chris is back. He sent us each a letter, and now Liam hates me because I deprived him of his father."

"Read them to me."

Barbara was uncharacteristically quiet after Jessica finished. When she spoke again, she was all business. "I'm going to need a copy of Liam's letter as well. Remind me. Is Chris listed as father on Liam's birth certificate?"

"No." Jessica rose and paced the small yard.

"No offense, but I have to ask this – you're absolutely certain Chris is Liam's father?"

"One hundred percent."

"So, here's the problem," Barbara said. "Chris has been off the radar for Liam's entire childhood so far. However, he could argue that he was incapable of meeting his obligations until now. He could petition the court to help him establish paternity, and he could then go on to request parenting time and even joint custody."

Jessica staggered and reached blindly for the nearest fence post. The old wood was rough and a splinter drove itself into her palm. She looked at it stupidly and dropped her hand to her side, shaking it impatiently, grateful for the distraction of the pain.

"That can't be right." She was aware as she spoke that it was too loud, too harsh. "You said I didn't need to worry. You said a single mother automatically has sole custody.

That's what you *told* me." She couldn't un-hear the pleading tone in her own voice.

"I know, Jess. And when I told you that, it was true. But the courts have changed their approach in the past ten years. Barring situations that involve violence or abuse, judges try to ensure a child has access to both parents. Chris never sent you any child support, right? Did he ever offer to help out?"

"Once, when I first told him I was pregnant. But that was back when I thought I could rely on my parents for support. So I felt comfortable turning him down. Is that bad?"

"It's not good. If he had never offered, you could argue he was purposely neglectful. But any judge who reads the letter you just read to me will interpret it as remorse and an attempt to make reparations. Which puts Chris in an excellent position to request partial custody."

Fury ripped through her, nauseating in its intensity. For a moment she couldn't speak. She tucked the phone between her ear and her shoulder so she could yank the jagged sliver of wood from her palm.

"Jessica? Are you still there?"

She watched a drop of blood well up from the wound as though it were on someone else's hand.

"What do I need to do to fight this? I'm willing to go to court if necessary. I'll do whatever it takes."

"Judges prefer parents resolve these sorts of disputes amicably. If you don't or can't and a judge gets involved, it's not likely to solve your problem. Unless you can demonstrate that Chris would be abusive to Liam or still has an ongoing addiction to illegal substances, your chances of success are slim to none."

Jessica sank slowly to the stoop, her legs trembling.

"I hate it that Chris is managing to come between me and Liam."

"Together, you and Liam will both get through this. I know it's not easy to imagine relating to Chris, but you must have had something in common once, right?"

"We were babies, Barbara. That's all we had in common. I was as stupid as Chris was. I didn't think through the consequences of my actions either."

"Wrong," Barbara snapped. "You didn't make the same decisions Chris did. Because when it came to Liam and his welfare, you would have done just about anything to keep your son safe. It's one of reasons I admire you, Jessica."

"I had help," Jessica said quietly.

"Your parents were more of a hindrance than a help."

"No. Not them. You. And your parents."

"Jessica, that's ridiculous. We all got back more than we gave you. Still do. If I couldn't talk to you every couple days I swear I'd go insane."

Jessica hung up feeling strangely lighter. It wasn't as though anything had been solved, but Barbara had always been good at putting things in context. Jessica took a deep breath and let it out slowly before knocking on Liam's door. No response. She shrugged away the sudden chill of fear and forced reason to kick in. The innate fear that Liam was just waiting for the right time to leave, that once again she would be left on her own, alone, unloved, was unreasonable. And unfair. He was probably outside playing basketball. Liam wouldn't go far without telling her.

Dr. Eisenberg had said once that just because some men had left Jessica didn't mean every man would. For the most part, Jessica managed to remember that. Liam would leave for real someday, to go to college, to make his way in the world. She accepted that. Wanted it for him. But occasionally the old fear ambushed her, slithering into the cracks of her consciousness before she had time to block it.

When Liam was little, it had been easy being his mom — despite the financial hardships, the uncertainty, and her fear of getting it wrong. Because as a boy, his face had been an open book to her. But recently, she had noticed a kind of reserve, as though he was withdrawing into a new version of himself. It was still Liam, but it was as if she was looking at him from some minor distance. Close enough to see his face but just too far to be absolutely sure of the message in his eyes.

She swung the door open, sure she would find the room empty. But Liam lay on his bed, asleep. Belatedly, she remembered how late he had been up last night. She stood for a moment, watching his eyelids quiver as he dreamed. With a pang, she noted he was cuddled up with Morty Moose. Morty had been a faithful companion to toddler Liam but rarely made an appearance these days. Gently, she closed the door again and tiptoed away.

SHE WAS NURSING a mug of coffee when Liam shambled out of his bedroom.

"Want cocoa?"

"How did we get cocoa?"

"I skipped out to the store while you were napping."

He tore a pouch of cocoa open and filled his cup with boiling water. She saw him pause mid-stir to register the cylinder of instant whipped cream and the bag of marshmallows on the counter. He shot her an unreadable look and busied himself topping the cocoa with a swirl of whipped cream. He slid into the chair opposite hers, cocoa slopping over the edge of the cup, and plopped three marshmallows on top. Her hand tightened on her own mug in anticipation.

"Nice bribe, Mom. But we still need to talk."

Despite, or maybe because of the tension in her throat, a laugh threatened to bubble up, but she managed to contain it. "That was my line," she said. "And you're right, we do. I owe you an explanation."

She had always loved Liam's eyes. He was born a thoughtful baby and his soft but persistent gaze had been a constant in her adult life. Now he looked down to poke at his marshmallows, but she knew he was completely focused on the topic. He wasn't going to let it go, and to be fair, he shouldn't. She ran her finger around the rim of her mug for courage and told him.

He sat silent for several endless minutes when she had finished. His gaze was fixed on the window beyond her, but she was pretty sure he wasn't seeing the branches waving in the sunlight. She looked at her hands, focusing her slightly crooked left thumb. She had broken it once as a child, falling out of a swing. Now it seemed emblematic of the moment. Mundane, but still a mark of irretrievable change.

"So he's a little bit right. You did tell him to leave."

She raised her eyes to Liam's, thankful beyond measure that his tone was more thoughtful than angry.

"I did. And I'm sorry I didn't tell you more about Chris sooner. I apologize, Liam."

"Okay." Liam nodded and took a slow sip of his cocoa. "Maybe that was a good decision when I was four. But I'm twelve, Mom. I've already learned about stuff like addiction and teen pregnancy in health class. Just knowing about other people's stupid decisions doesn't mean I'm going to make those decisions myself. Dumb ideas aren't contagious."

She bit back her instinctive retort. Because he was right about this too. She and Chris had made stupid decisions. She had just admitted to them. Still, it was entirely different hearing the label from her son. She was fairly sure Liam hadn't intended to embarrass her so much as to make his point about his own good sense. Which helped a little with the mortification of being given a dressing down by a twelve year old with a chocolate mustache.

"I agree," she said, trying to ignore the sudden heat in her cheeks. "I know you make good decisions most of the time. But my story is a good way to remember that no one makes good decisions *all* of the time. Mostly, Chris and I were well behaved, respectful to adults and good students. That's why our parents and teachers were so shocked when we acted out. But adults make mistakes too. And keeping you from knowing the full story about me and Chris was another poor decision."

"Do you still love him?"

She shook her head.

"Um. I think Chris may have the wrong impression of how much help you and I need. So he and I will probably have to talk about that."

"You don't *have* to marry him, right?"

"No, sweetheart. You know what Clara says — You can't force anyone to love you or to lend you money. I don't love Chris. I never did. I think we just liked each other and liked the idea of being in love. "

A look of relief flashed across his face. She suspected the prospect of so much change at once was as alarming for him as it was for her.

"Are we okay, then?" Her heart was in her throat.

"Sure. Like you always say to me, live and learn. Right?" He reached across the table and patted her hand. "Not to give you a swelled head or anything, but mostly you're okay as a mom. I mean, you don't make mistakes like this too often."

"Thanks. I think. Obviously, live and learn applies to me too." She blinked back sudden tears. To cover them, she rose to put her now cold coffee in the microwave. For the first time in hours, she noticed the fragrance of new growth in her garden, carried on a light breeze through the window screen.

"I don't even know what to call him," Liam said. He lifted his drained mug up and down, leaving a pattern of cocoa circles on the table top. "I don't know him well enough to call him dad."

"You could start with calling him Chris and see how that goes."

"I guess."

"Liam, do you want to meet your father?" Jessica's stomach clenched. She was pretty sure what the answer would be, and her body was already punishing her for having asked the question. Because maybe if she hadn't asked, she could postpone the inevitable. But it was too late now.

"Would you be upset if I did, Mom?"

She took a deep breath and shook her head. "No. If that's what you want to do, I understand."

It was peculiar to have to fix one lie by telling a second one. Or maybe there were levels of lies. Because this one, like the one before it, was the kind you told for love. And like the time she decided to keep her past secret from Liam, this lie was intended to protect. But she couldn't help feeling like the bird she had seen a portrait of once in a mythology book, pulling feathers from its own breast to pad a nest for its young.

CHAPTER 23

"YOU WERE HOME late last night." Aidy snagged another peeled potato from the bowl and began cubing it methodically.

Ronan concentrated on creating perfectly even cucumber slices. The silence demanded a response. He put the knife down, resignedly. He had ended up driving back to the Ulrichs to pick up a reluctant Bear, but Aidy didn't need to know that. Nor did she need a recounting of the polite but thorough grilling Hans and Clara Ulrich had subjected him to. He reminded himself to never again say yes when invited to sit down to a plate of freshly baked cookies. Although considering the quality of the cookies, it had been almost worth it.

"I went to Stella's," he hedged. "Did I wake you when I came in?"

"Nah. I was already awake." She patted her swollen belly. "The kid was busy tap dancing in the middle of the night. No point in even trying to sleep until dance class is over. Did you have fun?"

He grinned at her and channeled Groucho Marx, waggling his brows and tapping a piece of bell pepper as if it were a cigar.

"That's not what I meant," she protested, blushing. "It's just that it's hard to find fun stuff to do around here when it's off season. You're probably used to a Boston level of nightlife. I've been worried you would be bored. Or have you just been too polite to say so?"

"He's not that polite," Max growled, stepping into the kitchen to check the roasting chicken. He seemed satisfied and reached into the salad bowl to snag one of the cucumber slices Ronan had just added to the mix.

"Not my fault," Ronan retorted. "I learned my manners from you."

"Not my fault either. I learned my manners from Jock."

"It's nice of you and Aidy to offer to babysit Jane. That's next week, right."

"Right. It's nice of them to let us practice parenthood on their daughter for a week."

Ronan busied himself with vegetable arrangement to hide a smile. Max rarely sounded uncertain, but he did now.

"A two year old isn't the same as an infant," Ronan pointed out. "And Jane is a particularly bright —"

The doorbell rang.

"I'll get it." Aidy wiped her hands on her apron and headed for the front door.

"What's going on?" Ronan pitched his voice low. Shrugging, Max checked the chicken again.

"Max."

"Aidy invited Jessica to dinner. I reminded her the two of you don't get along. Every time I walk by your office I hear you squabbling. But she said maybe spending some time together outside of work would help with that.

Great. This wouldn't be awkward at all.

"Hi Ronan," Liam's face was alight with excitement. "It smells great in here."

"Hey, Liam." Ronan's eyes met Jessica's. He could read her discomfort in the tilt of her head, the careful set of her jaw. "Jessica."

"Hi, Max. Ronan." Jessica shot him a desperate look and grabbed a handful of silverware. She busied herself setting the table.

If she hadn't sounded so rueful last night, it would have been easier to leave. Ronan had hesitated for a good ten minutes under the dim glow of her porch light, even after she shut the door, wondering what they might be missing. But she had been right. Staying the night even without complicating matters by making love would have made things awkward. And he treasured the delicate thread of friendship they were reforming too much to risk it.

But it was one thing to have a sort of unacknowledged détente, maybe even the beginnings of a friendship between him and Jessica, and it was another thing altogether to be paired together in public. Not that dinner at Max and Aidy's counted as a major social event exactly. Still. At least Jessica seemed no happier with the situation than he was, although probably for different reasons.

He glanced at Liam, already busy whisking salad dressing under Aidy's direction. Liam was an earnest kid. A good kid. Maybe he would have been sweet natured anyway, but the foundation for Liam's character was in his raising. No matter how Ronan felt about Jessica, he had to give her credit for that. Because Liam was the kind of boy any man would be proud to call his own. So Ronan absolutely understood why Jessica had sent him home last night. The suspicion that Liam wouldn't approve had been enough to override any remaining desire Ronan had to stay the night. Didn't change what Ronan's body wanted.

He guessed that wasn't an issue for Jessica though. After that one awkward moment when she first walked in the door, no one would have guessed there was anything going on between her and her boss's brother. She treated Ronan with the same cordial charm she treated everyone in the room. Not one ounce less or more. It should have been enough. He brought the salad bowl to the table, slid into a chair and tugged his napkin from the napkin ring Jessica had just threaded it into.

"What's the point of those things, anyway?"

"Napkin rings?" She shot him a mystified look across the table.

"I mean I know they're decorative," he added, "but ultimately they seem pointless."

"I think some people use them to tell whose napkin is whose. You know, so you can use the napkins more than once." She sounded polite, a little distant.

"Gross. Then they'd get all crusty and disgusting." Liam plonked a platter of garlic bread on the table and sat next to Ronan.

"That's a custom from the days when people didn't have washing machines," Aidy said. "Back in the 1800's The Grand used to have an enormous collection of linens because laundry day happened about every couple months."

She set more platters on the table and waited for Max to take his seat at one end of the table before settling into her own seat at the other end. The conversation turned to the benefits of modern machinery. Absentmindedly, Ronan passed the salad to Max and listened to Liam chatter about cars of the future. Jessica sat across from him but avoided meeting his eyes. She had barely touched her food.

He reached his foot toward hers under the table and knew he had made contact when she twitched. But she made no other acknowledgment. Instead, she turned away from him slightly and asked Aidy about what it had been like growing up at The Grand.

He poked her foot again and was rewarded with a quick kick in the shin for his trouble – not hard enough to hurt, but still intentional. He purposely dropped his napkin and bent to pick it up, which gave him time to get rid of the idiotic smile that threatened to pop out. Teasing Jessica was the most fun he'd had in years.

He rose to gather the dishes and she did too. Maybe he should have been suspicious at that point because even if Max was always happy to avoid dish duty, Aidy usually put up a token objection. But instead she and Max invited Liam to walk around the Retreat Center with them and Liam, once his mother had given him permission, was delighted to go. The door shut behind them and the air became denser, more charged.

"Anything fun and exciting since I saw you last?"

"Neither. More in the vein of weird and disturbing. Liam and I received a couple letters from Chris – a kind of making amends deal. I guess he's clean now. At least that's what he writes in the letters. He said he's planning to move back to Demerest Cove to work as a youth minister, and he wants to build some sort of relationship with Liam."

"And with you?" He watched her carefully. The kitchen clock, normally inaudible, ticked loudly.

She rubbed her hand over her face. "I don't think so. God, I hope not."

"It's not a crazy idea," he said.

"Yes, it is," she insisted. "I never loved Chris. So I guess I'm guilty of using him. But I don't think the punishment for that has to be living with him, marrying him, like some sort of life sentence."

"No. Of course not."

A sudden giddy happiness ran through his veins. He busied himself with rinsing silverware to hide the idiotic grin that spread across his face. She opened the dishwasher and began systematically loading glasses and soup bowls into the top rack. He reached for a few more and handed them to her one by one.

"I didn't expect to see you tonight," he said.

"Aidy called today to invite us. It would have been awkward to refuse."

"I'm glad you came."

She flushed and turned toward the sink to scrape off a plate.

"Do you think they know?"

"I don't see how they could. They both already know we fight all the time. This dinner is supposed to encourage us to get along like civilized coworkers."

She let go her breath and eased the plate into the dishwasher. He watched her curiously.

"Would it matter?"

"Yes. No. I don't know." She shrugged her shoulders with a defeated air and turned to face him. "It's complicated."

"No, it isn't." The sense of sureness was so strong it felt nearly solid, an immovable truth. "It's simple. Do you like me?"

"Sure, I –"

"Do you want to spend more time with me?"

"Yes." She sounded hoarse and cleared her throat but did not elaborate.

"So what does it matter what anyone thinks?"

He was close to her now, close enough to touch her. But instead he reached past her and slid the platter he was holding into the sink. As he did so, she flinched. A part of his heart clenched at the sight.

"Why do you do that?"

"What?" Her fists were clenched, her tone suddenly belligerent.

"That. You flinch sometimes as though you expect me to hit you. Was it Chris? Did he hurt you."

"No," she answered quickly. "Chris wasn't like that."

"Then who?"

She blushed furiously and stared at the floor between them. It took all the restraint he had to keep his tone mild, to wait until she was ready to respond.

"My dad," she said finally, the words hanging in the air like smoke. "He didn't do it often and only when I acted up. I wasn't always an easy child."

As a teen he had assumed she was just shy and easily startled. But now the surge of rage was almost more than he could hide. At her father. At himself for not having guessed at the time. He waited a moment until he could be sure he was in control of himself before he spoke.

"I'll bet you never hit Liam."

"Well, no."

"No child deserves to be hit. Ever. Especially by a parent. Austin had no right to do that to you."

She reached toward him and patted him gently on the chest.

"It's okay. Therapy helped. And time. And maybe I do flinch occasionally, but it's sort of a vestigial habit, like a penguin flapping its wings. Trust me, if anyone ever tries to hit me again, that fool will walk away with a mouth full of loose teeth and a long-term stomachache. I took a self defense course a few years back."

"If I hear about it first, you're going to have to get in line," he growled. "Nobody hits my friend and gets away with it."

The yearning to grab the next plane to wherever Austin was now located and beat the man to a pulp was hard to resist so he indulged himself in the fantasy for a moment. Until it occurred to him that calling Jessica a friend had been a slip up. Maybe she hadn't noticed. Being friends was not the same as being lovers after all. He looked down at her face, still a little flushed but now maybe not so much from embarrassment as from her proximity to him. Or maybe that was just wishful thinking on his part.

Her lips were curved in a gentle smile and the hand she held over his heart radiated warmth. He marveled at the absurdity of her comforting him about her own history of pain. Slowly he reached for her and folded her into his arms, fitting her against his body until it felt like they were melded into one new shape.

"Friends, huh?" She shot him a mischievous look.

"Yeah. Friends." He tucked his fingers under her chin and bent down to touch his lips to hers. But he was a moment too late.

"Hey, Mom, did you know – oops!" The door slammed open as Liam halted mid-stride.

Ronan and Jessica sprang apart. Jessica reached for the forgotten platter in the sink and Ronan was left standing empty handed in the middle of the kitchen feeling unaccountably embarrassed. Jessica clearly wasn't saying anything, but the silence was too uncomfortable to ignore.

"Hey, Liam. See anything interesting?" Ronan cringed the moment the words popped out, but Liam seemed blessedly oblivious.

"I didn't know you had a hydraulic double scissors lift. Max said I could go on it and I did. I got it to go up to the loft level, and I even got to change out one of the dead light bulbs."

Ronan let go the breath he had been holding as Aidy came into the kitchen with Max close behind. It could have been worse. At least Liam had arrived first. Although Aidy was no fool. She knew exactly how long it took to clean a kitchen and he and Jessica were nowhere near far enough along.

"Don't worry about cleaning any more," Aidy said. "I'll put the kettle on –"

"You've been on your feet long enough," Max said firmly, shooting Ronan a meaningful look.

"Moon Shell is catering dessert, remember?" Jessica said with a smile. "Go sit down with your husband. I've got plenty of help here."

She ordered Liam and Ronan to unpack the contents of the bakery box she had brought with her and turned to attack the remaining pile of dishware with surprising ferocity. Ronan glanced at Liam as they carefully placed the delicate pastries on the silver platter. The boy looked subdued and Ronan's heart sank. Liam hadn't said anything about seeing Ronan kissing Jessica yet, but the kid had to be wondering about Ronan's motives. Which was only fair, since Ronan was beginning to wonder about them himself.

CHAPTER 24

WHEN JESSICA ARRIVED at the Retreat Center for work Tuesday morning Ronan was still in Boston researching colonial gardens. His absence should have been a relief because he often distracted Jessica with questions and general chatter. Maybe that was the problem. The usual banter, with its accompanying irritants, would have been restful compared to letting her thoughts drift back to that kiss.

Lying on Ronan's desk were the plans, some rolled in cylinders and one spread wide showing the building and garden from above. For the first time, she felt a pang as she looked at them. Except for the garden itself, there wasn't much left to do. Which meant, inevitably, Ronan would be leaving. No surprise there. It was what he did.

Which made her the worst kind of fool. Because when he kissed her at the carnival, she had allowed herself to imagine there might be a chance of something more. But that was impossible. Because there had to be equivalency for a relationship to work. The two people involved didn't have to be the same, socially or financially. But they did need to be equal.

Maybe once Jessica and Ronan had been equals of sorts, but not any more. Jessica had a high school degree, a failed business and a child. She was fiercely proud of Liam, but she had no illusions about the impact of single parenthood on one's value as a love interest.

In contrast, Ronan was well educated, even more handsome than he had been as a teen and preparing to launch what was likely to be a fabulously successful career as an architect. Not that he seemed too stoked about that.

She shut down the computer and stacked the loose papers on her desk into some semblance of order. Aidy had been pleased to honor Jessica's request for an extended lunch hour, which made Jessica feel vaguely guilty. But Barbara was visiting her parents for the day and had asked Jessica to meet her for lunch at the Ulrich's house. So in addition to her purse, Jessica had a crisp manila file that contained the letter

Chris had written to her and any other documents she could think of that might apply. Liam had refused to let his own letter out of his sight, even to photocopy it, and Jessica had been reluctant to insist.

It would be wrong to hope Chris had a setback. And unfair. But she could hope Chris fell head over heels for one of the waitresses at Lynne's party, married her overnight and got her pregnant right away. That would keep him busy and out of Jessica's hair until she figured out what her next move should be. On second thought, Chris was an awful fate to wish on an unsuspecting waitress. Jessica had the file in hand and was reaching for her purse when she heard a noise at the doorway.

"Jessica." Aidy's gaze was curious. "Your friend is here."

The file dropped onto the desktop from Jessica's suddenly nerveless hand. Chris was thinner than Jessica remembered – reasonable, she guessed, since football was a long way in his past and the impact of his addiction would surely have taken its toll on his body. But his face hadn't changed much. Even with his neatly trimmed brown beard, she would have recognized him.

Still, there were other differences from the Chris she remembered. His gaze was direct, his hazel eyes clear and unclouded. Even his skin glowed. But while she registered his improved appearance and was relieved, in a general way, at his apparent good health, she couldn't help noting the calculating look that flickered across his face.

"Jessica. Mother tells me that's what you call yourself now. Is that right? It's wonderful to see you again."

He stepped forward, holding both hands out as though to cup her hand in his. She wasn't impressed. The two handed shake was a typical clergy move but politicians and flirtatious men at parties used it too. It was a way to imply compassion and tender admiration without actually providing those things in any measurable form.

She kept her hands to her sides, resisting the reflexive impulse to reach out to him in return. If he wanted any more than the barest civility from her, he had a lot of work to do first. Including repairing the damage he had caused by sending those stupid letters. She doubted he was up for it.

"Chris." The chill in her voice was unmistakable.

Looking more resentful than chastened Chris tucked his hands in his pockets. He rocked back and forth on his heels, scanning the room as though assessing the quality of the goods before turning his gaze to her again.

"I sent you a letter."

"I received it."

She reached down for her jacket and put it on, hoping he would take the hint. When he didn't show any sign of leaving, she tugged her purse onto her shoulder and grabbed the file to make her imminent departure more clear.

"And to Liam."

"And he received it."

"Well?"

"He's thinking about what you said."

Chris's expression eased slightly and, although she still refused to feel any sympathy for him, it occurred to her it couldn't be easy for someone as self-centered as Chris to step into a life of serving others. It wasn't as though Chris had a natural aptitude toward empathy.

He had been willing to socialize with Jessica initially because she was top of the social heap in high school. But generally he had been the kind of guy who thought he was being gracious when he nodded at passersby in the hallway. Now that she herself was low on the totem pole, she suspected he felt the same about her.

"I can't stay, Chris. I have an appointment. Maybe next time you'll call ahead instead of just dropping by."

"That's okay. I can come with you and we can chat on the way."

He reminded her of a nursing home attendant calming a demanding patient in front of the patient's relatives. Jessica couldn't help envisioning how the conversation might have gone if he didn't have an audience. More demanding, she guessed. Aidy lingered in the doorway, her expression uneasy but determined.

Jessica squared her shoulders. "No. You can't."

Max's deep voice cut through the room.

"Jessica, before you go, I need your input on the garden design ideas Ronan just emailed me."

She felt a wave of gratitude toward Aidy who must have called him. It was good to feel, for a moment, that she had allies. She couldn't afford to get used to it, of course. Depending on other people to protect her was a recipe for disaster. Still, it was oddly comforting.

"But I —"

She didn't wait to find out what Chris was going to say, or how Aidy responded. But as Jessica strode away, trotting a little to keep up with Max's long stride, her flash of relief was mingled with an increasing sense of dread. Max looked angry, and she wasn't sure whether it was because he had been interrupted or because she had committed the ultimate sin of bringing her personal life into her work environment. Either way, she owed him an apology. She opened her mouth to do so just as they turned the corner of the corridor. Before she could begin, he rounded on her.

"Who was that?"

She sighed. No matter what she said, she was probably going to lose this job, she realized. She would survive it. She had to. But the unfairness of the situation was so nearly overwhelming she couldn't even feel anger yet. Fury would have been a comfort of sorts. You could count on anger.

"Chris Mullin. And I'm sorry. I didn't know he was coming here and if I had known, I would have told him not to."

Max's eyes were unreadable. "Aidy was worried."

"That's sweet of her. And you. But I could have handled him. He's — it's a little complicated. But I'll make sure he doesn't interfere with work again."

To her bewilderment, he looked angrier. "What, exactly, is your relationship with this Chris Mullin?"

"He's Liam's father. He just moved back to the island and he wants to share custody." The words dropped hard and stone-like. More real than they had been when she had read the letters and spoken with Barbara.

"That's not what I asked you."

She stared at him. He shrugged and led the way out the door to the open land slated to become the healing garden. Someone had left a set of folding chair stacked under the eaves. He set up two of them and gestured for her to sit in one. He sank into the other with a sigh.

"Does Ronan know?" he asked.

She could feel her cheeks flush. She opened her mouth to say something. Anything. And then closed it. He shook his head and raised his hand as if to ask for her patience.

"I'm out of line," he said. "Forget I asked. Your private life is private."

She swallowed and nodded, keeping her eyes firmly fixed on the tree line in the distance. "Are you going to fire me?" she asked.

She flicked a glance toward him and then looked away again quickly. She hoped he fired her quickly without a lot of rationalizations. She didn't have the energy for any more forgiveness today.

"Not unless you want me to."

The wave of relief was nearly tangible. "I don't. I love this job," she said hastily.

"Good. Because Aidy likes you. And so far you have been exactly as capable as I hoped you would be."

She tried to be surreptitious about loosening her shoulders. His exact use of words hadn't escaped her. Aidy liked her. He was reserving judgment. But his appreciation of her as an employee would tarnish quickly if Chris kept hanging around. And despite her promises, she wasn't sure how she would manage to keep Chris away if he insisted on popping in whenever he felt like it. And he was likely to. Chris had been a strategic player on the football field, and she knew he had recognized a vulnerability in her today.

By the time she walked back to her office, Chris had left. But the room still had an unsettled air. She looked at the architecture textbooks Ronan had stacked on the big central table. The certain lines swooping across the creamy surface of his open sketchbook. Say what she might about Ronan's personal failings, no one could deny his vision.

She hadn't heard from him since Sunday night. Not that Ronan owed her an accounting of how he spent his time. They were both adults with separate and independent lives. But still. The timing of his silence had not escaped her. She had been foolish to think that kiss under the carnival moon mattered. For all she knew, now that he was back in Boston, he would decide to stay there. It wouldn't be the first time he avoided being a friend by pretending ignorance of her pain.

And she had needed the reminder. It had been a near thing this weekend. It was too easy to forget Ronan's fatal flaw when she was with him. But she couldn't afford to do that. Not now. Not ever. She hoped he did stay in Boston. He would make some architectural firm very happy.

For that matter, he would probably make some woman very happy. She was surprised at how much she disliked the thought. Spending day after day with Ronan had reminded her of how much fun he could be. And then there was that incisive way he had of reading her, of *knowing* her. She guessed maybe that was because they had known each other so well once. But no. That couldn't be either. Because it had been years. Which made it impossible to understand why the knowledge he was leaving again was enough to make it hard to breathe.

CHAPTER 25

RONAN LEANED FORWARD against the rail of the ferry and breathed in the scent of sea, kelp and damp seasoned with a dash of diesel from the engine. The delicately drawn botanical lithographs at the Dunstable Library of Horticulture had taken him by surprise with their exacting sweep of pen lines and the lush colors. When a librarian had trundled by with a cart full of books, he'd looked up and was mortified to find he had lost an hour of perfectly good research time. He'd closed the drawer of Audubon studies reluctantly. It took a moment to realize he would have to loosen his hand from the knob of the drawer if he was going to search the stacks for an appropriate selection of books on garden plots.

He had intended to stay another night in his own apartment in Boston, but the contrast between the quiet of the library and the crowded Cambridge street changed his mind for him. As he stepped out of the narrow brownstone building onto the brick sidewalk, the growl of traffic, the pull and shove of pedestrians forcing their way to opposing destinations, the mingled funk of grime, exhaust, overcooked hot dogs and damp suddenly seemed too much to bear. He had minored in urban architecture – he should like it. He *did* like it. At least, he was pretty sure he would like it again once he was finished with the Demerest Cove project. As far as he was concerned that couldn't happen soon enough.

Because working side by side with Jessica was becoming a problem. He had been concerned initially that his teenage broken heart would influence his ability to work with her. But he had been wrong. It wasn't the memory of his teen love for her that was preventing him from thinking about her in a sensible fashion. No. This was an altogether different problem. He hadn't anticipated falling in love as a mature adult. And kissing Jessica at the carnival had been a terrible mistake. Luckily Liam seemed to have a sixth sense when it came to interrupting them before they made any worse ones.

The irony of it didn't escape him. And he felt doubly foolish. He had always disliked that snarky pronouncement:

Fool me once, shame on you. Fool me twice, shame on me. Now that it applied to him, he disliked it even more. Max's call hadn't helped. Maybe Jessica hadn't welcomed Chris's advances this morning, but the week wasn't over yet. Sometimes, hate and love were just two sides of the same coin.

Ronan turned to watch Boston Harbor disappear into the horizon and caught a glimpse of another passenger, a woman. If she hadn't looked so much like Jessica he might have ignored her. But the resemblance was uncanny, at least from a distance. He had always felt a bit sorry for Cookie Piers. Her husband so obviously despised her. And she seemed to spend all her time trying to live up to what she thought rich people did. He could understand it, even if he didn't exactly agree with her methods. He had been a boy when his father made a disastrous investment and lost not only his own funds but also Ronan's grandparents' savings.

Before the Durrell's personal financial crisis, Ronan's grandparents had been Demerest Cove elite. Ronan had never particularly cared about social status. If it didn't involve paper and pen, he wasn't much interested at the time. But he had a distinct memory of his grandmother's expression when she realized she had not, nor was she likely ever again to receive the usual invitation to the annual Club Gala. It had been just one of many such slights, but after the first, his grandmother never again allowed herself that stricken expression. At least not where her son and grandsons could see it. She had too much pride for that.

But Cookie's situation was different. Wealth, although critical for acceptance into the island's stratified social circle, was not enough. There were unwritten rules about who could fit in, and Cookie with her nervous laugh and obsequious manner, was the perfect outcast. She reminded Ronan of a little sister left behind by the older kids. She kept trotting after them, ignoring their disdainful glances and cutting remarks, trying to keep up. Even Ronan knew that was an approach destined for failure. Didn't stop Cookie though. He glanced back at her and was surprised to see her waving at him as though he were a long lost relative.

She was wearing a voluminous turquoise raincoat, presumably to protect her clothing from ocean spray. But she must have decided she didn't need it. He restrained a flinch as she removed it, partly because the free hanging sash came perilously close to tripping her. The other reason was the sequined midriff-baring outfit the raincoat had covered. She looked as if she were auditioning for the stage version of a Vegas waitress.

"Yoohoo! Ronan Durrell, is that you?"

He took a breath and smiled gamely, waiting until she tottered closer on her rickety heels before answering. "Cookie Piers, right?"

"You're even more handsome than I remembered you." She paused and looked up at him expectantly.

"And you look – very chic."

It was better not to lie. And he couldn't bring himself to say what she wanted to hear, that she hadn't changed a bit since he had seen her last, because that would be a whopper of mammoth proportions. She had always been slim, but now she looked emaciated. Her skin, leathery from years of assiduous tanning, pulled tight across her cheekbones, making her teeth look large and protruding.

"Oh, this old thing." She posed and pooched her lips forward, a teen taking a self admiring selfie. "You're such a sweetheart. I always wondered why none of the high school girls locked you down. Lots of them were head over heels for you. Anyone could see it."

He stared, startled into silence. With efficiency born of long practice, she hitched her arm through his and gestured toward the entry to the interior of the ferry.

"Buy me a drink and we'll catch up."

The thought of huddling over a sticky wooden table in the stale smelling ferry bar while Cookie Piers told all was simultaneously disturbing and oddly seductive. Despite his misgivings, he gave in. She was an unpleasant woman, but her knobby shoulders protruding from that ridiculously inappropriate halter top had a vulnerable air. And she was Jessica's mother.

The bar was deserted. No surprise since the breeze was so beautiful on deck. The bartender's surly air might have been a contributing factor too. He looked irritated at Ronan's request for a bottle of water. He was downright contemptuous when Cookie asked for a Sex On The Beach cocktail. Although, to be fair, Ronan thought dealing with people like Cookie all day long could get a bit wearing. He had only spent ten minutes with her so far, and he was already calculating how long it might take to swim to the island if he jumped overboard.

Cookie clutched her plastic cup of orange slurry, her fingernails long and painted neon blue. She stared out the window in silence for a moment before meeting his eyes. He realized he had expected some discomfort there, but all he saw was calculation.

"I hear you and your brothers are doing well. Lynne tells me you own The Grand now."

"Our company does. Sanderson Hospitality manages a number of properties in Boston too." He sat back and eyed her, waiting for the next question.

"And you're working for MacAllen. I know Ian MacAllen. We had a thing once."

There didn't seem to be a good reply to that, so he didn't make one. It struck him that with Cookie it was all about positioning. Which made sense given her past, but it was jarring to see her still acting that way. It seemed to him if you hadn't reached a level of comfort with yourself by the time you were in your sixties, you had a problem. It wasn't so much a matter of resting on your laurels, he decided. Nothing wrong with ambition at any age.

But Cookie had an air of perpetual dissatisfaction. Even as he sat directly across the table from her, she was eying another passenger. A business man, suitcase in hand, ordering a beer. Ronan cleared his throat and was amused at the way she immediately assumed a fascinated expression, staring into his eyes, her chin cradled in the heel of her hand. She batted her lashes.

"So, Cookie," he spoke before she could direct any more uncomfortable questions his way. "What have you been doing since I saw you last?"

"Oh. Well. When Austin and I split, I moved to Boca. I had to. I could hardly stay in Demerest Cove, could I?"

She sipped her drink and then carefully centered the cup on the small napkin it came with. When she looked up, he saw a flicker of something, maybe uncertainty in her eyes.

"Well, I couldn't," she said more forcefully. "I had nothing to live on."

"So why Boca?" He couldn't quite keep the fury from his voice.

"It's full of rich men." Her tone was patient but a little patronizing as though the answer was obvious. "I had to do something. Candy was no help."

He shook his head in disbelief. Of course she couldn't help you. She was in high school. And pregnant."

"You think I don't know that?" Cookie shot him an impatient look, as though he was being purposely obtuse. "I told her to marry Chris. It would have been a perfect wedding. The Mullins were rolling in money. But she was so selfish. There was no convincing her. So, in the end, I had to protect myself."

"By moving away and leaving your pregnant daughter homeless and alone," he said flatly.

"It wasn't my fault she wouldn't listen to anything I told her. You have no idea how difficult teenage girls can be."

"Probably not, since I haven't had the privilege of having a daughter of my own." His jaw was so tight he was having trouble getting the words out. "So why are you here now? Are all the rich guys in Boca dead?"

"Don't be crude." She shot him a reproving look. "Lynne invited me to her family do, and she was kind enough to pay my way, which is more than I can say for Candy."

He had a sick feeling in the pit of his stomach, but he forced himself to ignore it. He was pleased at the even tone he managed to achieve as he spoke.

"Your daughter is a phenomenal woman who has built a life for herself and has raised an amazing young man, your grandson, Liam. She calls herself Jessica now, by the way. Primarily, I think, because she had to remake herself when you abandoned her and a fresh name was one way to do that. She's a daughter any mother could be proud of. Does Jessica know you're coming to the island?"

Cookie waved her cup dismissively. The small amount of liquid remaining sloshed dangerously close to the edge.

"'Course. I told her ages ago." She enunciated with careful determination. He wondered how many drinks she'd had before she ran into him. "I don't see why you care. I shouldn't say this about my own daughter, but Candy's a user. She strung you along until she didn't need you anymore. She used Chris so she could strut around school on the arm of the football captain. Then, suddenly, he wasn't good enough for her. I took care of her all my life and look what she did to me. But now Chris is back, and it sounds like she has a second chance. And I'm here to make sure she doesn't blow it. For either of us."

He looked down at his hand and shook droplets from it. The bottle of water in his fist was crushed now, the bulk of its contents streaming over his fingers to the floor. He rose from his seat, deliberately silent. Cookie didn't deserve courtesy, as far as he was concerned. That ship had sailed. Dropping the bottle into the trash can, he headed for the door.

Jessica hadn't mentioned she was expecting her mother to visit the island. Even though given her relationship or, more exactly, lack of relationship with Cookie, that was big news, the kind of news that should have been front page over the fold. He couldn't define exactly why being last to know felt like a betrayal, a tiny rip in the delicate fabric that was their renewed friendship. But it did.

When the ferry pulled into the harbor, he was the first off the vessel, weaving between the small crowd gathered to meet the arrivals. Lynne wasn't there but maybe she hadn't intended to meet Cookie in person. Not that it mattered. At the moment, Cookie's fortunes were irrelevant. And her opinions should have been too, which made it all the more frustrating that as he slid into the Bentley, her words still grated at him. He would have to be more careful – he couldn't afford to be destroyed again.

CHAPTER 26

As Ronan began his left turn out of the parking lot, he checked traffic to his right one more time. A black SUV bore down on him, showing no signs of stopping. He swung the steering wheel sharply to the right, missing the SUV's rear fender by a hair. The SUV veered off the driveway, swerving onto the sidewalk and narrowly missing a lamppost before grinding to a halt. Ronan pulled to the side of the road and got out of the Bentley.

He strode across the street to the SUV and blinked. The driver's side door was open, but Chris Mullin sat staring through the windshield, seatbelt fastened, his knuckles pale as he clutched the steering wheel. The engine was still running, and Ronan could hear the audio system pumping out unfamiliar but earnest sounding music. The song selection changed to "Jesus Take the Wheel," a choice so utterly appropriate under the circumstances that he would have burst into laughter if Chris hadn't looked so stricken at the coincidence.

"Chris, you okay?"

Chris looked at him blankly for a moment.

"Do I know you – wait, Durrell, right?" The words came quick and sharp, the rat-a-tat pace of a self important businessman. "Your brother, Jock, played football a couple years before me."

Ronan nodded, wondering if Chris was on something. His pupils were unusually small, but then it wasn't as if Ronan had spent a lot of time looking into Chris's eyes. Maybe his pupils were always that way. Or maybe Chris had hit his head on the steering wheel. There was no sign of bruising but concussions were weird things. To be safe, he reached past Chris and turned off the ignition, removing the keys as an extra precaution. Carrie Underwood crackled into silence.

"I'm supposed to be picking someone up for my mother." Chris jabbed his index finger in the general direction of the dock. "Cookie Piers is coming to visit, and I volunteered to meet her when the ferry arrived."

"Okay." Ronan paused. "You almost hit my car before you drove onto the sidewalk, Chris. Are you feeling okay?"

"Of course I'm okay. Never been better." Chris blinked at him quickly and fumbled at the empty ignition for a full minute before realizing the keys were gone. Then he slowly pulled his hands toward his face and wiggled his fingers in front of his nose. Ronan's heart sank. No matter how Jessica felt about her mother, he was pretty sure she didn't want Cookie dead in a car crash. And Chris wasn't exactly safe to drive at the moment. Someone would get hurt.

"Come on out, Chris."

Chris scrambled out of his seat. "I don't think we should be settling our personal business here on the street."

Ronan stared, mystified. "Personal business?"

"Look, Rowan —"

"Ronan."

"Right. Rogan. I remember you had a thing for Jessica in high school. Everyone was a little in love with her back then. Girls envied her and boys wanted her, because let's face it, anyone who's going out with the captain of the football team has to be the cream of the crop, right?

"But like it says in Corinthians, 'When I became a man, I gave up childish ways.' You need to let go of those high school memories. And if you've been leading Jessica to think you're a better choice for her than her own son's father, well that's just wrong. As a mother, Jessica understands she has to think about Liam's needs now.

"Being married to me will put Jessica in the best position she could hope for on the island and will give our son the basis he needs to do well in life. Jessica's mature enough to see this will be the wisest decision for her and for Liam."

Ronan trained his eyes on the door handle until he could trust himself to speak.

"So, Jessica's on board with this?"

"Not yet, but once she understands the advantages I can provide for our son, she will be. And Cookie's influence will help with that. Girls listen to their mothers. That's why I made sure Mother invited her back to the island." Chris bounced frenetically from one foot to another while staring over Ronan's shoulder toward the ferry. "Where is Cookie, anyway?"

"Chris, are you on something?"

"Not at all!" Chris looked shocked and a little offended at the idea. "I'm clean and sober. I've been clean and sober for two years, three months, three weeks and two days. Frankly, I find it hurtful and offensive that you asked. Sobriety is a hard enough path to walk without old friends casting doubt on the hardest thing you've ever done in your life.

"You can't know how difficult quitting drugs is if you haven't been through it yourself. It was unbelievably painful at first, but then I found out about kratom and that changed everything. It's a South American herb, right? So you know it's healthy for you. I just had a cup of kratom tea before I left the house. It keeps me strong in my recovery by reducing my cravings for drugs."

Ronan raised his hands and took a step back. It was peculiar to feel apologetic toward a man who had nearly rammed into him. Never mind a self important idiot.

"No offence meant, Chris."

"None taken." Chris stepped away from the SUV and reached out to shake Ronan's hand. "One of the first things I learned in my studies at seminary was the pointlessness of holding grudges. You didn't know I'm a minister?"

"The scripture quotation might have given me a hint," Ronan hedged. The thought of Chris Mullin telling people how to live a moral life boggled the mind. The irony seemed to escape Chris himself, however, as he earnestly proceeded to detail his current situation.

"– two years as a youth minister. And after that, the sky's the limit, as they say."

Whatever had been affecting Chris initially seemed to have diminished in effect, but Ronan was still uneasy. Chris's pupils were average size now, and he was beginning to speak at a more reasonable clip. Maybe he wasn't taking drugs, but something still wasn't right. Ronan glanced over his shoulder and forced himself to stay where he was. Cookie was tottering ever closer, so he didn't have much time to lose.

"Maybe I should give you and Cookie a ride."

He gestured toward Chris's front tire. It might or might not be losing air, but the way the SUV's weight was now distributed, half on and half off the sidewalk, made it *look* like it was low. He hoped the ruse worked because he didn't have a better idea. Chris pursed his lips and stared at the tire critically as though sheer will might make it inflate. But by the time Cookie arrived, Ronan knew he had won.

Chris shook his head and gave the SUV one more disapproving look before turning to his guest with a warm pastoral smile. "Ms. Piers, or should I say Moth –"

"Cookie, darling! Call me Cookie! Anything else makes me sound old."

"Cookie, then." Chris continued to smile, but there was a reserve to his expression as he eyed Cookie's wardrobe. Or maybe Chris simply didn't like Cookie. Ronan could sympathize if that were the case. He wasn't sure whether spending the time with both of them while he drove them to the Mullin house was a prospect too horrifying to contemplate or whether they were both equally awful and would cancel each other out, like opposing sound waves. In which case the ride would be more pleasant than he anticipated.

There was no point in putting off the inevitable. He grabbed Cookie's enormous wheeled suitcases and headed for the Bentley. As he strained to lift the luggage into the trunk, he wondered how she had managed to drag them across the gravel parking lot on her own. Either she was stronger than she looked or she was powerfully motivated. Each one of the bags individually likely weighed more than she did.

It occurred to him as he ushered Cookie into the front passenger seat and gestured Chris toward the rear, that the last time he had driven unexpected passengers, they had been Jessica and Liam. He wondered what they were doing right now. Homework, in Liam's case, he imagined. There had been something about an end of year history project involving cotton balls. A diorama of an Arctic explorer, maybe?

And Jessica would be making dinner, or doing laundry, or finding glue to hold the cotton balls in place. His heart clenched at the image. The sensation of warmth, really. He wanted to be there with them. The sudden desire surprised him with its intensity, urgency even. It was good the Mullin's estate was in the opposite direction.

He put on his right signal and had begun to turn when Chris said, "You want the left turn. Jessica's house is that way."

Ronan pulled to the curb and shook his head, confused. "Cookie's staying at your mother's house."

"That was the plan," Chris said in an indulgent tone. "But Mother expected at least some of the invitees to respond with their regrets. If she had asked me, I could have told her to expect full attendance. But she had no idea so many of our family members and friends wanted to welcome me home."

"But I'm Lynne's best friend," Cookie protested. "She invited me especially. I traveled here all the way from Boca. There must be some mistake. All the way from Boca," Cookie repeated with a depth of feeling that implied she had walked the whole way.

"I know and I'm sorry," Chris said. "Mother is simply devastated. But on the bright side, you'll be able to spend more quality time with Jessica than you expected. And with my son, Liam."

His son. Ronan shook his head again and pulled away from the curb. Not "our son" or "her son" or even "your grandson." His son. Chris didn't deserve Liam. And Liam had done nothing to deserve Chris either. The unfairness of it burned. He tried to keep his tone casual.

"I'm assuming you called Jessica to let her know when to expect her mother."

"That's not necessary," Chris said. "Timothy teaches us that anyone who does not provide for their relatives, and especially for their own household, has denied the faith and is worse than an unbeliever. I'm sure Jessica will live up to my expectations for a good Christian woman."

Ronan's knuckles were white on the steering wheel. Chris was wrong in more ways than Ronan could count, but in one way he was right. Ronan had no good excuse for intruding into Jessica's private life again, particularly since he knew there was no future in it. It wouldn't be fair to pretend otherwise, especially when he factored Liam into the equation.

The best thing would be to keep his relationship with Jessica strictly professional from now on. On the other hand, he had to balance the obligations of the friendship they had once shared and the delicate relationship they had cobbled together over the past week against his own foolish issues. It wasn't Jessica's fault he had fallen in love with her. And his stupid feelings didn't excuse him from the obligations of friendship.

His heart clenched because he hadn't considered the possibility until now that perhaps he couldn't have her as a friend any more, especially if he loved her. Although friendship suddenly seemed like too small a word. Or maybe too broad a term. Loving her would mess things up, make their interactions stilted, and he didn't think he would be able to bear that. Which was why it would be better to cut his losses.

Maybe once waiting around for the other shoe to drop had been the only plan available to him, but he had more options now. He would be finished with the garden plans by the end of the week. Then he could direct his attention to sending out more job applications. The thought of moving toward something positive should have cheered him. Which didn't explain why he wanted to wipe the smug look off Chris's face. There was no point in being jealous. The dude was an idiot. Besides, it wasn't as though Ronan had the option of marrying Jessica himself.

Because the bottom line was nothing had changed since high school. There was no mistaking their chemistry, both emotionally and physically, so it wasn't that she didn't enjoy Ronan's company. It was that he was just a bit of a good time without strings. Her life plan over the long term didn't include him. Again.

She hadn't told him Chris was talking with her about marriage. Or that her mother was coming back to town to join the Marry Chris Campaign. Maybe Jessica would marry Chris. Maybe she'd end up marrying some other guy. But Ronan had never been in the running and he never would be. Jessica just hadn't bothered to remind him of that yet.

CHAPTER 27

SOMETHING ABOUT THE way Ronan stood on her porch, framed by the screen door, made Jessica uneasy. He entered when she beckoned but stayed near the doorway as she turned away to slide the chicken into the oven.

"I saw your mother on the ferry."

Jessica froze. In the tumult of addressing Chris and his letters, she had completely forgotten her mother's call. She nodded, her mouth suddenly dry. She yearned for the familiar anger – she needed the strength and protection of it now. But instead there was just a sense of stillness. Not the tranquil kind. More of a dead quality to it, as though everything were wrapped in a coating of fiberglass.

"Did she – is she okay?"

"I think so. She brought a huge amount of luggage for a few days' stay."

If anything he seemed to be choosing his words with even more care now. She found herself getting irritated about that, which was a relief of sorts. Some feeling was better than no feeling. She reached for the refrigerator and yanked out salad ingredients. She hadn't intended to make salad but keeping her hands busy and chopping crunchy things into teeny tiny pieces seemed like a good plan.

"That's Cookie. An outfit for every occasion." She tried to sound flip but it fell flat. She tore the wrapper off a head of lettuce and ripped at the leaves, jamming them into the salad spinner.

Ronan cleared his throat. "I also ran into Chris."

"Did you."

There it came, finally. The white anger she had been yearning for. She scrubbed at the carrot in her hand with vicious concentration before fumbling for the peeler.

"He, uh, was planning to give Cookie a ride from the ferry."

"What?" The peeler slipped from her hand and clunked into the sink.

"But his car broke down and I offered to help out."

Carefully, she put the carrot on the cutting board and turned to look at him. She refused to make Ronan the scapegoat. It wouldn't be fair – this wasn't his problem, after all. And if he had sounded the least bit worried about her approval, she would have found that decision easier. Minimally she should have read discomfort on his face. But instead she had the sense he was waiting for something from her. An explanation, maybe. For what, she had no idea.

"That was kind of you." She leaned back against the edge of the sink and folded her arms.

"Just normal courtesy," he said. "And a sense of social responsibility. How sure are you Chris has kicked the habit?"

Her throat tightened. "You know what, Ronan? I don't need this," she snapped. "I have a life to attend to. A son to raise. Bills to pay. My plate is full. You'll be back in Boston in a few days, but I have to stay here and keep picking up the pieces and cleaning up the messes. Which," she held up her hand, "I don't mind doing. Because I took that responsibility on thirteen years ago and I will continue to take it with the good and the bad parts until I die. I just hate the implicit criticism."

"Mom?"

Liam poked his head out his bedroom door, his earnest face flushed, his glasses slightly askew. At that moment she loved him with an animal-like ferocity.

"Oh, hi Ronan. I didn't know you were here. Want to see how my science project came out?"

"I do," Ronan said. "Just give me a couple minutes more to talk with your mom."

"Cool. Are you staying for dinner?"

"Well, I'm not –"

"No. He's not," Jessica said sharply. "Dinner in five minutes, Liam."

Liam's door clicked shut. When she turned back, Ronan looked rueful.

"What?"

"You think you're mad at me now."

"Get to the point, Ronan, I –"

"They're waiting outside in my car. Lynne can't host your mother after all, so Chris was planning to drive Cookie over here and drop her off."

"Outside. In your car." The information just wouldn't compute. The thought of Chris finally meeting Liam was disturbing enough. But knowing Cookie was just outside was making it hard to breathe. And this time the fear wasn't just for Liam, it was for herself too.

"But that's not – I can't."

Ronan was at her side with his palm under her elbow before she had a chance to assimilate what he was telling her. She shook him off impatiently but didn't object as he pulled a chair toward her and urged her to sit.

"We can put her up in The Grand," he said quickly in an undertone. "You don't have to –"

"Yoohoo! Anybody home?"

And Cookie was there, on the other side of the screen door. Thinner, for sure. Older too. Jessica felt a stab of anguish at that. Which made no sense because getting older was a good thing, at least in her own experience. But she knew how hard her mother had fought against the subtle signs of aging. And somehow, despite the futility and ultimate silliness of Cookie's lifelong focus, Jessica couldn't help feeling sorry that all her mother's struggles had resulted in this.

Cookie's hair should surely have been showing some signs of gray by now, but she must have dyed it. As a result there was an odd contrast between the bright blonde strands and the leathery skin of her face. Her eyes were almost fevered, darting anxiously to and fro with an intensity that reminded Jessica of an unrealistically ambitious small fish tossed in among a bunch of sharks. Maybe there were external differences, but the core of Cookie hadn't changed much.

"Mom, I –"

She broke off, unsure of what to say. She could hardly refuse her own mother shelter, but there was Liam to think of. Once she had yearned for a relationship between Liam and his grandmother, but now that contact was imminent, protecting Liam from Cookie had to be the first order of business. Her thoughts raced frantically. She would have to take Ronan up on his offer, although she didn't want to think about how long it would take to pay off a multi night stay at The Grand. But before she could act on the plan, Liam popped his head out of his bedroom again.

"Hey, Mom, my project's almost done. Should I finish the rest after dinner? There's just this one piece of wire I can't get to bend right. Maybe Ronan could – oh, hi."

Before Jessica could stop him, Liam stepped into the living room. He needed a haircut and his shirt was tucked into his jeans on the left side but not the right. Her heart clenched at the dearness of him at the same time she was furious at her inability to prevent him from walking toward danger. Liam reached the screen door and unlocked it before Jessica had fully risen from her seat. It was rare she had occasion to regret drumming social etiquette into Liam, but this was one of those times.

"Welcome to our home. Come on in."

Cookie stared at the room's well-worn furnishings with a surprised air. Jessica's stomach clenched with a mingling of shame and indignant pride. Shabby, her mother would be thinking. Not shabby chic. Shabby chic had the benefit of costing money. But at least it was hers, Jessica thought defiantly. She braced herself for the inevitable comment.

"You must be Liam," Cookie said. "My bags are in the car. Be a dear and go get them for me, would you?"

"Not now," Jessica snapped.

Liam looked surprised, but she strode past him to the door. Chris was behind the Bentley, fiddling with the trunk catch. Fumbling, she relocked the screen door and closed the wooden one and locked it too for good measure.

"How about we leave the bags in the car for a bit so you and your grandson can get acquainted," Ronan said.

His tone was friendly, but there was an undercurrent of command in his voice Jessica hadn't expected.

Liam's face lit up with joy. "Really?" His voice cracked. "Are you – wait, which grandmother are you?"

"This is my mother, Liam." Jessica's throat was tight enough to make speaking painful. "Cookie."

"Oh." He shot Jessica an uncertain glance. It tore at her heart. Liam was intuitive enough to read between the lines. His pause wasn't about the social niceties of greeting a relative. It was about loyalty. To her. It wasn't until the doorbell rang that she remembered Chris. And then it was too late because Liam was already at the door.

"Oh. Hi. Welcome to our home."

Chris left the monstrous suitcases where they were and stepped into living room, extending his hand toward his son. "You must be Liam."

Liam shook hands and smiled politely. "Are you friends with my grandmother?"

"Better than that." Chris smiled beatifically. "I'm your father."

The blood drained from Liam's face. He took a step back, stared at Chris, then turned on his heel and fled out the back door. The screen door slammed before Jessica could catch it. She tore it open and raced after her son but forced herself to halt when she saw him. Liam stood facing the corner of the fence, kicking at the soil. His shoulders bunched under his worn T-shirt with every kick. She looked back to be sure no one had followed her. Ronan must have run interference. She guessed it was the least he could do after bringing Chris and Cookie to her home in the first place.

Cautiously, she stepped closer to Liam. From the back she could see the shape of the man he would be. Tentatively, she reached out and put her hand on his shoulder. He stopped kicking but didn't move.

"Liam," she whispered.

He turned suddenly and curled into her embrace, tears running down his cheeks. She held him until his sobbing eased. Only her fury kept her from dissolving into tears with him. When he stepped away from her, she looked toward the house. Ronan stood just inside the screen door blocking Chris and Cookie's view. She would have appreciated the gesture more if he hadn't initiated the whole crisis. She had an image of standing in front of a tennis ball launcher, unable to avoid being hit by ball after ball. First Ronan, then Chris, then Cookie. It wasn't exactly Ronan's fault. But she couldn't ignore that his had been the first blow to her predictable life. She turned her back to Ronan and focused on Liam.

"Are you okay?"

"Yeah, I guess." He shuddered. "You should have told me they were coming."

"I had no idea. Believe me, I'm as shocked as you are. But I can tell them to leave."

"No, I – it's okay if they stay. I mean I guess I want to get to know them. It's just a lot all at once, you know?"

She did know. And the weight of the damage she had done by allowing things to go the way they had was like a stone in her heart. Perpetual guilt was a requirement of parenthood, but this was harder.

Ronan helped with dinner conversation and Cookie chattered away too. Mostly about fashion, but you couldn't have everything. Chris seemed uncharacteristically subdued. Maybe it was a delayed reaction to meeting Liam. Jessica hoped so. It would be nice to think he felt some emotional connection.

But when they had settled in the living room with cups of coffee and Liam had excused himself to finish his homework, conversation slowed to an uncomfortable silence. Jessica glanced at Ronan and took the leap.

"Mom, I understand Lynne doesn't have room to put you up, but Ronan has offered you a room at The Grand while you're in town."

"But I want to stay with you," Cookie protested. "We need to talk about your future. Now that Chris is becoming a minister, he's looking to settle down. And he's willing to consider a woman with a child. That's not all that common. I should know. Plus we need to go dress shopping soon. Lynne's event is on Saturday," she added. "I'm sure you'd be welcome."

"Indeed you would," Chris said. He folded his hands over his stomach and smiled placidly. It was good Jessica had put down the coffee cup. She couldn't afford to break a mug every time her mother said something infuriating. There wouldn't be anything to pour coffee into by tomorrow morning.

"Mom." She waited until Cookie met her eyes. "We are not discussing my love life right now. I work for a living, so I can't go dress shopping during the day. I'm not attending Lynne's party as a guest. And I don't have an extra bed for you here."

Cookie tightened her lips and looked around the room as if for a clue to the riddle Jessica had posed. There was something lost in her gaze.

Liam clumped into the room and dropped to the couch. "Grandma can stay in my room if she wants. It'll be fun."

Jessica registered the shift from Cookie to Grandma at about the same time she realized she had been outmaneuvered by her own son.

"Where will you sleep?"

"On the couch. And you don't have to worry, Mom. I won't play any video games. Promise."

CHAPTER 28

RONAN FINISHED ARRANGING carrot sticks on the platter and reached for a bell pepper. Jock, Charlotte, their daughter, Jane and Charlotte's elderly spaniel Jerry were outside taking Bear for a walk, and Aidy was absorbed in the intricacies of making potato salad. Which meant Ronan might be able to avoid having any awkward conversations during dinner. A precocious toddler and two dogs pretty much eliminated any real discourse. Worked for him.

He cut the pepper into strips exactly the right size for a two-year-old hand to hold. Jane was old enough to enjoy dipping vegetables into dressing now. It was amazing how quickly she had grown into a walking, talking kid. But he still felt that same protective urge he had when he had first met her, a blue eyed cherub with a broad toothless grin. He guessed that fierce need to keep her safe would stay with him even when she was an adult.

"Wonan! Wonan!"

Between joyous barking, hugs, exclamations over Jane's latest seashell, and a delicious dinner, it was some time before Ronan had the opportunity to chat with Jock. As freeing as it was to have a place of his own, Ronan missed the daily contact he had enjoyed with Jock when they had shared an apartment.

"You feeling any better?" His brother leaned back in the leather armchair with a happy sigh, cradling a mug of coffee.

For a moment Ronan wasn't sure what Jock was referring to. Then the light dawned. The last time they had spoken, Ronan was reeling from being fired. It was surprising to realize how far away that moment seemed now. Less significant, somehow. Certainly less painful.

"Much." He nodded. "I'm done with the building plans for the event space. I've still got to do some research on historical garden design before I tackle the healing garden. Although I got a head start on understanding some of the issues by digging a vegetable garden for Aidy. Turns out seventy-five percent of what I thought was garden soil is in fact rock."

Jock grinned. "No surprise there. Rocks are the main indigenous crop of New England."

"Yeah, well. My back didn't thank me. But Aidy did, so that's what counts. What's new in the world of Sanderson Hospitality?"

Jock handled the legal end of the family property management business. Their conversation veered to the intricacies of managing the properties of their latest client, an old woman in Florida who had inherited seven decrepit multi-families in Somerville. It was soothing to focus on something pragmatic like ancient heating systems for a change. But then the topic naturally segued to the remaining renovation plans for The Grand. And then to the event space.

"Max said he hired an events coordinator already. How's she working out?"

Tricky, tricky – he probably should have seen that one coming. Jock could be subtle when it suited him. On the other hand maybe it was just a casual question, and Ronan was falling into the common trap of thinking everyone was interested in his business. He shot Jock a surreptitious glance and sat back, trying to look casual. His brother seemed entirely focused on taking a bite of a cookie from a platter they had rescued from the kitchen. Jock was disturbingly perceptive at times, but thankfully this didn't seem to be one of them.

"Good. She's – good."

Okay, well, that sounded odd. He considered adding something more but rejected the idea. If he started listing Jessica's positive attributes now, it would only sound more awkward. He took a bite of his own cookie and his eyes widened appreciatively. Molasses with a gingery bite encased in a crisp coating of sugar.

"Wow. Is this Grandma's recipe?"

"Yep." Jock grinned. "Max says if he keeps baking at this rate, he and Aidy will both gain four hundred pounds. I told him I'll take the baked goods off his hands, if only to protect his health."

"It's the least you can do," Ronan agreed, relaxing. "All for one and one for all, I say."

Jock's eyes sharpened. "Who is she?"

Ronan stiffened. "Sorry?"

"The new coordinator. Max said she's a local, but I don't remember a Jessica Piers. Is it her married name?"

"No. Uh. No. Jessica was Candy Piers back when you would have known her."

"Huh. Didn't you and she have something going on back then?"

"I don't – it was a long time ago." He hated how weak he sounded.

"Blonde, right? I do remember now. I always liked her," Jock said. "Not for me," he added hastily. "Candy was a cute kid, though. And the two of you couldn't seem to stay apart for more than an hour at a time. Of course that was a long time ago."

Ronan shrugged. Anyone who said women were gossips hadn't met any men. Especially if those men felt they had a moral responsibility to guide their little brother through the rocky shoals of life no matter how embarrassing or ill advised the conversations. He cringed at the memory of the time Jock and Max had decided he needed to know more information about sex than health class in fifth grade provided. In retrospect it was more amusing than embarrassing since his brothers hadn't known much more than he did about the topic.

Embarrassment aside, Ronan wasn't going to go down this conversational road with Jock. He wasn't sure he wanted to go down it with anyone. What was the point? For all Ronan knew, Jessica's mother would push all the right buttons. Again. Despite Chris's sullen demeanor on the ride home last night, Ronan couldn't ignore the fact that Jessica hadn't rejected him outright. And now Chris was back in town for good. And the three of them could live through high school all over again. Except Ronan wasn't going to come out and play this time. He was done.

And it wasn't a tragedy, after all. Liam needed a father and providentially Chris had reappeared at exactly the moment a boy needed a male role model most. Maybe Chris was a pompous self-righteous idiot, but he wasn't a mean or vindictive person, and he was definitely motivated to make things right. Or at least right in the way he conceived of the term.

So it would be great for the three of them if things worked out. Ronan knew he should hope they did work out. But somehow he couldn't bring himself to be that selfless. Because whether he liked it or not, he had fallen just as hard for Jessica this time as he had for her all those years ago when she had still been Candy. At least now he had a viable escape route in place. And a solid support structure until one of the jobs he applied for came through.

"Jessica and I are different people now. You know how it is – you grow up," he said, shrugging. "She's got a son. Nice boy, Liam."

He felt a pang as he spoke because the bit about being different people was true about Jessica. There was a seriousness to her now, a sturdiness of purpose he had never associated with her as a teen. It didn't replace the sweetness and sharp wit he had always relished. In fact, it infused her with a depth he hadn't envisioned when he had first known her. Different but also the same.

And maybe he had changed too. But not as much as he wished he had.

"So, she's married?"

"No."

Jock frowned.

"But you still like her?"

"We're just friends."

"Good. Because a kid changes things. As you know."

Ronan rolled his eyes. What was it about being the youngest that gave everyone permission to give him advice? And at what point would he be considered old enough to be an equal? It crossed his mind briefly that this would be an important side effect of being employed again.

"I do know kids change things, Jock. I don't think I'll ever forget the look on your face when you brought Jane home. Horrified doesn't begin to describe it."

Jock gave him a long look but mercifully the two year old topic of their conversation came running into the room joyously waving what looked like a piece of road kill. While Jock was engrossed in convincing Jane to trade what turned out to be a well-chewed dog toy for the one remaining cookie, Ronan slipped out of the room and made for the back door. If he moved quickly he could be out in the garden before anyone noticed. Unfortunately, Charlotte was still in the kitchen. She was emptying a dust pan and stopped him just as he reached for the door knob.

"Ronan, could you take out the trash? I don't want to leave Aidy with a messy kitchen."

"Where is she?"

"Outside, showing Max where she wants things in her vegetable garden. She told me you dug it up for her."

He shrugged. "Least I could do."

Smiling, she tied the bag shut and handed it to him. "In case you weren't aware, we voted you brother-in-law of the year."

"I didn't know there was a competition. Do I need a tux for the award ceremony? "

She grinned. "Aidy's hoping you stay on here for a while. At least until the baby comes."

His heart sank. It wasn't that he didn't enjoy Max and Aidy's company. But for his own sanity, he had to leave. The sooner, the better.

"If my job applications don't get any bites, she may get her wish."

"Any exciting opportunities?"

"Not exciting, exactly." He resisted tugging at his collar with his free hand. Surprising how warm it had suddenly gotten. Maybe it was residual heat from the oven. "But they do pay well."

"I guess that's the most practical way to look at it. Particularly if you'd be doing something you don't like."

He blinked. "Why would you think I don't like architecture? I've been studying it for years."

"Maybe you liked *studying* architecture. But the whole time you worked at MacAllen, you were miserable. Today is the first time I've seen you relaxed since you left school."

He was saved from responding by Max and Aidy's return. Bear and Jerry raced to welcome them with the effusiveness normally reserved for people who had been gone for at least twenty minutes. In the ensuing hubbub, Ronan slipped out the door and headed for the office. He felt a little selfish going for a walk without Bear, but once in a while it was nice to be outside and not have to focus on rabbits, or squirrels, or whatever the dog might be interested in.

Plus he was feeling, well, spiteful. Maybe angry too. It was hard enough making sacrifices for people you loved. The least they could do was to accept those sacrifices graciously. But no. First Max and then Charlotte had as good as excused him from following the career plan he had decided was best for all of them. And Jock was no better.

What on earth gave him the right to tell Ronan who he should and should not relate to? Although, to be fair, Jock hadn't warned him off Jessica, exactly. More, he had warned Ronan not to toy with her. Which was so far from the reality of the situation it would have been laughable if it weren't so painful. If anyone was toying with affections, it was Jessica.

The clouds that had been dripping sullenly throughout the day had finally gone off to sea and freed the moon to glow unobstructed. But without the tapping of drops on the windowpane, the office felt particularly silent that evening. Ronan poked through the cardboard tubes of plans aimlessly before settling into his chair to catch up on email. Fifteen minutes later, after eliminating dozens of promotions for everything from art products to dog toys, he saw it. Domain Architects from New York had responded. Not a form letter.

He scanned it quickly at first, then again more slowly with a deepening sense of disbelief. It was an invitation to meet with the head of the firm. Kobi Ellis had been impressed with Ronan's portfolio and wanted to speak with him personally. Would Ronan be able to travel to New York City sometime in the next week? Without giving himself a chance to back out, he placed the call.

He sat back and dry scrubbed his face. He would have to tell Max. At least the plans for the building were complete. Researching historic garden layouts for the Retreat Center was intriguing but once Ronan had the information in hand, he could finish the plans on his own time and send them to Max from New York. Assuming he got the job, of course.

But he was going to try hard to get it. He needed to stop making excuses and actually take on the goal he had set himself all those years ago when his father died and the world had come crashing down. Chris might be an idiot, but he was right about putting away childish things.

CHAPTER 29

JESSICA WAS UNUSUALLY quiet the next morning. Ronan sneaked a look at her as he wandered toward the coffee pot Aidy had insisted on installing in their makeshift office. He didn't actually want coffee, but it was a good conversation starter. He had the uncomfortable feeling something had changed between them. There was a kind of distance this morning in her, in the way she looked or didn't look at him, even in the way she nodded and filed the papers he handed her.

"Want some?" He gestured toward the pot.

"Hmm?" She looked up, her gaze abstract and then returned to studying her spreadsheet. "Oh. No. Thanks."

Great. Now he was saddled with a lukewarm coffee he didn't even want, and he was still no further toward reaching through that wall she was slowly building.

"Everything going all right with your mother?"

It had been two days now and every time he asked, she fobbed him off. It was almost as though she had decided to cut him out of her life, or at least out of the parts of her life that mattered. Which should have been a relief under the circumstances, but oddly, wasn't.

She rolled her eyes. "Three people, one bathroom. Plus Liam's project was too big for the bus and Cookie wanted me to drop her in town so she could shop for an outfit for the party. At least I could use coming to work as an excuse to avoid joining her. Let's just say work is shaping up to be the most relaxing part of my week."

"Liam seemed pretty happy to meet his grandmother." Ronan held his breath. This felt like walking through a minefield.

"Yeah. He did." Her face softened. "But I worry."

"That he'll be hurt."

She nodded.

"If it's any consolation, I think she likes him."

"Sure. Until she finds someone better. She wanted to stay at my house, God knows why. But she did. So she realized she would have to be polite to Liam to secure her lodging arrangements."

He blinked. That was a cold assessment. On the other hand, Jessica had once known her mother very well. So he couldn't discount her reasoning. Still his admittedly brief interaction with Cookie had made him wonder if the older woman hadn't changed, mellowed a bit with age. She had a calculating air, sure, but there was something, well, vulnerable there. Sort of like an injured hawk. Maybe some of her aggressiveness had to do with disguising a weakness.

Under the circumstances, it was strange Cookie had wanted to stay with Jessica, especially once Ronan had offered a room at The Grand. Cookie had always impressed him as a person who valued the sorts of amenities upscale venues offered. Jessica's cottage wasn't the sort of place Cookie would normally be caught dead in.

Unless the two women had been in touch more than Jessica admitted. But in that case, Cookie's visit wouldn't have been a surprise. And Jessica's shock had been too clear to be faked.

"You think I'm being unfair to my mother, don't you?" Jessica's tone was sharp.

He shrugged uncomfortably. "Not completely. Cookie caused you a lot of pain over the years. And she destroyed your trust in her. So I can see why you would question her motivations now. But I did offer her a place to stay at The Grand and you repeated the invitation. And she refused. No offense, but a suite at The Grand would have been a lot more elegant than your cottage, certainly more roomy. And it would have been free."

She watched him, an impassive expression on her face, but did not interrupt. Still, he wondered whether he should back off now. This tentative friendship they had was worth preserving. On the other hand, lack of forthright communication was part of what had destroyed their friendship years ago. And maybe a friendship that couldn't withstand honesty wasn't a real friendship.

But even if what they had now wasn't the real thing, the idea of losing it was acutely and surprisingly painful. Which in and of itself was disturbing. He couldn't afford another broken heart. With the same woman.

"Your point?" Her tone was cool, her glance dismissive. She stood and straightened some files and slid them into the tray on her desk.

"My point is, I'm wondering why she insisted on staying with you. I'll grant you, it's a weird way to try to build a bridge after all these years. But I can't figure out what other reason she could have to reach out so persistently."

"Cookie? I can think of several reasons." She ticked them off on her fingers. "She wanted to impress on her friends that she can still manipulate me. That gives her something in common with Lynne – they both have troublesome offspring whom they are trying to "civilize." Second, she can complain to Lynne about the poor quality of the accommodations, and they can bond over how low class I am. Third, and this is my real concern, she could pretend she is concerned about Liam's welfare and use him as a lever to pressure me about Chris. Mom would love, and I mean love, to be related to Lynne by marriage."

"Liam's welfare?" He was mystified. "But you're an excellent mom to Liam. Don't get me wrong, I think Liam would have turned out a fantastic kid no matter what, but the fact he's so well adjusted is all down to you. Look how generous and sweet he was once he got over the shock of meeting her and then Chris. He's going to make an amazing man."

She nodded quietly and puffed out a breath. "Barbara's a family law attorney now. She thinks Chris wants custody, at least partial custody." She held up a hand at his instinctive protest. "She says the courts lean toward joint custody between birth parents as long as there isn't any realistic risk to the kid."

If it weren't for the tremor in her hand as she adjusted the pens in the cup and unnecessarily realigned her computer monitor, she might have convinced him she was at peace with the idea. He wished she wasn't quite so self-contained for once. It would have been easier if she cried, or screamed, or even threw something.

He put the coffee cup down before he crushed it. Rounding her desk, he stared down at her in disbelief. "But Chris is an addict. He freakin' deserted you before Liam was even born. I'd say he has less rights than pretty much anyone on the island at this point."

She shook her head. "I know. I reminded Barbara of all that, but she said since he's been clean for so long – "

"He says he's been clean. And he told me he's using some sort of herbal concoction called kratom tea to control cravings, but he looked high when I saw him on Tuesday. Why do you think I drove him and your mother to your place that night?"

She shook her head. "You said his car broke down."

"There wasn't time to tell you more before Liam came in and all hell broke loose. Chris ran his car off the road and onto the sidewalk." His fury at the injustice of the situation spilled over. "This is insane. We'll call my brother. Jock doesn't practice law much anymore, but he knows lots of people in the legal community. He'll connect us with the best family law attorney in the state."

She shook her head. "We could, but I trust Barbara. Even so, I did some research online. Everything I found backs up what she said. On top of that, fighting it would be expensive –"

She held her hand up to prevent him from interrupting, "– and ultimately a waste of time. But most significant of all, Liam wants to spend time with his birth father. Maybe the novelty will wear off once they get to know each other. Or maybe Chris will move on. But in the meantime, how can I say no?"

"Great." Ronan leaned forward over her desk, his hands fisted on the cold surface. He was out of line at this point, but he didn't care anymore. He had to do something, any-thing, to break through her tight control. "So when Chris drives up to your home, high on crystal meth, you're just go-ing to wave goodbye to Liam and wait for the phone call from the police telling you which emergency room to drive to to pick up the bodies? Or are you planning to let Chris move in with you so you can experience the full joint custody experience? That would be a fulfillment of a lifelong dream, right? Not to mention your mother's social aspirations. Sounds just about right."

In one swift move her hand swung up. He caught it just before it smacked his cheek. The blood drained from her face, and for a moment he thought she might pass out. Instead, she wrenched her wrist from his hand, grabbed her purse and fled.

Well. That had certainly gone well. Maybe he should have gotten drunk first and kicked a blind kitten. He knew he was being petulant, but he stomped out of the office anyway and headed toward Max and Aidy's house. The great thing about Bear was she liked him all the time. Even when he was being a jerk.

Aidy and Max had taken Jane to the city for the day. The plan was to go to Aidy's obstetrical appointment and then to visit the duckling statues in the Boston Garden. For some reason no one could determine, Jane had a particular fondness for Lack, the third duckling in the row of statues, and she loved the Swan Boats. Jerry stayed behind with Bear to keep him company, but even with two dogs in it, the house was extra quiet. The sort of quiet absence creates.

Instead of going to the mudroom for Bear's leash, Ronan strode into the living room and sank onto the couch. The energy from his temper had dissipated, leaving him hollow and a little sick. Bear nudged at his hand. Absently, he stroked her, tugging at the burrs she had somehow managed to collect since he brushed her last night. His ring tone wasn't loud, but it startled him anyway. It was a New York number. He took a deep breath and touched the green icon to accept the call.

"Ronan Durrell, please."

An older woman, by the sound of it. Professional and crisp. He could hear the hum of voices in the background.

The clatter of something being dropped and cheerful laughter.

"Speaking."

"Mr. Durrell, I'm following up on behalf of Mr. Ellis at Domain Architects."

He made a point of breathing slowly, evenly. She would tell him Ellis wasn't interested in meeting him. It had all been a mistake.

"I know this is short notice, but Mr. Ellis had a cancellation and he is most interested in discussing your folio with you as soon as possible. Would Monday afternoon at two o'clock work for you?"

"Yes." His voice seemed to be coming from far away. "Two o'clock Monday would be fine."

"That's wonderful." Her voice was warm with pleasure. "Will you be staying overnight in New York after your appointment? We have a standing reservation at a hotel nearby for some of our more important clients. You would be our guest, of course."

He blinked. "Thank you. I mean, that's very generous."

"No trouble at all." He could hear her smile through the phone. "Mr. Ellis is looking forward to meeting with you."

He hung up and stared at his phone. This was good news. Not good – amazing news. He would have to tell Max and Jock. He needed to review his portfolio. And he'd have to go back to his apartment to pack. But he'd leave Bear on the island.

He was suddenly filled with energy, a kind of urgency. Bear, who associated energy of that sort with chasing a ball was already shifting from foot to foot with anticipation. Even Jerry had caught the mood and ambled expectantly toward the door.

"All right, you troublemakers. Let's go chase some squirrels."

Ronan tucked his phone into his pocket along with Bear's leash and headed out toward the Retreat Center. If he was going to leave the island on Sunday he had to get back to work. And it might not be a bad idea to take copies of his plans for the event space and its accompanying garden with him to New York too. They were the best work he had done so far.

Maybe there had been nothing to salvage in his friend-ship with Jessica, but he would never know now. And maybe that was for the best. It wouldn't be fair to either him or to Jessica to keep pursuing this whatever-it-was they had. A kind of death match dance with no winners.

CHAPTER 30

JESSICA SLAMMED HER car door shut with more force than necessary. Sunlight streaming through the windshield had heated the cracked faux leather upholstery so her seat was too warm for comfort. She rolled down the window and sat staring blindly at the trees that rimmed the parking lot. She tugged her raggedy ponytail out of its elastic and tried to fix it. But bits of hair kept slipping out of her grasp. Scowling, she gave up and dropped the elastic into the crowded console bin.

She hadn't been able to sleep well since her last conversation with Barbara about custody. On a rational level, she understood Barbara's advice. Making a goodwill gesture by allowing Chris some contact with Liam might reduce the risk of his asking for partial custody.

It wasn't a great decision. But it was the best of several bad ones. Which was the most she could hope for under the circumstances. Still, learning to live with it was painful, and it didn't help to have Ronan second guessing her. He had no right to say those hurtful things, to scare her with horrifying imagery when she was already terrified. It wasn't as though he was going to be around to pick up the pieces when things went south as they inevitably would.

She clasped the top of the steering wheel and leaned forward so she could rest her head on her hands, her hair draping around her face like a privacy curtain. She eyed the grit laden floor mat and imagined Chris had not come back to the island. Cookie had not moved into the cottage. She could feel her shoulders ease under the image of her former life. Stressed, maybe. But not on the level it was now.

It was harder to remember life without Ronan though, which was troubling. It shouldn't have been so difficult. Ronan hadn't been around for Liam's birth, for any of the usual markers of life with a child, for any of the events that had framed Jessica's life since he had left her behind. But the days she had spent with him over the past two weeks were so vivid she had a hard time dismissing them. She gave in to the warm sunshine on her shoulders and closed her eyes.

She was running through the woods, her feet surefooted on the uneven path of packed earth. And then the path curved upward and she was running faster, suddenly aware there was someone, something behind her. She could hear it panting. Or maybe that was her own breath straining against her ribs as she pounded forward, twisting and leaping between trees, over stones. But the panting thing was nearer now, and she was no longer sure she could outrun it. There was shouting in the distance, but she knew with dull certainty whoever was coming to help would not make it in time. The thing's hot breath caressed her cheek.

She woke with a start and raised her arm to fend off Bear. The dog's front toes scrabbled for grip at the open window, her great furry head poking into the car as she continued to aim an industrious tongue at Jessica's face. Jessica grabbed for her collar, but the Newfoundland seemed determined to finish the task she had set herself.

"Hey!" Ronan's shout went unheeded until he made it to the car and pulled the dog down. "You okay?"

She took a moment to wipe the well-meant slobber from her cheek with her sleeve before answering. "If there was any remnant of breakfast on my face, it's gone now."

"I'm sorry."

She could tell by the tone of his voice, he wasn't talking about Bear. Or, at least, not just about Bear. And she was sorry too. Sorry for him. Sorry for herself.

"I shouldn't have said what I did," he added. "I was out of line. I know this situation must be exceptionally hard for you."

She had returned her hands to the steering wheel. She stared blankly at her white knuckles without responding for a moment. She didn't want to look at him. Because looking at him would mean two things. First, she would forgive him. Second, she would start to cry. And neither of those was an option if she was going to keep her head together in the long run. Finger by finger she loosened her death grip on the steering wheel and then nodded.

"It is hard," she said. "And you were out of line. But I shouldn't have lost my temper."

"Can I make it up to you?"

She sighed. "Not necessary. I just need work to be separate from home stuff right now."

"That's fair." He hesitated. "But I would like to take you and Liam out for lunch on Saturday. If you're free, that is. A kind of celebration for finishing the plans for the building."

Startled, she lifted her eyes to his. She knew he had been researching garden plans, but she hadn't realized he had actually finished the plans for the event space. Her quick burst of joy on his behalf was accompanied by an equally sharp jab of sorrow. He wasn't talking about a celebration. It would be more of a gracious thank you kiss-off. Because once the plans were complete he would have no more reason to stay on Demerest Cove. The thought of sitting politely across a table from him as they both didn't say what they were feeling was more than she could bear. She swallowed. At least she had an unimpeachable excuse.

"Sorry, I can't. Carl called this morning. His brother was in a car accident and Carl's flying out to be with him this afternoon."

"Oh, no!"

"Apparently the brother is going to be okay, but recuperation will take a while and his family is pretty shaken up. But on this end, it means I may have to take some of my vacation days earlier than anticipated to cover the events Carl was going to manage. Including the Mullin party this Saturday afternoon."

She didn't know how she would explain the change in staffing to Lynne. But if Lynne wanted her party done properly, she would have to lump it. And if Lynne told all her friends to stop doing business with Moon Shell, well, the business was closing in a few months anyway. Jessica meant it when she had assured Carl that family came first during their conversation that morning. And she was glad he had taken her at her word. Didn't mean it wasn't going to be awkward on Saturday.

"Of course. I'll help," Ronan said.

Great. What she needed for Saturday was more stress. "Probably not a good idea. I'll handle it on my own."

He nodded. She could see him withdraw right in front of her. He leaned forward, and she had a fleeting hope he would graze his fingers against her cheek. Instead, he clicked her door open and held out his hand to help her out of the car. The gesture was an old-fashioned courtesy. But the personal warmth of his gaze had slipped away behind his usual cool mask of gracious charm.

It bothered her too much. Maybe because the way he had looked at her a moment ago had been so caring, so distinct to her. Nobody else looked at her that way. A person could get dependent on that kind of attention, even addicted. Probably better not to expose herself to it too often. Because the more dependent she was, the harder going cold turkey would be. And going cold turkey was non-negotiable. She turned to grab her purse and got out of the car, purposely fumbling with her purse strap as she rose so she could avoid putting her hand in his.

RONAN CURLED HIS fingers and tucked his hand into his pocket. There was no point in standing there with his hand held out like a beggar. The ludicrousness of the situation struck him. Back home, he was surrounded by women who wanted him. But here the only woman he wanted, maybe the only woman he had ever wanted, Jessica, didn't want him. She hadn't wanted him when he was a struggling high school student. And even now, when for all intents and purposes, he had made it through his preparation for adult life and was facing a bright future, she wasn't interested.

She couldn't have made it clearer than she had just now. And he felt like a fool. If there was one thing he knew, it was that you couldn't *make* a person like you. Which was what made families so special. They had to like you. Although, on second thought, he guessed that wasn't true either. There didn't seem to be much love lost between Jessica and her mother. Understandable under the circumstances, he guessed. It would be difficult getting past being abandoned as a pregnant teen.

What was impressive about Jessica was that she had managed to build an alternate family for herself. The Ulrich's clearly considered her another daughter. Max and Aidy were already protective of her. Hell, even Della liked Jessica and until now he had been pretty sure Della didn't like anyone.

And then there were the other things Jessica had accomplished. Liam was, well, Liam. Not much could be improved on that score. And she had even started her own business. And now she was going to do amazing work in her new position. Her self-sufficiency was admirable. But it made him feel like an extraneous puzzle piece in the vast and complex jigsaw puzzle that was her life.

A dark cloud scudded over the sun and the shadow it cast touched his skin with a faint chill. Jessica walked next to him, but slightly ahead. He couldn't see her expression, just the line of her jaw, a tendril of hair brushing at the ridge of her ear as she strode, the slightly crooked vulnerable line of her part.

He wanted her. His heart pounded with the intensity of his desire. Not just physically although yes, definitely that. He loved the challenge of her, the way he had to work to figure her out. With another woman it might have been frustrating, tiresome even. But with Jessica, it was more like climbing through undergrowth in a forest. Hard work with a high risk of sustaining scratches from thorns. But every now and again, there was a glimpse of the vista waiting for the hiker who made it to the next level of forest. It would never be easy with Jessica. But easy was boring. It wasn't that he enjoyed fighting. But he wouldn't have wanted a woman who needed a relationship in order to assess her own value. Not that it mattered in this case.

"Jessica." He said it quietly, feeling the sound of it on his tongue. Sweet with a bitter residue, because after all, how else could an impossible beautiful dream taste. "I told Max I'm leaving Sunday."

She slowed and turned to face him.

"I see." There was a tightness to her tone, but her face gave no hint of emotion.

"I can check in with Liam before I go."

"Not necessary." Her lips tightened and she looked away.

"I mean I'd like to."

She shifted slightly and shoved her hands into her pockets and studied her feet for a moment before responding. "Ronan, I – I think it would better if we kept this a work friendship and left it at that. It's not your fault I've got Chris and Cookie to deal with in the same week. But it's a lot. And not just for me. For Liam too."

He studied her for a moment. "You okay?"

She puffed out a breath. "Not yet. But I will be eventually. At least that's what I keep telling myself."

This so exactly mirrored his own sentiments he nearly laughed. If they hadn't been such an awful pair they would have been a perfect match. "You said you think Cookie is leaving on Sunday too, right? So that should be a relief."

"I guess." Jessica shrugged. "I hope. She hasn't been specific, and I need some time alone with her if I'm going to succeed at pinning her down. She keeps changing the subject every time I bring it up. But Liam can't sleep on the couch forever."

"I'm probably going to be heading into Boston the same time she is. Want me to escort her to the ferry that day to make sure she actually gets on it?"

She shot him a grateful look. "That's – I'd appreciate it. Are you doing more garden research?"

He paused a little too long before responding.

"No. I have a job interview. In New York."

CHAPTER 31

JESSICA KEPT HER head high as she headed toward the office. But when she reached the doorway she walked right by it, down the hall and into the bathroom. Her stomach was in knots. She locked the door behind her and leaned against the sink, trying to breath. Gripping the edges of the vanity, she dropped her head so she didn't have to see her reflection in the mirror. It was bad enough to feel as though her heart was shattered, she didn't have to see it written on her face. He was leaving.

And maybe she should be grateful. She did love him of course, she had loved him since that autumn day he had walked into her classroom and tripped over his shoelace on his way to his desk. She suspected that love would never fade. But being *in* love with Ronan was a disaster.

True to form, he was running out when she needed him the most. And it wasn't a spur of the moment thing – going to a job interview in New York on Monday meant he had sent the application out at least a week ago. Her heart hardened at the realization, and she recognized her flash of resentment for the envy it was. Shaking her head, she forced herself to meet her own eyes in the mirror.

She should be glad Ronan was headed to New York. She *would* be glad. He deserved a chance to show the world the depth of his talent. So it was a good thing he was leaving. Better for Liam too. Liam needed the kind of normalcy and predictability she had yearned for as a child, but Chris's arrival and even Cookie's continued presence threatened that. Having Ronan around would just confuse Liam more.

And definitely better for her too. She didn't think she could bear to live through the exact mirror image of her past. Thirteen years ago, even if she hadn't believed she was too good for a poor boy like Ronan, everyone else on the island had. The irony of the reversal would have been funny if it weren't so painful.

The last thing Ronan needed was an undereducated single mom dragging him down. Maybe he wouldn't acknowledge the problem at first, but when he moved up the ranks in the NYC world of business, she would be a liability. People would be polite on the surface, just the way they were here, but when they thought she wouldn't notice those same polite people would exchange looks. The kinds of looks that said, "What does he see in her?" And she would be in the same situation she was in on the island but without the resources of supportive friends.

So maybe Ronan was being self serving, but in a way he was doing her a favor. His taking the step of leaving before their friendship deepened into something neither of them wanted was the best thing for everyone involved. The fact that the benefit to her and Liam was secondary to Ronan's needs hurt, but she would get over it.

Her cell phone rang. She reached for it, intending to ignore the call if it wasn't Liam, but her finger slipped and brushed against the "accept call" icon.

"Cand – Jessica, this is Chris. Chris Mullin."

His timing was stunning. For a moment, she considered dropping the phone into the toilet. But replacing it would be expensive and Chris wasn't worth it. She had to ask, even though she had a sinking feeling she already knew the answer. "Chris, how did you get my number? Did my mother give it to you?"

"Of course she did."

"She had no right to do that."

"Don't be silly," he said. "Your mother wants Liam to have a normal family, and she's trying to make sure you and I heal our relationship. That's why she agreed to come all the way to the island when I invited her."

"We have no relationship," she responded automatically. But then she replayed his last sentence and her heart grew cold. "You invited her. That makes more sense. I should have realized Lynne would never invite Mom to a party, much less pay for her travel. How long have you two been planning this?"

"Oh, a few months. Maybe since Christmas. She sent Mother such a lovely card, and I decided to reach out and provide counsel. Cookie is a good woman. She wants what is best for you and for Liam."

The betrayal was a tiny wound, but it bled anyway. And, like a paper cut, it managed to hurt more than a deeper wound would. "Cookie wants what is best for Cookie," she retorted.

She was pretty sure the silence that followed was one of disapproval, but then he sighed.

"We need to talk, Jessica."

"About?"

"About Liam. I want to get to know him. And I think it's time I acknowledged him publicly as my son. I don't have to tell you how significant that would be for his social status on the island."

She rolled her eyes. Chris still managed a combination of small mindedness and hubris that would have been laughable if it hadn't posed a threat to Liam.

"Chris, I can't talk now. I'm at work." She stepped out of the bathroom and walked toward the office so it wouldn't be a lie.

"Then let's chat this evening," Chris said. "I'd like you and Liam to come to Mother's party on Saturday."

Her grip on the phone relaxed infinitesimally. She didn't have to worry about this one. Lynne hated Jessica and she refused to –

"Mother thinks it's a good idea," Chris continued. "She says –"

Jessica stopped in her tracks and gently hung up on the call. Chris would think she had walked out of cell phone range. The island had lots of places with spotty reception. When the phone began to ring again, she muted it and let his call go to voice mail.

Unlike Ronan, Chris never backed off unless it suited him. It wasn't so much that he was tenacious – more that he was spoiled and determined to have his way no matter who was hurt in the process. Other people's feelings didn't have much significance to Chris. Although to be fair, she thought he was interested in Liam's welfare. It was just that he cared for Liam as an adjunct of Chris himself, rather than as a distinct entity.

She glanced toward the open office door. She didn't want to go in there – her anger at Chris and Cookie was holding her together pretty well for the moment, but it wouldn't last. And she didn't want Ronan to see her cry. She hesitated, but when she didn't hear any noises from inside, she bit her lip and started walking. The room was empty.

She sank into her chair and stared about the office, suddenly conscious of how deserted the administrative wing was. Max and Aidy were in Boston, and evidently Ronan had left the building after their conversation. Not that it mattered. It wasn't as though he had any reason to stay.

Absently, she picked up the troll doll Liam had given her years ago for her birthday. She kept it on her desk as a reminder of how proud he had been to buy her a gift with money he earned himself doing chores for Clara and Hans. But today she was having a hard time recalling the eager joy of five-year-old Liam.

The garage sale find sported a threadbare biker outfit, shocking green hair and the typical impudent wrinkly troll smile. But a previous owner had given the troll a flat top haircut, probably with the optimistic expectation the hair would grow back. As a result, the doll had a kind of worn, tough girl look.

Jessica swallowed. Normally the doll's rakish expression and spunky persona made her smile. But today being indomitable seemed out of reach. Putting it back on her desk, she turned it to face away from her. That was better. This way she didn't have to look at that stubbornly grinning face.

She blinked hard and scrubbed away the dampness on her face irritably. She didn't want to be tough. She was tired of being tough. But it wasn't as if she had a choice.

The memory flooded back. She had been stocking shelves at Hans's hardware store when she overheard Ronan's grandfather telling Clara that his youngest grandson was leaving the island that day to go to college in Boston. Clara hadn't probed when Jessica said she was too tired to work that afternoon. But Clara always had seen through high school girl lies.

The sky had been overcast but the breeze was warm with the stubborn heat of late August in New England. Nonetheless, on her way out the door, Jessica grabbed her denim jacket. Her belly was beginning to swell under her T-shirt and the jacket would hide it. Barely. By the time she reached the pier, her hair was damp and a rivulet of sweat from her temple had trailed down to her collar bone.

The moment she saw Ronan, she ducked behind a crate. Now she was here, she wasn't sure why she had come. It wasn't as if he would want to say goodbye to her – not after what she had done. But she couldn't leave. He might see her.

He wasn't bringing much with him, just a duffle bag. He wore a knapsack too, but that would be full of art supplies. She blinked back tears as she watched him hug his father and his grandparents in turn. Then Ronan and his brothers boarded the ferry and faster than she could process, the whistle blew, and the ferry pulled away from the dock. It was surprisingly graceful for such an ungainly looking vessel.

After the rumble of the engine and the cheerful shouted conversations between passengers and their loved ones faded, the deserted pier was filled with a hollow silence. Wavelets smacked against the footings of the pier and a lone seagull circled above briefly before heading off to better scavenging grounds. Jessica had never felt lonelier in her life.

The ferry was growing smaller now, alone in the vastness of the sea. Slowly, Jessica walked toward the end of the pier. Swimming was prohibited in this area of the coast, not only because of the jagged rocks that lurked below the surface of the water on either side of the central channel the ferries used but because there were often rip currents.

She took another step forward and stared at the gray blue swells on the horizon. It wouldn't be an easy way to go, but nothing was easy anymore. The thought of release was seductive. It wasn't as though anyone would miss her. The Ulrichs, sure. But they had each other. They'd get over it.

The toes of her sneakers poked over the edge of the last plank on the pier and Jessica held her arms wide, letting the wind push against her face. Maybe this was what gulls felt like when they flew. Maybe, in her next life, she would be a gull. But just as she began to lean forward into the wind, she felt it – a tiny string of bubbles inside her. The tracing of a tiny hand against the inside of her belly. And just like that, Liam had saved her life.

Jessica leaned back in her desk chair and stared out the window blindly. Maybe Liam was saving her from herself again. Because the pain of losing Ronan was just as bad now as it had been thirteen years ago. But this time she knew how to use her responsibilities to distract herself from it.

At least she hadn't told him she loved him this time either. Small mercies. His knowing would have been more shame than she could bear, so that was some small consolation. And at least he was leaving the island soon.

CHAPTER 32

AN EMPTY SCHOOL bus rattled past Ronan as he drove the Bentley toward Jessica's cottage. He was pretty sure Cookie would still be dress shopping, and Jessica was still at work. Which meant Liam would be home alone. He had to tell Liam in person. It wouldn't be fair to leave it to Jessica to break the news. Maybe too, he wanted to cast his leaving in the kindest light possible.

Jessica could hardly blame Ronan for building his career and supporting his brothers, but he had a nagging feeling it would be better to get in with his version of the story first. He wasn't sure why it mattered so much. After all, if he got the job in New York, he would likely move there, which meant he would be unlikely to visit the island again for some time and even then those visits would be sporadic. His chances of seeing Liam again were slim.

Ronan's heart clenched at the thought. It wasn't so much that Liam expected him to stick around – it was Liam's lack of expectations that made the upcoming conversation so painful to contemplate. Maybe he should ask Max to take Liam under his wing once Ronan was gone for good. He forced himself out of the car and closed the door with a definite snap, mostly to signal his own determination to himself.

He flashed on an image of Liam sitting a little forward in the driver's seat so he could reach the accelerator. His cheeks had been so pale his freckles had stood out and the look of sheer joy in his eyes had been luminescent. He loved Liam, he realized with a jolt. He was an extraordinary boy and would grow into an extraordinary man. It hurt Ronan to know he wouldn't be around to see that.

There was something ludicrous in the way he slowed his pace to a reluctant trudge as he neared the porch steps, like a little boy heading toward a well-deserved scolding. He took a deep breath and knocked. For a moment he had a wild hope Liam had stayed at school for an orchestra rehearsal. The desire was so strong he had convinced himself it was so and turned to walk back down the stairs before he heard the click of the door opening.

"Hi, Ronan."

Ronan turned at Liam's dull tone. Jessica couldn't have told him already. Could she? It didn't seem like the kind of thing she would do over the phone.

"Want to come in?"

Cautiously, Ronan followed Liam into the cottage. Liam gestured toward the couch and, without a word, took a seat on the floor, picked up a video game controller and focused on Super Mario. Ronan waited until Liam got past a tricky part before speaking. "I didn't know they still made Super Mario World."

"They don't," Liam said. "I got it at a yard sale. Not all the games in the set worked, but this one and Super Mario Kart do."

Ronan sat silently watching Mario jump, spin and stomp on his enemies. He remembered soothing himself with the game the summer after his mother died. His father had uprooted them from their family home and moved them to Ronan's grandparents' house on Demerest Cove. At least that was the way Ronan had thought of it at the time.

As an adult, Ronan understood how bereft his father must have felt at the loss of his wife, how overwhelmed to have to care for three grieving sons on his own. And how much he must have needed the emotional and financial support of his own parents. But as a twelve year old, Ronan had blamed his father for ruining what was left of his middle school life. And burying himself in video games had been a good way to sublimate that pain.

"Ronan, what do you do if you like someone but they don't even seem to know you're there?"

Wow. Right in the gut. But this wasn't about Ronan and Jessica, of course. He cleared his throat. "Stephanie?"

Liam nodded, his eyes glued to the action on the television screen.

"She seemed pretty interested in you at the carnival."

"Yeah. Well, I guess not. I asked her to the end of year dance and she said no."

"Did she already say yes to someone else?"

"No. She just doesn't like me."

"Is that what she said?"

"Dude." Liam dropped the controller and turned toward Ronan, face flushed. "It's obvious. Can we just drop it?"

The irony didn't escape him. He waited a beat before responding. "Until she says, "I don't like you, Liam," right to your face, you can't know for sure."

"Sure," Liam muttered, his thumbs busy on the controller again. But his shoulders were more relaxed. Hope did that, Ronan knew. He shrugged his own shoulders but didn't feel any discernible loosening.

"For what it's worth, I don't think you are going to have any trouble finding girls who like you. Women tend to look for men who are kind and considerate."

Liam glanced at him and then looked back at the game. For a kid with such an open quality, he wore an atypically unreadable expression.

"Mom isn't going to be home until five-thirty."

"Yeah. I –" Now that he had an opening, he wasn't sure how to start. "I wanted to tell you I'm heading to New York on Monday."

"Cool." Liam focused on the screen. Once Super Mario had stomped all over a particularly troublesome enemy, Liam paused the game and shambled toward the kitchen. "Are you going to see the Ghostbusters' Fire House? If I ever go to New York, that's one thing I have to see." He opened the refrigerator door. "Mom got me orange soda in honor of me getting an A on my book report. Do you want some?"

"No, thanks," Ronan said. "Liam, I'm not just visiting New York, it's a job interview. And if I get the job, I'll probably have to start right away. But maybe once I get settled in, you and your mom could come out to visit. We could see that fire house together."

Liam didn't respond. Instead he focused on pouring orange soda into a glass and carefully screwing the top onto the bottle.

"I don't think so." His tone was polite, thoughtful even, but definite. "I don't think that would be good for my mom. Or for me."

Ronan, who had risen in expectation of making a smooth exit, sat back down on the couch. Liam was right, of course. Still, it was one thing for Ronan to acknowledge the unsolvable conundrum of his relationship with Jessica. It was quite another for Liam to be so assertive about it.

"Why not?"

The moment the question was out of his mouth, he was sure of the answer. Chris. It had always been Chris. He could hardly blame Liam for having hopes of what meeting his birth father might result in. One of those hopes had to be that Chris and Jessica would marry.

Liam shrugged silently. He took a slow sip of his soda and set the glass down on the counter but made no move to return to his game. "I don't want to be rude," he said finally. "But I think you should leave."

Ronan stood, trying not to look forlorn. Liam was wrong – probably. Ronan was pretty sure Chris didn't have a snowball's chance of success with Jessica. On the other hand, what did he know? Maybe this time she would actually marry the guy. It would certainly please her mother, and whether she admitted it to herself or not, pleasing her mother mattered a great deal to Jessica.

He shook his head wordlessly. Nothing had changed. Nothing. There was no point in waiting around to hear Jessica tell him she didn't love him and never would. He didn't need to hear it again to know it was still true. Maybe she would marry Chris. She could do worse. At least Chris was trying to do the right thing.

That was Ronan's responsibility too – to do the right thing. So he would walk away from the only woman he had ever loved. Again. Because doing so was the best thing for everyone – his brothers, Jessica, Liam, even Chris. The pompous twit. There were worse things, Ronan guessed. Although at the moment he couldn't think of any. Breathing wasn't easy just now.

He waved halfheartedly at Liam and wished him luck with Stephanie before stepping out onto the porch. The last time he stood out here alone had been the night after his date with Jessica. He wasn't sure you could call it a date, exactly. More of a happenstance, a promise, a kind of shining possibility. He remembered the scent of damp night air, the gnats throwing themselves fruitlessly against the glass porch light. Not a great image, now he thought about it.

He drove carefully, stopping at each stop sign even if no other car was at the intersection. Behaving normally took all his focus and energy because the pain was savage. Maybe Liam was right. But that didn't change the howling emptiness that had now taken the place of his heart.

He was vaguely aware the sun was shining. Normally he would have relished the dogwood tree on the corner with its breathtaking fall of flowers, the bustling hurry of a pair of birds fluttering into its branches with nest building supplies, the whiff of salt in the breeze. Spring had always been his favorite season but now he wondered why he had ever enjoyed it.

They had studied T. S. Eliot's "The Waste Land" in high school, he and Jessica. At the time he hadn't seen the point of the poem even as Jessica dissected it for him. His focus had been on the feel of her breath on his cheek as they bent over the thick textbook together, the smooth line of her bare arm. She had a freckle on her right wrist. He had longed to touch that freckle with the tip of his finger, to trace the lines of her palm. To press his lips to the pulse there. That hadn't been an option then. And now it never would be.

He could still hear Jessica's soft voice reading the opening lines to him in an undertone, her manicured finger tracing under each line.

April is the cruellest month, breeding
Lilacs out of the dead land, mixing

Memory and desire, stirring
Dull roots with spring rain.
Winter kept us warm, covering
Earth in forgetful snow, feeding
A little life with dried tubers.

Eliot was wrong. April wasn't the cruellest month. May was. But he was right about the rest. Because it was safer, better, to stay covered and forgetful. Ronan had made the mistake of falling in love with Jessica years ago and it had been painful. But this time was worse. Much worse.

CHAPTER 33

THE COTTAGE SMELLED a little funky, so Jessica opened the windows as soon as she put the grocery bags on the counter. There was no sign of Liam, but the door to his bedroom was closed which meant Cookie was in there. Jessica flicked the oven on to preheat and started yanking items from the bags. Cookie didn't eat much, but the grocery bill had been significantly higher this week. Probably because Jessica was buying fancier food than usual. She scowled at a can of chopped tomatoes. Normally she only bought store brand.

There was no point in trying to impress Cookie, so she wasn't sure why she was making the effort. Cookie had always relied on a housekeeper to provide food and, on those rare occasions the housekeeper was off, she relied on takeout. Cookie was hardly a culinary expert. Jessica shoved the can into the cupboard and was fumbling in the paper bag for another when she heard the tap of her mother's heels.

"Liam, is that you? I thought – oh, Candy."

Jessica rolled her eyes but resisted commenting on the Candy/Jessica thing. It was Friday afternoon, but Sunday morning seemed terribly far away. She yearned for her mother to leave, and the moment she felt the yearning, so powerful it was tangible, she felt guilty. Because Liam and Candy were actually enjoying each other's company in ways she would never have envisioned. Liam spent hours chatting with his grandmother. And Cookie was having a great time reacquainting herself with old friends on the island.

It seemed the only person who wasn't delighted with Cookie's visit was Jessica. Some nights she felt like the only adult in the house especially when it came time to call lights out. Liam would protest good naturedly and Cookie would call her a party pooper. And later, when Jessica was lying in bed, trying to escape her thoughts of Ronan long enough to fall asleep, she would hear her mother next door humming to herself and she would press her fists to her ears to keep the sound out. She knew she should feel grateful. For years she had wished her mother would reach out, would be a part of Liam's life. But as anyone who read fairy tales knew, one had to be extraordinarily careful with wishes.

"Did you find a dress, Mom?" Jessica tried to keep her tone friendly and light. Liam would not have been deceived, but Cookie was not as observant. Or maybe she just didn't care.

"First I looked in Delilah's, you know that new little place on Main? But there wasn't anything quite right. So then I checked Philipe Marche's, but everything there was a little too-too. I really was about to give up, but a girl's got to keep the faith, right?"

Jessica nodded and checked the refrigerator for the chicken breasts she had defrosted last night. That was odd. She moved items around with increased confusion. She remembered pulling the meat from the freezer before going to bed. She had put it in the blue bowl she always used for defrosting. But it wasn't in the refrigerator.

Cookie chattered on, her face suffused with a triumphant glow. "So then I went down to Water Street. I had no idea the harbor area was becoming so chic. If you haven't been down there recently, you should go. Adorable. And that's where I found it. The cutest little sundress with a keyhole neckline and it was on sale, marked down to two ninety-nine. They had a couple things you would like too, so you should check it out. It's the little shop on the corner, called *Apparently*."

Jessica stared at her mother blankly. The shops on Water Street were appallingly expensive. They catered to summer folk with bursting wallets and no self discipline. Some of the shops even had piers attached to the buildings so customers could tie their yachts nearby when they came to spend the day on the island. As an island resident, Jessica approved. Demerest Cove's businesses depended on tourist money. So she guessed it was a good thing for the economy Cookie had spent the money.

She understood Cookie's excitement on a visceral level. As a teen, she would have known about *Apparently* even before Cookie did. Shopping was all about the excitement of the hunt, the thrill of the catch. Cost had been irrelevant back then except for a way of demonstrating how little the price mattered.

But the experience of putting milk back into the dairy case at the supermarket because she couldn't afford it was seared into Jessica's memory. Three hundred dollars would have been a fortune back when Liam was a baby. Even now, it was a shocking amount of money to spend on one garment. And it wasn't as if Cookie needed another article of clothing. There must have been several appropriate dresses in the massive suitcases that now took up most of the floor space in Liam's room.

"I don't need anything at the moment," Jessica hedged. "But I'll be sure to keep that store in mind if I do."

Jessica turned back to the freezer. She expected to find the chicken breasts on the shelf, looking as smug as frozen chicken could look when it should have been defrosted. But there was no package of chicken there. And apparently Cookie hadn't gotten the message.

"Of course you'll need something to wear on tomorrow. It's not just any party. And I looked in your closet yesterday, Candy – you've really let your wardrobe slide. I told the manager at *Apparently* to expect you tomorrow morning, so she put a few of the nicer dresses aside for you."

Jessica could feel a tiny spark of temper now, warm and dangerous. "You – Mom, you can't just –"

"Oh, pooh. No need to thank me. You'd look pretty again if you just put in the effort. And it'll all pay off when Chris proposes, you'll see. Under the circumstances no one will expect a long engagement, so a June wedding would be perfect."

"No."

"You're right," Cookie said, after a pause. "Fall weddings are lovely too, and that way we'll have more time to plan."

"No, Mom. Look, I – we need to talk."

She gestured toward the couch. Cookie gave it a doubtful glance. Liam had scrambled for the school bus that morning and had left his sheets and blankets in a rumpled pile. Cookie waited to sit until Jessica transferred the pile to a kitchen chair.

"I'll be at the Mullin's house tomorrow, Mom, but not as a guest. Lynne hired my event planning business to run her party, so I'll be behind the scenes making sure everything runs smoothly. But even if I were going as a guest, you need to understand I'm never going to marry Chris. I don't love him."

Cookie looked mystified. "But don't you want Liam to have the things he needs? And what about me?"

The cold fury flashed again, a little larger this time, blue flames licking hungrily. Jessica scrambled to her feet and looked down at her mother. "I'm sorry, what?"

"Well it's not all about you, Candy." Cookie gestured impatiently. "Since your father left me, I've been managing but it hasn't been easy. There are so many single women in Boca, it's extraordinarily difficult to find an available man with the right income. It's easy for me because I've been keeping my looks up. And I don't allow myself to be distracted by unimportant things like whatever you do with yourself all day. It takes a lot of work to stay desirable. You have no idea how lucky you are to have a perfectly acceptable, wealthy man like Chris who actually wants to marry you."

There was a tinge of envy in her tone. Pursing her lips together, Cookie flicked a minute dust particle from her slacks and shifted her leg away from a threadbare spot on the couch cushion. Jessica watched her silently, considering and discarding ideas for a retort. Because in the end, what was the point. It was as though somewhere along the way, Jessica and Cookie had stopped speaking the same language. So no matter what she said, Cookie would be incapable of comprehending it.

Sometimes Jessica wondered what she might have become if Liam hadn't come along. Probably she would have gone on to college, maybe followed her dream into academia. She would have met a man. But there her daydream always stopped. Because the man looked like Ronan. And Ronan was an impossibility. And because the fact of Liam was so tangible, so un-ignorable.

For a while she had grieved her loss of social status almost as much as her other losses. She had been the undisputed queen of the high school, not just because of her appearance, although her lithe physique and her swath of long blonde hair had been the envy of all her friends. But she had been a good student too, a golden girl who won the admiration and praise of her teachers. "Candy Piers will go far" was the consensus.

But life had changed her, in some ways for the better. In other ways, not so much. She had come to accept herself as the scrappy, hardscrabble person she had become. A rumpled loner with a reputation for being unfriendly. And as far from being physically desirable as she was from that other Jessica, the one called Candy.

On the other hand, her life had given her skills and knowledge she would never have gained in the charmed imaginary life Candy might have led. She hadn't done it alone. Without the Ulrich's she might not have made it to adulthood at all, and raising Liam had taught her everything else she knew.

She was no longer in her mother's social class and probably never would be again. But she wasn't sure that was a bad thing, at least in terms of character development. At least she didn't lie and manipulate people. She crossed her arms and prepared to give her mother a piece of her mind.

"Hi Grandma! Hi Mom! Whoops —" Liam's tuba case thumped against the door frame as he angled it into the living room. "I'm starving. Is that dinner?"

The blue bowl filled with oozing raw chicken was on top of the bookshelf, nested tidily between a ceramic pitcher and Liam's second grade school picture. Jessica's face burned. She had heard her phone vibrate late last night, just as she was cleaning the kitchen, and for a moment she had been sure it was Ronan texting her. And in the totally predictable but blinding disappointment of finding it was only a school advisory, she had forgotten all about the chicken. And somehow, now, it felt providential.

"You know what – no. We're going to Hans and Clara's for dinner tonight."

CHAPTER 34

AS SHE DROVE toward the Ulrichs' house, Jessica's anxiety ratcheted up. Which made no sense. Clara had been delighted to hear they were coming for dinner. She probably would have been a bit less delighted if Cookie had been coming, but as it turned out, Cookie was expected at the Mullin's house for some sort of pre-party get together. So at least there was that. Still, as Jessica let the engine idle in the Ulrich's driveway, she considered just dropping Liam off and heading back to the cottage instead. There were several cars in the driveway already so Hans and Clara wouldn't miss her. The thought of time alone in her silent home was tantalizing.

The sun was setting, and the windows of the old house glowed with rosy reflected light. Slowly, Jessica turned off the engine. Through the windshield, she watched as the door opened. Hans stood in the doorway, smiling. He ushered Liam in, hugging him with one arm and holding open the door with the other. She expected Hans to follow Liam into the house, but instead he came out onto the porch, carefully closing the door behind him before heading toward Jessica with a serious expression on his kindly face. Staying in the car seemed childish, so she got out and leaned against the closed door, trying to look nonchalant.

"*Zissele.*"

The first time Hans had called her that, the name had slid off his tongue like a caress. He had stumbled upon Jessica vomiting up her breakfast and had gently wiped her face with a warm wet washcloth that felt like heaven. It had taken a few weeks before Barbara explained *zissele* meant "little sweet one" in Yiddish. Jessica had felt so far from meriting the name she had almost asked Hans not to call her that, but she hadn't been able to bear the thought of hurting his feelings. Now she tried to contain the hot flood of tears, but they fell anyway. He wrapped a comforting arm around her shoulders as he fumbled in his pocket for a tissue. But all he pulled out was a handful of washers and a lag nut and she found herself laughing through her tears at his look of consternation.

"I'm okay," she said. She was pretty sure that was true until, to her horror, another sob came pushing up and out.

"*Zissele*, what's wrong?" He patted her on the shoulder but his sharp gray eyes appraised her. "Is everything okay with Liam?"

"Liam's fine, Hans," she said. Although now she thought about it, Liam hadn't been his usual talkative self recently. Even his enthusiasm for visiting the Ulrichs had been a bit muted. But maybe he was having a delayed reaction to meeting two new family members in one week. Or maybe he was just reflecting her own lack of energy since her last conversation with Ronan. Maybe she was coming down with something.

"Liam says your mother is visiting." He peered into the car and shook his head. "You could have brought her along."

"Mom had other plans."

Which was accurate as far as it went, but the truth was she hadn't joined Liam in pressing Cookie to come with them because bringing Cookie into the warmth of the Ulrich's home would have been like dripping spoiled milk into fresh. And because casual bigotry cloaked in witty banter had been common in the Piers household, among her parents' friends and even occasionally at school.

As a child, Jessica had known Barbara was Jewish in the way she knew Marley had asthma. It was a kind of condition you didn't mention so the sufferer wouldn't be embarrassed, but also so you wouldn't have to hear any uncomfortable and boring explanations. All the other elementary school students had known for sure was that Barbara brought big crackers to school for lunch for a week every spring, which was peculiar and she didn't celebrate Christmas, which was downright weird.

So when Barbara brought Jessica home, Jessica had expected to feel sorry for the Ulrichs. She hadn't expected to envy them. It had taken a while to get used to the rhythm of the Ulrich's household, their casual use of Yiddish in daily speech, their observance of holidays she had never heard of.

214 | ROSE GREY

But the toughest thing to adjust to had been the intensity of care and warmth they enveloped her with.

"We would have been glad to put her up in one of our bedrooms." That was how Hans did it. He just kept being kind until you had no choice but to cave. "You know we have no shortage of space. It must be a tight fit in the cottage."

"I hadn't expected to host her," Jessica admitted. "When Lynne ran out of space and couldn't host her as planned, Ronan even offered Mom a room at The Grand. But for some reason I can't understand Cookie wanted to stay with us. Maybe she's discovered some latent maternal instinct at least relative to Liam. And Liam's eating it up."

She hated that Cookie could still make her feel bitter even after more than a decade. She stopped mid-breath. That was wrong thinking. Cookie had no control over Jessica's pain – not really. That was Jessica's choice. She could choose to let that pain influence her life, or she could choose to reduce its power over her.

Because she couldn't fix Cookie. And no amount of scolding her mother or catching her out in misbehavior would change that. Cookie might be damaged goods or she might be irretrievably selfish. In either case, there was nothing Jessica could do about it. The air left her with a whoosh, and she was filled with an extraordinary sense of peace.

"And there's something else." She took a deep breath. "Chris Mullin is back."

He nodded. "Barbara told us. Don't look at me like that," he added, shaking his finger. "She was worried about you. We all are."

"My wellbeing is not the point. Liam's is."

Hans turned so he stood next to her, leaning back against the side of the car. "That is true. For you. You are Liam's mother so it's only reasonable that your focus is on him. But Clara and I are concerned about you, Jessica. That's our job."

"I'm fine." She looked at him, surprised because it was suddenly true. "Or I will be fine once Cookie leaves. And the business with Chris will work itself out somehow."

He looked unconvinced. "If you want to take care of Liam properly, you have to take care of yourself. No one person has the obligation to carry the whole world alone. This is why we have family and friends. So we can share our burdens. Clara made your favorite kreplach for the chicken soup. She's worried about you too."

She patted his shoulder. "I should have called. I just didn't realize life was going to get complicated so quickly. But Cookie is only here so she can go to Lynne's party tomorrow. She'll be leaving on the ferry Sunday morning." Her breath caught.

"So you were crying because everything is fine and dandy," he said. "And you are looking forward to watching your mother leave on the ferry Sunday morning."

And there it was. Worse than Cookie leaving. Even, God help her, worse than the idea of Chris being a part of Liam's life. Because the image of Ronan stepping onto the ferry again, made the tears spring to life again. Angrily knuckling her eyes, she stumbled after Hans. She couldn't allow her heart's desire to rule. She wouldn't – that way led to catastrophe.

Clara seemed to intuit the situation at a glance but clamped her lips together and said nothing. Instead, she allowed Jessica to recover her composure unobserved by scurrying back and forth from kitchen to table with arm loads of platters and tureens. Maybe the Sabbath was technically a day of rest, but the atmosphere in the kitchen was one of military precision. So Jessica managed to avoid the inevitable reckoning until they were cleaning up.

"Is it that young man?"

From the first, Clara had made it clear she considered Jessica one of her own although it had been a while before Jessica had grasped what that meant. So the question, slipped between comments about Liam's accomplishments and Barb's children, shouldn't have taken her by surprise. Still, she took a moment to respond.

"You mean Chris Mullin?"

Clara shot her a scornful look. "Not him. The nice one. The boychik with the big dog."

Jessica turned away to hide the rush of heat she felt burning her cheeks. She tried to keep her tone casual. "Ronan. No, we're just friends."

"He doesn't think so." Clara finished wiping the big casserole dish and slid it onto its place on the shelf.

Jessica's felt a sudden lump in her throat at her matter of fact tone. It wasn't true.

"He loves you."

"He told you that?"

Clara folded the dish towel neatly and hung it to dry on the oven door handle before responding. "He didn't have to. It was obvious when he talked about you. Hans's eyes used to look like that – still do sometimes. But maybe you don't feel the same way about Ronan?"

Jessica sank into the nearest chair, ignoring the handful of flatware in her hand. "He's leaving," she whispered.

Clara frowned. "Did you have a fight?"

"No. I mean, it didn't feel like one. But it's obvious I'm not right for him. He has a life to lead off the island, a career to pursue. Even if I wanted to compete with other women he's likely to meet, I couldn't. And I wouldn't. Because he deserves to have the best, and I'm not it."

Clara leaned forward, her palms spread flat on the table and glared at her. "What are you talking about? My children *are* the best."

"But I'm not –"

Jessica stuttered to a halt. The year the Ulrich's had taken her in, Clara had been deeply concerned that Jessica was dangerously despondent. So Clara squeezed a Christmas tree between the bookcases laden with Jewish texts in an attempt to cheer her up. In retrospect, the generosity of that act still took Jessica's breath away, particularly since Clara's parents had lost most of their family during the Holocaust. But Hans said Clara insisted it was a matter of *pikuach nefesh* – the overriding obligation to save a life, even if it meant bending religious rules.

And now Jessica felt stunned, humbled and vaguely fool-ish. Because the Ulrichs weren't simply polite, or overly hos-pitable. They *loved* her. But even more significantly, they loved *her* – Jessica, messy life, bad decisions and all. Dazed, she ran her palm over her eyes. How could she have been so blind?

She looked up. Clara's eyes sparked with fury and she was saying something emphatic about foolish life choices, but Jessica couldn't make sense of it. Because the words beating with the tattoo of her pulse were, "He loves you."

CHAPTER 35

RONAN SLID THE file into the bottom of his empty suitcase. It almost didn't matter what else went into it, but the file was critical. Dully, he slid the dress shoes Max had loaned him into plastic bags and put the bags on top of the file. They would be too wide, but that didn't matter. He looked back and forth between the two dress shirts he had brought and shrugged. He put both of them into the suitcase. Maybe by the time he got to New York he would have an opinion about which to choose. Right now, the decision seemed insignificant. He tossed in a couple changes of underwear and socks and he was done. Which left him with exactly nothing to do until Sunday morning.

The worst part of being told off by a dignified twelve year old was that any energy Ronan had managed to drum up for the Ellis interview had dissipated. Even after taking the day off to prepare additional materials to bring with him, he couldn't seem to summon up much enthusiasm. All that was left was a kind of hard determination, probably not an attractive trait for this particular position. Kobi Ellis was looking for passion, excitement, a kind of delight Ronan wasn't sure he would be able to manufacture in time for their first meeting.

He glanced out the window toward the Retreat Center and scowled. Aidy had insisted on knocking off an hour early today so she and Max could go out for a Friday night date. She said their remaining days as a free wheeling couple were limited so she wanted to take advantage of the time they had left. They had invited Ronan to join them but he had declined.

He didn't regret it now. They were a cute couple and they deserved a little alone time. Still, once the rumble of their car faded into the distance, Ronan was struck by the loneliness of his own life. At least his dog loved him.

He whistled for Bear and headed out the door, taking a measure of comfort in the excitement she displayed at the most mundane of pleasures. He had friends in Boston, of course. He probably had a few on the island too, if he ever bothered to look them up. And there were his brothers, sisters-in-law and Jane. Plenty of people. Occasionally it felt like too many, in fact. So his sudden sensation of isolation was irritatingly illogical.

He never doubted Max and Aidy loved him and enjoyed spending time with him. It was the same when he was with Jock and Charlotte. But there was always that moment as he entered a room they were in when he felt the couple-ness of them, not just the fact they were married, but that they were bound to each other by invisible cords of communication, spoken and unspoken.

He had an inkling how that must feel, to be part of something greater than just himself in the most visceral way possible. And that inkling of understanding was the worst part. Because that heart connection with the one person he wanted most – that wasn't possible.

He scowled and quickened his pace, heading toward the Retreat Center. Across the meadow would have been more direct but also more visible. He wasn't in the mood for socializing with anyone. The administrative wing should be deserted by now, so with luck he could get a jump-start on plans for the healing garden.

But as he approached the building from the rear, he was surprised to see a large group of people wandering the grounds carrying pads of paper. As he stepped from the woods and wended his way through the crowd, an older man approached him. His hair was a mass of gray curls, his eyes piercing blue and he held a clipboard in one calloused hand, a pen in the other. The lanyard around his neck bore a name-tag. Leonard Eskin.

"Here for the class? It's free."

Ronan's head shake was instinctive, but he smiled. "What's the class about?"

"Nature sketching. Not really a classroom event. More experiential. Although I'm glad to give input as needed. It's really intended as more of a meditative experience than an exploration of craft. If you don't mind my saying so, you look as if you could use a little down time."

Ronan wasn't sure whether to be offended or amused. By the time he had decided on the latter, Leonard had already handed him a pad and a charcoal pencil from a box of supplies on a nearby picnic table.

"Give it a shot," Leonard advised. "It's not about perfection. Just about paying attention."

Ronan nodded politely. He would dump the pad and pencil once he was out of Leonard's sight and would make his way into the building. There was no point in insulting the man. But the crowd of attendees had begun to settle around him, some to the ground to draw the tiniest of flowers between blades of grass, others onto scattered folding chairs to depict trees, birds, even the Retreat Center itself. As the hum of conversation died down, he could hear the scratch of pencils amid the soughing of leaves in the gentle breeze. The sound pulled at him. He loved that sound.

And the fibrous smell of drawing pads newly opened. Without stopping to think, he opened his own. Just one drawing, he promised himself. Just one. He stepped blindly to an unoccupied bench and sank onto it. His rib cage felt tight as he fumbled with the pencil. But the moment the charcoal tip touched the white cream of the page, he was lost.

It was almost like vomiting, a kind of urgent expulsion of images. A nun curved over her drawing pad. A young man, freckle-faced, with a dreamy expression, staring up at the canopy of leaves. Leonard, leaning over the shoulder of a plump skull-capped rabbi to peer more closely at whatever was on the page.

And it didn't stop with the people around him. There was Liam frolicking with Bear on the beach. Jane's face, alight with discovery. Aidy leaning over the back of an armchair to see what Max was reading. Charlotte standing on her toes to clean the wall mirror in her dance studio. Jock frowning into the engine of his truck. And Jessica. Her chin on her knees as she stared into the surf. Her face crinkled in laughter as she assessed a slice of pizza. Her shoulders slumped wearily as she swept the high school cafeteria.

"Your wife? She's lovely."

It took a moment for Ronan to register Leonard's voice. He pulled himself away from focusing on the turn of her ankle. There was something wrong there, but he hadn't managed to fix it yet. "No, she's not. I mean, yes, she's beautiful. But she's not my wife."

He looked up from the pad. Leonard was sitting next to him on the bench. The eager artists had all disappeared, which was weird because who ran a class for fifteen minutes. "Where is everyone?"

"They left an hour ago for another class. Weaving, I think."

Huh. It occurred to Ronan the sun was surprisingly low. He reached for his cell phone and looked twice for confirmation. He had been sitting on the bench drawing for two hours. He cast an apologetic look at Leonard. "I didn't mean to keep you."

Leonard shrugged. "You needed to be here."

Ronan rubbed his forehead with charcoal smudged fingertips, aware he must look shell shocked. He certainly felt shell shocked.

"I've been on the island for a while," Leonard continued. "Eight years now. I'm surprised I haven't met you. I thought I knew all the artists on Demerest Cove."

"I'm not an artist," Ronan said automatically. "I grew up here but I moved away to study architecture."

"Don't try to kid a kidder, son. And if you believe you aren't an artist, you're kidding yourself, which is worse. This," he tapped the pad firmly, "is not amateur work. There's an implicit story. More than that, you've caught emotion here. No amount of schooling can teach that. What on earth are you doing chaining yourself to the ground when you could be touching heaven with a pencil?"

"Earning a living." It had felt like the right thing to say when he said it to himself. But Leonard's silence made the words seem contrived. "I can't support a family as an artist," he added.

"I don't see why not." Leonard's tone was sharp. "I did. And quite nicely too."

Ronan wondered if this was how a shipwrecked man felt. That moment when it was no longer a matter of simply surviving the next swelling wave, the next smash of froth. Because at the edge of the horizon there was a ship. And for the first time, a sailor had actually waved.

And maybe, as was usually the case, the sailor didn't actually see him. And the ship's engines would keep rumbling as the huge vessel disappeared again into the distance. But for the first time, it occurred to Ronan that waving back was not only an instinctive survival mechanism but a kind of obligation. At least, that was what Leonard was implying. Because maybe the sailor did see him.

Ronan rubbed his thumb against the charcoal absently. "You probably started young," he said finally.

"What do you think you are? An old man?" Leonard's tone was withering.

"Well, no. But I've invested years of my life into learning how to be an architect. I can't just walk away from that."

"Why not?"

Ronan started to respond but closed his mouth when nothing clever came to mind. In Boston, he had considered himself strategic and ambitious. The way an adult should be. He had planned his future carefully, from his career path to his social life. And the gears of that process ran smoothly, so even if he wasn't exactly happy, he could get some satisfaction from observing the notches fitting neatly into each other as the wheels revolved. But now it was as if beach sand had gotten into the mechanism. And no amount of cold strategy was going to fix it.

Because the truth of the matter was, he couldn't ignore what Leonard was saying. There was something deeply distressing and dreadfully right about the feel of the charcoal in his hand. It was as though he had been holding his breath for years and had finally allowed himself a sip of oxygen. The thought of holding his breath again, this time for a lifetime, was more than he could bear. He swallowed and put the charcoal down on the bench beside him.

"Do you think – I mean, could you teach me how?"

CHAPTER 36

THE CATERING STAFF for the Mullin party was down by two, which was one reason Jessica was in the vast kitchen arranging sushi rolls on a platter. The other reason was to postpone running into Lynne for as long as she could. Carl's absence was a perfectly good excuse, of course, but she didn't look forward to the look of mingled distaste and disgust that would play across Lynne's face. Still, the conversation was inevitable because along with Cookie, she had also dropped off Liam at the front door before driving around back to park near the service entrance.

"Try to give in to Chris on the things that don't matter, so you can justify taking a stand on the ones that do matter," Barbara had advised. "How is Liam doing with all this? It has to be stressful on him.

"Liam seems okay, I guess," she had responded.

Jessica felt uneasy now, recalling the conversation. Liam had been unusually subdued for the past day or so. As a new mom she had learned to pay attention to her instincts when Liam was an infant, but she had been ignoring them recently, maybe because Cookie's constant presence had distracted her. She would make sure to talk with Liam this weekend, once the party was over and Cookie had left. The wrenching feeling in her heart at the thought of the ferry dock did not take her by surprise this time. She guessed that was a good thing.

"Jessica? Maybe just go to the dining room and fold the napkins instead."

Clive, of Clive's Chives, gestured toward the squashed sushi roll in her hand. "You okay? You looked miles away just then."

"Yeah, I'm fine. Sorry."

This had to stop. She had been making stupid mistakes all day. She had arrived at the Mullin's later than she would have liked because she had to circle back to the cottage to pick up her file of notes. And then Liam reminded her she hadn't picked up the floral arrangements on Friday. She was lucky the florist had been willing to open up the shop early. And now this.

Scowling, she grabbed for a dishtowel to scrub the sticky mess from her fingers, but a corner of the towel was wedged under a display stand piled high with Clive's signature savory scallion scones. Clive lunged for the save, the tips of his fingers grazing the edge of the tray, but to no avail. Jessica clapped her hands to her mouth and stared wide-eyed as two dozen scones rolled off the wide counter top and bounced across the floor.

"Oh, my God, I'm so, so sorry."

Clive pointed toward the door, his face thunderous. She draped the towel over the edge of the sink and slunk out of the kitchen. Carl had made a point of hiring their most experienced staff for the day. Mahmood, who was a math tutor during the week and was always happy to pick up extra weekend cash, was draping the folding chairs with elegant fabric covers while Cheryl, normally a town administrator, arranged them around the cafe tables scattered throughout the generously sized rooms. They had already moved the big dining room table to the wall where it was draped in linen, ready for the abundant display of food Lynne had ordered. The napkins were neatly folded, placed in artistic swathes on each end of the broad surface.

Ideally, there was a moment like this before an event began, the gentle hum of work getting done in no particular hurry but with purpose. Normally Jessica enjoyed the sensation, but today she wished there was something urgent she needed to do, anything to keep her hands busy. On the other hand, given her performance in the kitchen, it would be better for all concerned if she didn't touch anything that mattered. She shoved her hands into her pockets and glanced out the long windows that overlooked the garden. Liam and Cookie sat on a bench under an arbor, Liam chatting animatedly and Cookie nodding. Jessica waved, but the sun was pouring in and she suspected he couldn't see her standing there.

His neck looked vulnerable between the padded tweed shoulders of his new secondhand sport coat. The jacket wasn't cut right, but it was the only one the thrift store had even close to his size this time of year. Cookie, wearing her elegant finery, had looked as if she wanted to comment but in the end had held her tongue because Liam was so obviously proud of his new look. As a little boy, Liam had been fascinated by the legendary King Arthur, in particular he had loved the description of the King's prized cloak of invisibility. She smiled at the memory of Liam wrapped in a blanket, scuttling to his bedroom with a handful of cookies all the while insisting she couldn't see him because of his magical cloak. He had grown so much since then. The sense of loss she expected at the thought never came. Instead, she was suffused with gratitude and a little triumph.

She checked her own reflection in the ornate mirror between the windows. The first time she put on her standard party planner attire, black slacks, black tunic, she had fallen in love with the anonymity it granted. Unlike Liam's blanket, wearing work clothing at a fancy dress party actually worked because when guests looked her way, they looked right through her. It wasn't exactly magic, but it made her feel safe. Although she would feel a lot safer once the Mullin party was over. And as though she had summoned her with the thought, Lynne appeared in the mirror behind her. Jessica made an effort not to look startled. She had been relying on Lynne's noisy high heels to function as an early warning system. But she had overlooked the thick oriental carpets that covered the wood floors.

"I thought I made it clear I didn't want you here."

Jessica sighed. There was no way she was getting out of this unscathed. On the other hand, Lynne wanted a smooth running party and Jessica was the professional whose business Lynne had hired. There had to be some way to make this work. She didn't have to look to know Cheryl and Mahmood had slowed to watch the interaction.

"Mrs. Mullin," she said. "Is there someplace we can talk privately?"

Lynne looked as though she wanted to refuse, but she too must have noted the sudden silence in the room. Or maybe she just wanted to say things to Jessica she couldn't say in public. Without a word, Lynne turned on her heel and strode away. Jessica followed through the elegant living room, across the entrance hall and into the small study that overlooked the front drive. She closed the door behind her and turned to face Lynne.

She had seen Lynne occasionally, since the last time they had met in this room. But Lynne seemed smaller now, as though her meanness had compacted itself into something altogether more fragile, the way a sturdy leaf could become skeletal after a hard winter. It hadn't occurred to Jessica until now that the intervening years must have been hard on Lynne too. Not that it excused Lynne's behavior. But still.

"I'm guessing Carl didn't have time to call you," she said. "He had a family health emergency and had to leave the island suddenly."

"He did call," Lynne said stiffly. "Why Carl hired you in the first place I'll never know. But I specifically told him I didn't want you here today. I don't understand why you insisted on coming when you knew you weren't wanted. Don't you have any sense of pride at all? Or do you have another motivation for being here today?"

Jessica's jaw dropped. Her first inclination was to walk out – just gather up Mahmood and Cheryl and Liam and leave. But, to her surprise, the idea didn't provide the relief she expected.

"I can't afford pride," she said. "And I don't leave customers in the lurch."

"I'm not a fool," Lynne shot back. "I saw your son sitting in my garden. My Chris may have taken a shine to your little brat, but anyone can see the boy looks nothing like him. I don't care what your mother and Chris cooked up between the two of them."

Jessica's heart sank. "What does my mother have to do with this?"

"Don't pretend you don't know. When Chris called her with his fool-headed idea of making you an honest woman, she couldn't wait to get on board. 'Oh, Lynnie. We'd be family.'" Lynne's voice rose in a passable mimicry of Cookie's coaxing tone.

"That's not —" She wanted to say it wasn't true, but the words stuck in her throat. And the truth was, it sounded exactly like the sort of thing Cookie would do. But it hurt less than she might have expected. She studied the paperweight on Lynne's desk, a bronze hawk with a vicious looking set of talons. Beautiful in its own way, but not something she would want to live with.

Lynne waited a beat and then continued. "Cookie may be one of my oldest friends, but I swear sometimes the lights are on but nobody's home in that head of hers. I didn't get Chris to where he is today just to have him ruin his life by marrying the likes of you. So you can just get that idea out of your head, missy."

Lynne stood shielded by her thick oak desk and glared at Jessica, her whole body quivering. Indignation, probably. She reminded Jessica of a drenched infuriated lap dog. Maybe an elderly Yorkshire Terrier — the kind that yapped all the time but inside was terrified. Jessica looked around for a chair and sat in it.

"What are you doing?" Lynne snapped.

"Waiting for you to sit down so we can talk like normal human beings."

Jessica felt unnaturally calm as she waited. Huffing in annoyance, Lynne finally sank into her desk chair. Once Jessica was sure Lynne was settled and paying attention, she held up one finger. "First, Chris is Liam's father. However, if Chris wants to spend time with Liam, he's going to have to pass a paternity test. Primarily because I'm not allowing you anywhere near my son until we all agree Chris is his father."

Lynne opened her mouth but closed it again as Jessica raised a second finger. "Second, I will not marry Chris. Ever. We were friends briefly in high school. But I didn't love him then and I don't love him now. And third —"

She raised her hand and shook her head warningly. Lynne, who had leaned forward to object, sat back again with a sulky expression.

"Because of your hatred, you've missed out on twelve years of Liam's childhood. That is your loss, not his. But if you find you do want to spend time with your only grandson, you will need to convince me you will be kind. Note, I said kind, not generous. Liam doesn't need your money. But he would appreciate your love."

She waited a beat and then continued. "Lastly, I own Moon Shell Events. Don't you ever, *ever*, refer to Carl as my boss again."

Jessica waited for a time to see if Lynne would respond but finally rose. As she touched the door handle, Lynne spoke.

"Is –" she cleared her throat and tried again. "Is it true?"

"That Chris is Liam's dad? One hundred percent true."

"I didn't, that is –"

But Lynne didn't have the opportunity to complete her thought because Cookie was at the door, her expression tinged with fear.

"Chris took Liam for a drive," she stammered. "I mean, Chris wouldn't do anything to harm him, so I'm sure Liam's fine. I just – Chris was driving awful fast – he ran over one of the tulip beds on the way out."

CHAPTER 37

SUNBEAMS DAPPLED THE wood floor, shifting back and forth as a breeze moved the limbs of the dogwood tree near Ronan's bedroom window. The sun was high – Ronan guessed he had slept late. Although since he hadn't managed to fall asleep until three in the morning that wasn't surprising. The scent of coffee drifted into the room, and he could hear the faint clatter of a dish being scraped, Max's low tones and Aidy's gentle response. He sat up and swung his legs off the edge of the bed, relishing the coolness of the floor beneath his bare feet.

He looked at his toes as he wiggled them. Small miracles. He had forgotten what those felt like. But now as he glanced around the room, he remembered being eleven – the tingle of excitement at the start of each new day, the sense that anything might happen and that if it did he would make the most of it. He looked at his suitcase and then looked away. He wanted to hold on to the unaccustomed sense of promise for just a little longer.

Ronan poured himself a cup of coffee and stuck a couple waffles in the toaster before turning to look at Max more closely. His big brother was glowering. Trouble in paradise? Probably not. Aidy had patted Max on the shoulder as she left, muttering something about catching up on laundry. Ronan slid the waffles onto a plate and snagged the bottle of maple syrup as he headed to the table. Max waited until Ronan had eaten the first waffle before slapping the sketchbook on the table top.

Ronan froze, his brain racing frantically. He had intended to tuck the sketches somewhere deep, in the bottom of his knapsack, maybe. But he had been so distracted by his conversation with Eskin, he must have forgotten. He commanded himself to look casual, to find something flip to say. But his body wouldn't obey. Because despite the necessity, he felt it would be a betrayal to minimize last night's experience.

"How long has this been going on?" Max sounded strained.

"I, uh." Ronan took a breath. "It's not like I'm having an affair."

He meant to be witty, but it came out flat. Because Max and Jock had every reason to believe he was no longer interested in art. Primarily because that was what he had told them. Repeatedly. To be fair, it was what he had told himself, day after day. Until it seemed true.

"It's nothing serious," he added. "Don't worry. I'm not changing careers."

"That's exactly what I'm worried about," Max exploded. "Dad always said you were contrary, but I had no idea you were so ungrateful."

Ronan's heart plummeted. He put his fork down, his appetite gone. "Don't make this harder than it is," he ground out.

"What the hell is hard about it?" Max threw his hands in the air. "Cancel the appointment and get on with your real life."

"What appointment?" Ronan was mystified. Eskin had offered to meet with him, but they hadn't made any firm plans. How could they when Ronan might end up living two hundred miles away? What would be the point?

Max spoke through gritted teeth. "The appointment with Kobi Ellis. Cancel it."

Ronan stared. He was hearing it, but it made no sense. Chris had lectured him about giving up childish things, but Chris was about twenty years too late. Because when Ronan's mother had taken ill, his world had begun to fall apart. Losing Jessica, and then losing his grandparents in quick succession had reinforced his sense of the precariousness of life. But his father's business losses and subsequent death had hit him in a different way. Not harder but maybe a more effective blow.

"I can't. That would be crazy."

Instead of speaking, Max tapped the sketchbook.

"You know what it's like when people take foolish risks with their careers." The words poured out like acid. "Everyone suffers. I thought Dad hung the moon. He used to tell me stories about all the cool connections he had in business. About how important it was to take a gamble sometimes. Until he lost Grandpa and Grandma's savings and his own in one swoop.

"You of all people should remember what that was like. Your wedding was ruined. Jock's engagement fell apart. Without you and Jock working two jobs, I would have had to drop out of college. We slept on the freakin' floor, Max. For months.

"Dad wanted to have the fun of risking it all and winning, but he lost. Everyone in the family paid for his love of a gamble. So don't you dare call me selfish for doing what I have to in order to pull my weight. Because if there is one thing I learned from Dad's example it was the necessity of putting family needs before my own."

Max shook his head. "No. You have it wrong."

Ronan leaned back in his chair and folded his arms. "Oh, really."

Max sighed. "Okay, look. I could lecture you on the importance of risk taking in business. I actually took a seminar on that exact topic for my master's degree. And relative to Dad's business acumen, you probably didn't know this but he was only one of hundreds of people who got sucked into that one. Many of them were even more experienced than he was. You could say they should have known better, I guess. But that wouldn't be fair. Because all of us take risks, Ronan. And we should, not because we are gamblers but because without risks we have no hope of advancing our ultimate goals. Hell, love is a risk," he added with feeling. "Whether it's doing what you love or committing to one person."

"And if you love someone, you make sacrifices for them," Ronan said.

"Sure. But the sacrifice should make sense. I love carrot cake. If Aidy's health and wellbeing depended on my not eating carrot cake, I would give it up without a second thought. But would it make sense to give up something I enjoy preemptively, just in case she might develop an allergy to it?"

"But that's not the same," Ronan protested.

"You're right," Max said. "Because my ability to eat carrot cake is not a gift from God. No one's heart will be lifted up if I take another slice." He opened the pad and traced his fingers over the sketch of Liam at the beach.

"Being an artist is a risk, Ronan, but in your case, I don't think it's a big one. And I think it's imperative for you, for your soul. But even if it were a risk – so what? We all take risks every day. Charlotte opened a dance studio. Risky, but ultimately I think it will succeed. And if it doesn't, she'll try something else. The Retreat Center was a risk too. Hell, when you and I and Jock started Sanderson Hospitality, all we had was spit and hope. But look at it now."

Ronan leaned forward to rest his elbows on the table. He heard what Max was saying and also what he wasn't. Max and Aidy were taking a big risk too. It must have taken enormous strength to try for a baby again after the miscarriage. He wasn't sure where they had found the courage.

"But we spent money on tuition." It was a weak argument and he knew it.

Max rolled his eyes. "Don't be ridiculous. We get it back every time you advise on renovations and building plans for the business. You won't lose that skill just because you pursue your passion." He shoved the sketchpad across the table to Ronan. "Now go make that phone call."

Ronan hung up the phone unutterably lighter. Bear danced around him happily, sensing a walk was in the offing. Grinning like an idiot, he grabbed her leash and ushered her out the door. He was nearly out of earshot when he heard Aidy calling him. She waved and he turned back. She was holding his cell phone he belatedly remembered leaving on the kitchen table.

"It's Jessica."

Something in her tone alerted him.

"Is she all right?"

"I didn't want to pry. But she called you twice."

He took the phone but didn't bother checking the messages. He scrolled through his contacts twice before managing to stop the list of names at hers.

"Ronan, thank God." Jessica's voice was strained. "It's Liam. He's with Chris and no one seems to know where they went."

He ran for the Bentley as she spoke, ordering Bear to stay with Aidy and fumbling with the keys before managing to jam them into the ignition. He cursed as he drove, cursed Chris for being so irresponsible, cursed the fact that Liam didn't have his own cell phone yet, cursed the curving roads for preventing him from driving faster.

The Mullin's long curved driveway was filled with cars as were both sides of the street. He pulled past and searched frantically for a spot to leave the car. He finally settled on a barely legitimate open space near a stop sign and raced back toward the house.

There was something surreal about seeing a party going on as usual under the circumstances. Guests wandered calmly amid the beds of early blooming spring bulbs, champagne glasses in hand. He ignored them and headed for the house, slowing to a fast walk as he neared the front door. There was no need to knock, the door was ajar. He could hear the chatter of more guests inside over the gentle rills of a harp.

He stood in the entryway for a moment looking for Jessica. Not in the living room. He dove into the crowd, forging his way toward the back of the house. But the sturdy looking chef pointed him back toward the front, a closed door off the entry. He didn't bother to knock. Lynne sat behind her desk, jabbing angrily at a cell phone while Cookie perched on a window seat, looking anxiously back and forth between her best friend and her daughter.

Jessica had turned when he opened the door. She looked lost and it nearly broke him. It was as though the toughness she had always depended on had failed her and now she had no armor left. Gently, he reached for her. She stiffened in his arms and then gave a great shudder as she buried her face in his chest.

"We'll find him. He's going to be okay." As he spoke he felt the futility of providing comfort. He had no idea where Chris might have taken Liam. Maybe someplace harmless, like the movies, or even just for a ride. But the fact Chris hadn't asked permission worried Ronan. And the memory of his behavior at the ferry dock chilled Ronan's heart.

CHAPTER 38

BREATHING REQUIRED ALL her attention. It seemed as though there wasn't enough oxygen in the air. And then Ronan made her sit and shoved her head down between her knees. Which, in another life would have been mortifying but now, as she looked at it from a clinical distance, seemed reasonable. Because embarrassment was secondary to finding Liam. Everything was secondary to that, even her anger. She could always yell at Liam later. She would give anything to have the opportunity to yell at him.

Ronan was talking in sharp tones. It was hard to interpret what he was saying, sort of like tuning into a short frequency radio station at irregular intervals. She sat up and ignored the wave of dizziness on the theory that if she behaved normally she might be able to cue her brain to think normally. It didn't do much good. She could smell the sharp stink of fear on herself. Images of Liam hurt in a car wreck, bloodied and unconscious kept weaving through her thoughts.

She felt a hand squeeze her shoulder. Not Ronan's. She looked up, momentarily distracted, expecting to see her mother. But to her surprise, it was Lynne, offering her a bottle of water. Instinctively, she shook her head to refuse it, but then took it anyway. She couldn't afford to faint. Ronan leaned against the desk frowning, his cell phone to his ear. His solidity was a kind of comfort because everything else in the room still seemed a little out of focus.

"About half an hour ago, officer." He shot an inquiring look at Cookie, who nodded unhappily. "A big, black SUV, license —"

Lynne recited the numbers in a crisp tone, but it clearly cost her to do so. Jessica couldn't dredge up much sympathy for her, but she respected Lynne a little more than she had.

"Yes, sir," Ronan continued. "His mother is right here."

Numbly, Jessica took the phone and recited Liam's height, weight, age and physical characteristics as well as her cell phone number. When she described Liam's sport coat, her voice broke. As soon as she hung up, Ronan took his phone back and called Max and Aidy. Jessica guessed, given his responses, they were planning to begin a search of their own. That was a kind of comfort too. She clutched her own phone, checking it reflexively to make sure it was on, that the ringer volume was on high. And then Ronan was kneeling in front of her, cupping her hands in his. His skin was warm on hers, his expression determined.

"I want to go out to see if I can find them, but I don't want to leave you until I know you'll be all right here."

To her horror, her eyes overflowed. She was shaking now and she couldn't seem to stop. She didn't trust herself to say anything so she bit her lip and nodded. He studied her for a moment and shook his head. In one smooth move he scooped her up in his arms and carried her out the door.

"What's your best guess?" he asked, pulling away from the curb.

"I don't know. He's got a new job as a youth pastor – maybe he wanted to show Liam the church. Days of Joy, I think he said."

Ronan made a U-turn and she could feel the engine surge. His jaw was clenched, and he muttered something she couldn't hear as he drove. She couldn't blame him. This had to be a major distraction when he needed to be preparing for his big interview.

"This is kind of you," she said quietly.

Ronan stared at her with a furious expression. Jamming on the brakes, he yanked at the steering wheel, pulling the car to the side of the road. "It is not kind of me," he snapped. "Why do you think I'm doing this – as a good deed of the day? Damn it, woman, I love you. And I love Liam. I don't understand what it's going to take to convince you of that."

He glared at her and put the car in gear again. She blinked, opened her mouth to say something, anything, and shut it again because her phone was ringing and she couldn't seem to move the icon to accept the call. It was as if she was wearing gloves. Frantically, she stabbed at the touch screen and just before it would have gone to voice mail, the phone picked up the call. Ronan pulled the car back to the curb.

The voice on the other end was too quiet to hear. She fumbled with the phone, but the volume was turned up as far as it would go and still, the words were inaudible. Ronan grabbed the cell phone from her, setting it to speaker mode.

"This is Doctor Eliason from Island Medical Center. Is this Ms. Piers?"

She swallowed and tried to speak but nothing came out. If it was the medical center something very bad had happened.

"Is Liam – is he okay?" The muscles in her throat were so tight, it hurt to speak. The length of time between the question and the answer seemed elastic, a kind of endless stretching. And then the doctor spoke again and Jessica knew she must have misheard, so she asked him to repeat it.

"Liam is just fine, Ms. Piers. He has a few bruises but nothing serious. He's a lucky and resourceful young man. You should be very proud of him."

She looked at Ronan. She guessed her face was probably as pale as his. Doctor Eliason said to drive carefully since Liam was in no danger of anything except being spoiled by the staff, but Jessica was consumed by a visceral need to see him, to touch him, to make sure all of him was intact. Ronan seemed to be feeling the same since he drove as fast as he could without exceeding the speed limit.

The medical center waiting room was deserted – even the reception desk was unoccupied. Ronan reached around Jessica and hit the bell. It took a moment for the intake nurse to appear but when she did, she smiled broadly.

"You must be Liam's parents."

Jessica glanced at Ronan. She started to correct the nurse but something in his face stopped her. Instead, she nodded. "Can we see him?"

Liam sat on a gurney, legs dangling as he dipped a spoon into a bowl of green gelatin. He grinned as they came in. "Hey, Mom. Hi, Ronan. Guess what? Turns out some kinds of tea are like a drug. Mrs. Oberson in health class is going to freak when she finds out. She's always drinking tea."

RONAN WATCHED AS Jessica tenderly inspected her son, frowning over the bruise on his forehead before enfolding him in a tight hug. Then she climbed onto the gurney next to him, holding his hand while he continued to eat the disgusting green stuff with every evidence of enjoyment.

She hadn't responded when Ronan told her he loved her. She wasn't obligated to love him back. He wasn't even sure how Liam felt about him. But it had sure felt good to say he loved them – both cathartic and final. A kind of closing of a circle. Sometimes that was enough. Maybe it would have to be.

He watched them as Liam told the story. How Chris had wanted to show him the youth wing of the church where he would be working. How excited Chris had been and how fast he had been driving because there wasn't much time before the party and Chris said he had an announcement to make. And then they had neared the church and Chris had missed the turn.

"It's a good thing I was wearing my seatbelt," Liam observed, suddenly solemn, "because when the airbags went off, it would have hurt a lot worse. And my glasses flew off, which is bad because they broke, but good because Doctor Eliason said they could have hurt my eyes. Kind of ironic, right?"

"So did someone call an ambulance?" Jessica asked.

"No one was there and I couldn't call 9-1-1 because Chris forgot his cell phone," he said, pausing to lick the last of the gelatin off the back of the spoon. "And Chris was acting weird because I think he hit his head somehow. So I found a box cutter in the glove compartment and cut the airbag off the steering wheel. And I made Chris get into the passenger seat and I drove us to the Medical Center. Mom, could I have some more of this? It's really good."

Ronan sank into a chair, stunned, as Jessica left to hunt down more green gelatin.

"That was really brave, Liam. I hope you know that."

"I didn't feel brave at the time," he said. "Mostly I was just scared."

"That's what makes it brave," Ronan said.

"I guess." Liam sounded doubtful. He glanced toward the door and then back at Ronan. "I thought you were leaving."

"Do you want me to?" Ronan didn't breathe for a moment. He would stay regardless. But he needed to know.

Liam waited a beat and gave him a long assessing look, neither friendly nor unfriendly. "Are you going to marry my mom?"

"If she'll have me. And if you want me to. I mean, I'd like to."

"I think you should," Liam said in a judicious tone. But his shoulders eased and he sighed as though he had been carrying an enormous weight and had only now been permitted to put it down.

"Should what?" Jessica was back with another bowl of the stuff.

"Marry us," Liam said.

"Sorry, what?"

"Well, marry you," Liam said. "He can't exactly marry me."

Jessica's eyebrows shot up and Ronan nearly lost it.

She patted Liam's knee. "Ronan's leaving tomorrow for a job interview in New York City, which he'll probably get because he is super talented. But I know he'll be back to visit. Once Aidy has her baby, he'll be visiting the island a lot." She smiled apologetically at Ronan.

He held her gaze as he spoke. "I'm not leaving. I'm staying on the island, and I'm going to be an artist. Do you love me?" The question escaped him unexpectedly, but once it was out there it dangled like a breath. He watched her frown.

"What kind of question is that?"

If she didn't want him, he needed to know. Now. It wouldn't change what he did. He would still become an artist. He would still see Liam occasionally and interact with Jessica when he saw her at the event space. The thought of being just a side bit of their lives, while better than nothing, was a bitter pill to swallow. But he wouldn't leave her behind. Not again.

She walked toward him and stopped just before her knees touched his. He braced himself as he looked up at her, but instead of the impatience he expected to see in her eyes, there was something else. Eagerness, light, joy. And as she cupped his face in her hands, there was a glint of tears there too.

"I love you, Ronan Durrell."

Liam cleared his throat. "Underage kid in the room, folks."

"Get used to it," Ronan growled, pulling Jessica in for a kiss.

CHAPTER 39

"**I DON'T SAY** this often, but you were right." Cookie added another rosebud to the bouquet and frowned.

"About?"

"About not marrying Chris. Lynne is mortified and with good reason. That kratom tea he was taking is practically poison. He's lucky he got away with a warning from the judge. And that girl who he's with now? The man has no taste at all."

"Sherry seems sweet to me," Jessica said. "And addiction counseling is a great career."

"But the two of them running off to get married in Aruba looks ridiculous. For that matter I don't understand why you and Ronan are in such a hurry to get married. People will think you're pregnant. You aren't pregnant again, are you?" Cookie stopped fussing with the bouquet long enough to give Jessica an assessing look.

"No, Mom."

"And if she was, would that be so terrible?" Clara countered. "Jessica makes beautiful babies. Besides, once you find the person you love, why waste time."

Jessica reached for whatever was pulling her hair but Barbara slapped her hand away and wriggled the combs holding her updo in place until the pain eased. Jessica sighed with relief. It was bad enough she had allowed Clara to persuade her dressing up like an actual bride was a good idea. There was no point in being uncomfortable along with feeling like a fraud.

"You're good at this." She smiled at Barbara's reflection over her shoulder in the vanity mirror.

"Yeah. If the lawyer thing doesn't work out, maybe I can open my own bridal hair arrangement business. Is the dress ready, Mom?"

"Hanging in its garment bag," Clara said. "What time is it?"

"Twenty minutes."

"No problem," Clara responded, "It won't take long to put it on."

"It's just me." Aidy slipped into the room, closing the door behind her. "I brought the veil." She held the delicate misty confection up for Jessica's inspection.

Jessica gasped.

"Like it?"

"Perfect. The bead work is gorgeous," Clara declared firmly. "Now let's get our beautiful bride dressed."

Jessica took a deep breath and let it out. The moment Clara, Cookie and Aidy had learned of the wedding, any plans she and Ronan had for a simple ceremony in the town hall were clearly out of the question. Aidy had begged them to hold the wedding in the new healing garden. She said it would be good luck plus provide an excellent trial run for the catering staff. Cookie and Lynne had taken charge of what they considered the necessities of a social event on the island – engraved invitations, champagne, flowers and a photographer.

And Clara flatly refused to let Jessica get married in the simple outfit she had planned on. When Jessica protested there was no point in spending money on a dress she would wear only once, Clara had offered her own wedding dress. The gown waited undisturbed in storage since it had been too small for Barbara, who took after her father. Clara said it would fit Jessica with a few adjustments.

But now Jessica wondered if she should have insisted on seeing the dress. Clara had become quite secretive after taking Jessica's measurements. The upside was Jessica only needed to wear it for an afternoon, so if it was old-fashioned, it wouldn't matter. Because what mattered was the love Clara had sewn into it.

Still, there was a tiny seed of reluctance growing in her at the thought of what was probably a confection in white – the sort of dress made to showcase an innocent virginal bride in the first flush of womanhood. And she was not. She looked at her hands. Cookie had insisted Jessica have a manicure before the big day, but no amount of oils and massage could successfully disguise the calluses on her palms.

This was a big mistake. Not the part about marrying Ronan. Not that. Just the rest of it – the pageantry, the ceremonial nature of it. Years ago, she would have walked down the aisle a triumphant queen. But now it felt wrong to wear the fancy clothing, the updo, the veil. Those things would look like a pathetic attempt to disguise the messed up, dinged and dented person she had become. She contained her flinch at the sound of the garment bag zipper.

But the dress was not what she had envisioned. No froth or frufru. It didn't look like a wedding cake at all. Hesitantly, she reached out to stroke the smooth fabric. She looked up and found Barbara grinning at her.

"Nice, huh?"

"This was your wedding dress?" Cookie looked at Clara with dawning respect. "Is it –"

"Chanel," Clara said. "My mother was married in it. I was too. But I think it will suit Jessica better. She has the lines for it."

There was a dreamlike quality to stepping into the gown. It felt as though the weight of history in its grandeur and individuality were combined in the motion. Barbara grinned, and Aidy's eyes sparkled as Clara and Cookie did up the buttons in the back. Jessica was itching to see what they saw now, but Clara wouldn't let her turn toward the full length mirror until every last button was done.

When she finally was allowed to look, she froze. In her experience, most brides looked beautiful despite their dresses, not because of them. But this dress made her look, well, sexy. The fabric clung and molded itself to her hips, her waist, her breasts. The minimal sleeves began off the shoulder and the sweetheart bodice was simply adorned with a pair of silk roses.

"No, Bear. It's not for eating. Nooo!"

Jessica flicked her eyes toward scuffling sounds behind the door and considered her options. If Bear managed to get in, the dress would suffer and to her surprise that suddenly mattered. A lot. She wanted to see Ronan's face when she walked down the aisle in it, the way his eyes would widen, his breath would quicken.

There was a muffled woof and Jane's shriek morphed into an "Oooh" as Charlotte hustled her into the room, slamming the door behind them. Charlotte handed Clara a shoe box and settled into a chair, pulling Jane onto her lap.

"Very nice," Clara pronounced.

"I hope you like them," Charlotte said. "They're excellent for dancing in. Good traction and surprisingly good support."

Jessica stared. The delicate pearl beaded pumps were more than nice. They were Cinderella shoes.

"The dress is old, the shoes are new," Aidy muttered. "The veil is borrowed. We forgot something blue."

"More to the point, we need jewelry," Cookie said.

She unhooked her own earrings and removed her diamond bracelet, handing them to Barbara who passed them to Jessica.

"You don't have to do that, Mom," Jessica said.

"Yes, I do," Cookie said. "But I don't have a necklace and that neckline requires one."

Jane wriggled off Charlotte's lap and ran toward Jessica, nearly tripping in her haste. Jessica caught her and set her upright before she could fall. Jane smelled like baby soap and Jessica's heart clenched.

"You could wear dis," Jane said. "See, it's blue."

Without waiting for a response, the little girl pulled her macaroni necklace over her head and proffered it to Jessica then nestled closer as Jessica inspected it.

"I used all my blue paint in the whole jar," she said.

"And you used ziti noodles. My favorite."

"Me too! But one bwoke."

"Pasta can be fragile," Jessica agreed. "So I will have to be extra careful."

"No," Cookie said as Jessica reached up to slide the necklace over her head.

Jessica looked at her mother.

"Not like that," Cookie clarified. "Here, let me."

She twisted the strand and entwined it with a strand of white ribbon and some bits of baby's breath left over from the bouquet. When she was done the necklace looked intentional, adventurous. A kind of intermingling.

"Don't cry." Barbara sniffed. "You don't get to cry today."

RONAN SLID A finger inside his shirt collar and loosened his necktie's choke hold. The guests chattered cheerfully from their seats below. The platform wasn't high but he still felt surprising exposed. He wondered how Jessica was doing. He had caught a glimpse of her as Clara and Cookie hustled her into the bride's room. She had looked like a condemned prisoner. At least he had Liam with him for comfort.

"You have the rings, right?"

"I couldn't have lost them in the last twenty seconds, dude. I've been standing right here." Liam grinned at him and patted his jacket pocket for emphasis.

"I know I said it before, but thanks for this," Ronan said. "For all of it. For letting me marry your mom. For letting me be part of your life. For being my best man."

"Sure."

"And I said this too, but I know Chris will always be your real dad."

"Birth dad." Liam looked at him reprovingly. "Get the lingo right."

"Got it."

"I like Chris when he isn't taking that stupid herb stuff. I wouldn't mind spending some more time with him. But a real dad is the one who stays around. Goes to tuba concerts. Teaches you stuff."

"I can do that."

But Liam's response was lost in the swell of the processional music and the rustle of clothes as the seated crowd turned.

Jock came first, with Charlotte at his side. Then Max with Aidy. Hans and Clara were next. As each couple approached they separated and aligned themselves next to him. The men at Liam's right, the women to Ronan's left. Cookie walked up the aisle. As matron of honor, Barbara came next.

The crowd chuckled as Jane walked slowly up the aisle. Her brow was furrowed in concentration as she dropped rose petals from a tiny white basket one at a time, watching each velvety petal flutter to the ground before reaching for another. As she reached the front she looked up and waved.

"Oh hi, Wonan! She's weally pwetty, wait and see!"

Jane settled into her assigned seat patting down her dress with a happy sigh. The tone of the music changed and he looked toward the back again. The expectant mutter of the crowd faded away. There was a breeze. It puffed against his cheek, his hand, and the scent of carnations from the garlands draped over the chair backs. He glanced at Liam. At Jock and Max. And then to his left, at Aidy and Charlotte. His. And now, their circle would be even more complex and stronger for it, the way a delicate strand of fiber was strengthened by being braided with another equally delicate strand.

Then Jessica stepped into view, framed by the trellis. And his breath left him. Because this was love. This was joy. This was the promise he had longed for. She looked uncertain for a moment but then her eyes met his, and he felt the familiar click of connection, visceral and solid. She smiled tremulously and stepped forward. Closer, and closer still, until her hand was in his and they turned together to face the future.

EPILOGUE

"DON'T LIE."

The coffee slopped over the edge of the mug as Jessica slapped it down in front of Ronan.

"What are you talking about?"

"What I am talking about, Ronan, is you pretending everything is fine and dandy."

Jessica watched him squirm. Good. Now they were both miserable. There were few things that made a person more irritable than Braxton Hicks contractions on top of feeling like a beached whale. She glared at him for good measure.

"You've been a basket case this week," she added, "so don't try to pretend otherwise."

"I should never have scheduled the exhibit for this month."

"You said the timing was ideal. The height of the tourist season. And Island Arts Gallery is a prime location for the monthly art walk crowd."

"Sure, but I didn't anticipate this." He gestured toward her belly.

A sense of stillness came over her. "You didn't *anticipate* this? What did you think was going to happen?"

"Not – you know that's not what I meant. All I'm saying is once we knew we were expecting a baby in August, we should have rescheduled the exhibit. What if you go into labor early?"

She bit her lip and blinked back tears. Stupid hormones. And stupid nightmare. The image of standing on the pier watching Ronan's ferry disappear into the mist was starting to be a regular occurrence at two in the morning. And it was terribly unfair because Ronan had been a rock since that horrible wonderful day at the health center. But he looked so worried now, she had to swallow an awful urge to laugh. She reached across the table to pat his hand, half reassurance, half apology.

"Liam came late so there's no reason to suspect this little one will arrive three weeks early. Dr. Hazel told you not to worry so much, remember?"

"Of course I worry," he snapped. "I love you."

Then she did laugh. "I love you too, Ronan. And I promise not to give birth in the gallery tonight. Is Kobi Ellis really coming?"

Ronan nodded.

"And Leonard will be there early, right?"

Since Ronan's decision to pursue art full time, Leonard Eskin had been a loyal and energetic champion. Tonight's exhibition, Ronan's first official showing of his work, was largely a result of Leonard's connections and encouragement. Ronan had labored overtime to ensure his work was as good as he could make it. But now the day was finally here, there was more dread than anticipation in his expression.

"What if it's no good?" He spoke so quietly, at first she wasn't sure whether she had heard him correctly. And even then, she thought she must have misunderstood.

"You mean the setup for the exhibit?"

"My work," he spoke louder now. "What if my work is second rate? What if I am second rate? What if I made a terrible mistake changing careers? Talk about self-centered. How can I hope to support you and Liam and a new baby when I can't even produce a quality product?"

She shook her head. "Leonard says –"

"What if Leonard is wrong?"

"He's not wrong," she said firmly. "And don't you look at me like that. I may not know art, but I know you, Ronan. You don't have the capacity to be second rate. And even if you were a second rate talent, you would find a way to make a first rate product. I believe in you, Ronan."

"I know. And I'm grateful for it. I just –"

"You're afraid you'll let us all down."

His lips tightened and she caught the flash of fear in his eyes.

"You won't." She held his gaze. "It's not just that I believe in you. I trust you."

He took a deep breath and let it out slowly. "I don't know what to do."

"Eat your breakfast," she said sharply, "and get over to the gallery. You have picture hanging to do, and I want to check in with the event space office before I pick up Liam."

RONAN SCANNED THE room. Jessica stood near the refreshment table, her cheeks flushed as she chatted with Kobi Ellis. She was beautiful, his wife, even more now than she had been when he first lost his heart to her. He loved her grit, her inner steel core, as much as he loved the soft curves of her body.

Liam and Chris stood nearby inspecting a sketch. Chris draped an arm over Liam's shoulder as he leaned in to hear his son's comment. Sherry, the addiction counselor, had turned out to be a good influence. Chris wasn't relying on his herbal remedies anymore, and he seemed a lot more even-keeled now. Didn't mean he got to drive Liam home from his new job as a counselor at Days of Joy Summer Day Camp though. Or anywhere, ever, as far as Ronan was concerned. Still, it was good Liam and Chris's relationship had a chance to grow organically.

Max and Hans were deep in conversation. The noise of the crowd made it impossible to hear about what. Given Han's hand gestures, it probably had something to do with plumbing. Jane demonstrated a pirouette and then shook her head patiently as Aidy and Clara attempted to copy the move.

Cookie hadn't made it although she said she would visit once the baby arrived. Lynne's party felt like a lifetime ago, but apparently one of Lynne's cousins and Cookie had hit it off. Since then, Jessica's mother had been living with Herman in Las Vegas. She had promised to invite Liam to stay with her for a week but so far hadn't followed through. Ronan guessed they'd cross that bridge when they came to it.

So much of life seemed to be like that. Waiting. Wondering whether you would be enough when the test came. He had thought by setting goals he could control what tests he would face, prepare for them, guarantee success. But he hadn't predicted a second chance. Couldn't have envisioned losing his heart again. And maybe that was the whole point. Not being sure. At least he was going to give that risky road his best shot. Terrifying? Absolutely. But full of promise too.

Jock and Charlotte, clasped hands swinging gently, strolled toward him. Charlotte let Jock's hand slip from hers long enough to give Ronan a fierce hug.

"It's beautiful, all of it," she said, her face alight with pleasure.

Jock slapped him on the back. "Leonard says you're sold out."

Ronan felt the blood drain from his face. That couldn't be right. He had kept his hopes reasonable. Three sales was the goal. Four would be a fabulous night. He shook his head. "I'm sorry, what?"

"Look at the dots, bro. Better get that charcoal moving. You've got nothing left in inventory."

Ronan swallowed and stared. Each piece in view had a neat red dot on the lower right corner of the frame. Dazed, he looked toward Jessica. She was standing in the middle of the room now with a peculiar expression on her face. Charlotte was saying something but the sound of her voice faded as he walked toward Jessica. He put his arm around her and placed his other hand on her belly.

"You okay?"

"I think my water just broke."

"YOU'VE ALREADY MET me and Daddy. But wait till you meet your big brother Liam. He's going to love you to bits. And then there are Uncle Jock and Aunt Charlotte, Uncle Max and Aunt Aidy, and Hans and Clara and Aunt Barbara and Uncle Salim and Uncle Zack. Your grandmother Cookie is a bit of a challenge, but she'll love you too in her own way. And there are cousins too, Barbara and Salim's little boys, Ethan and Ezra, Charlotte and Jock's little girl Jane and Max and Aidy's baby boy, Oliver. And Charlotte's pregnant too. So there will be lots of kids to play with. And dogs too."

Emma yawned hugely and pursed her lips. Jessica heard a scuffling in the hallway and a whine accompanied by a laughing shushing sound. She smothered a giggle when Bear's head poked around the door frame. The health center was small and the rules were more flexible than they would have been in a large city hospital. Still, dogs weren't normally allowed in the building unless they were therapy animals. On the other hand, Jessica was the only patient in the tiny maternity ward and the first to actually give birth there in some time, so maybe the staff had decided to overlook the transgression.

Bear scrabbled on the slippery tile floor, pulling Liam behind her on the other end of the leash. But midway to the bed in which Jessica cradled Emma, the dog halted. Slowly she crept forward, one paw at a time until her great muzzle hovered over the infant. Gently she sniffed Emma from head to foot and then from foot to head, stopping occasionally to aim a licking tongue at Jessica's face and hands. Satisfied, the dog flopped to the floor with an unmistakable grin.

Liam shifted from one foot to the other. Once Jessica began to show, he had been a little awkward about the whole baby thing, not jealous so much as embarrassed. Understandable, she guessed. Still, she had worried that might impact his long-term relationship with Emma. She proffered the baby. "Do you want to hold her?"

"She's awful small – I should probably wait until she's bigger." He clasped his hands behind his back, but she could see the flicker of longing in his eyes.

"Nah." Ronan appeared behind Liam. "I used to worry about that when I first met Jane too. But babies are pretty tough. Want me to show you how?"

Jessica watched as Ronan settled Liam into the chair. Then he took the baby from her arms and nestled her in Liam's, demonstrating how to support the vulnerable head and neck. Together, they curved over the tiny bundle of pink blanket. They were hers, these two. One, the man she had loved as a boy, the other, the boy on the precipice of manhood. A wave of tenderness overcame her.

"Oh, Mom." Liam's face was suffused with awe. "She's super cute."

Ronan sat beside her and put his arm around her waist. With a sigh of contentment, she leaned into his embrace. The family would descend on them soon – Max and Aidy, Jock and Charlotte and Jane, Hans and Clara, Barbara and Salim, Zack, all of them with their stubborn kindness. Her family now. Tears filled her eyes as she watched Liam chat with his baby sister.

Ronan shot her a concerned look. "You okay? Want me to call the nurse?"

Her laughter bubbled over and suddenly she felt light, a bird loosed from a tether. Happiness, yes. But there was something else too, a kind of sureness. She knew exactly where she was going and who was going with her. She cupped Ronan's face in her palms and drew him close, but before her lips could graze his, Liam cleared his throat.

"They're crazy about each other," he muttered to Emma. "But you can hang out with me when it gets too obnoxious."

THE END

About Rose:

Online reviews are crucial to an author's success. If you enjoyed The Closer You Get, please consider leaving an online review. Even a few lines can have enormous impact and would be most appreciated.

Rose's first two books in the Durrell Brothers Trilogy, Waiting For You and All Of Me are available in ebook and paperback form on Amazon and at other online book retailers. Her romantic suspense Hot Pursuit and her standalone contemporary romance, Not As Advertised are also available from major e-bookstores as both ebooks and paperbacks.

Rose's idea of an emergency is realizing a long weekend is coming and the library is closing in an hour. She loves finding cool seashells, knitting sweaters which start out right but inevitably turn out too large, and petting stray dogs. She lives in Rhode Island with her husband and cheerfully admits to the sin of boundless pride when it comes to her four grown children.

Say Hi!

Rose blogs about books and writing on her website. She loves visitors, so drop in. You can also visit her on Facebook or send her an email.

Blog: *http://rosegreybooks.com/blog*
Website: *http://rosegreybooks.com*
Facebook: *https://www.facebook.com/rosegreybooks/*
Email: *rosegreybooks@gmail.com*

If you want to receive an email when Rose publishes her next book, join here: https://rosegreybooks.com/newsletter/. Rose will never share your email address and you may unsubscribe at any time.

Single woman in search of…well, a plumber would be good for a start.

Waiting For You

Durrell Brothers Trilogy, Book 1

When Max Durrell books a room at The Grand, Aidy Jones, hotel manager, signs up for a dating service. Aidy knows what she needs and Max Durrell isn't it. Her ideal man is attractive enough to have children with but not attractive enough to fall in love with. Ideally, he'll also have some roofing skills.

Max Durrell has returned to Demerest Cove to accomplish a lifelong dream. The Grand isn't on the market yet, but convincing the eccentric owners to sell should be a piece of cake. His brothers will take care of the transaction. Max's job is to flirt with the owners' daughter so she doesn't interfere.

Flirting is easy. It's the friendship that's the problem. He can't help enjoying Aidy Jones and while he'll never fall in love again (Been there. Bought the tux. Bride never showed up.) he is falling in like with her. Deeply in like.

But any day now, the sale will go through. And once Aidy learns Max is the one tearing her beloved hotel away from her, she'll never want to set eyes on him again.

To purchase **Waiting For You** visit online retailers or Rose's website, http://rosegreybooks.com. While you are there, sign up for the newsletter. It's fun to be the first to find out about upcoming books!

Two blue eyes. One toothless grin. And Jock Durrell's heart is gone, gone, gone.

All Of Me

Durrell Brothers Trilogy, Book 2

Jock is having a lousy week. Learning he is a father has been a shock but it's the lack of sleep that's killing him. The kid is five weeks old and cries all night, every night. He needs childcare. Yesterday. He's hoping for Mary Poppins.

Charlotte Aubin is good at getting hired. Staying hired is more of a challenge, especially since she knows nothing about babies. But most worrisome is Jock himself. He's kind. She hates that in a man - it's so much more deceitful than open hostility. Falling for the baby may be unavoidable. But falling for Jock would just be stupid. No man can be trusted, especially when it comes to love.

But Charlotte's past follows her, endangering everyone she holds dear. Will she flee to safety? Or risk it all for the man who has stolen her heart?

To purchase **All Of Me** visit online retailers or Rose's website, http://rosegreybooks.com. While you are there, sign up for the newsletter. It's fun to be the first to find out about upcoming books!

He may be every woman's dream, but she can't wait to see the last of him.

Hot Pursuit

For the first time in her life, Jenny Rasmussen has things organized the way she wants them. Her toy store is flourishing, her sister and niece are happy, and her love life is nonexistent. Jenny has seen firsthand the damage love can do and she wants no part of *that*, thank you very much. But the moment she meets Special Agent Beau Rivers, Jenny's well ordered life spirals out of control.

Beau knows trouble when he sees it. The defiant, spitfire he is charged with protecting definitely falls into that category. But Beau is determined to do his job, even if Jenny dislikes him. Good thing the dislike is mutual since, in his line of work, love can be fatal to a career. But more than Beau's job is at risk. Jenny's life is at stake and the threat may be coming from within his beloved FBI.

To purchase **Hot Pursuit** visit online retailers or Rose's website, http://rosegreybooks.com. While you are there, sign up for the newsletter. It's fun to be the first to find out about upcoming books!

Mel loves her job. Too bad it's breaking her heart.

Not As Advertised

When Blue Hill Elementary School's new hire crashes into his life, Paul Stokowski is not pleased. The pretty violin teacher is a distraction he can't afford. Still, when she pleads for his help, Paul can't turn her down. After all, under the circumstances, the woman won't be in town long.

Mel Stone banked everything she has on her dream job and she's not going down without a fight. So when she learns the school committee members thought they were hiring a Mr. Stone, it's a no brainer - she cuts her hair and dresses like a dude.

But as she settles into small town life, Mel feels increasingly guilty about her deception. Worse still, she is falling in love with the only person in Blue Hill who knows her secret, a man she is sure would never be interested in her as anything other than a friend.

To purchase **Not As Advertised** visit online retailers or Rose's website, http://rosegreybooks.com. While you are there, sign up for the newsletter. It's fun to be the first to find out about upcoming books!